"The Scalebearers" by Sweet

Published by Sweet Discords LLC

www.storiesbysweet.com

Copyright © 2021 Sweet Discords LLC

All rights reserved. No portion of this book may be reproduced in any form without permission from the publisher, except as permitted by U.S. copyright law.

Cover Art by Polina (Dr.Graf)
Cover Design and Book Layout by Sweet

ISBN: 978-0-578-34696-0

Printed in the United States of America

1st Edition

The Scalebearers

BY: SWEET

For Content Warnings, please scan the QR below or visit:
www.storiesbysweet.com/content-warnings

TABLE OF CONTENTS

Map	pg. 6-7
The Scalebearers	pg. 11
Before	pg. 13
Chapter 1	pg. 17
Chapter 2	pg. 33
Chapter 3	pg. 54
Chapter 4	pg. 77
Chapter 5	pg. 90
Chapter 6	pg. 107
Chapter 7	pg. 131
Chapter 8	pg. 149
Chapter 9	pg. 165
Chapter 10	pg. 176
Chapter 11	pg. 211
Chapter 12	pg. 224
Chapter 13	pg. 239
Chapter 14	pg. 266
Chapter 15	pg. 285
Chapter 16	pg. 298
Chapter 17	pg. 326
Chapter 18	pg. 352
Chapter 19	pg. 361
Elsewhere	pg. 399
Acknowledgements	pg. 401
Glossary	pg. 403
About the Author	pg. 406

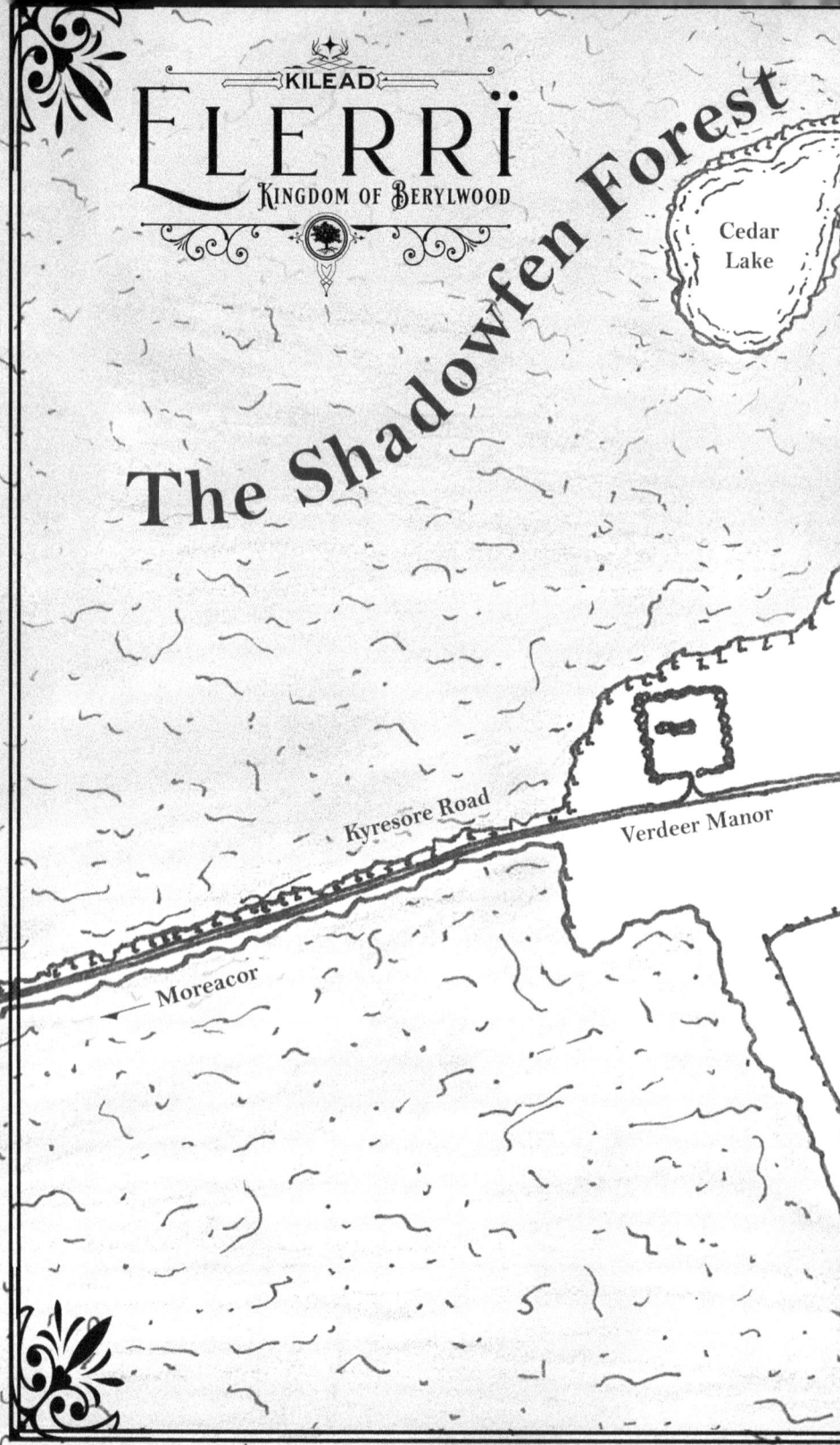

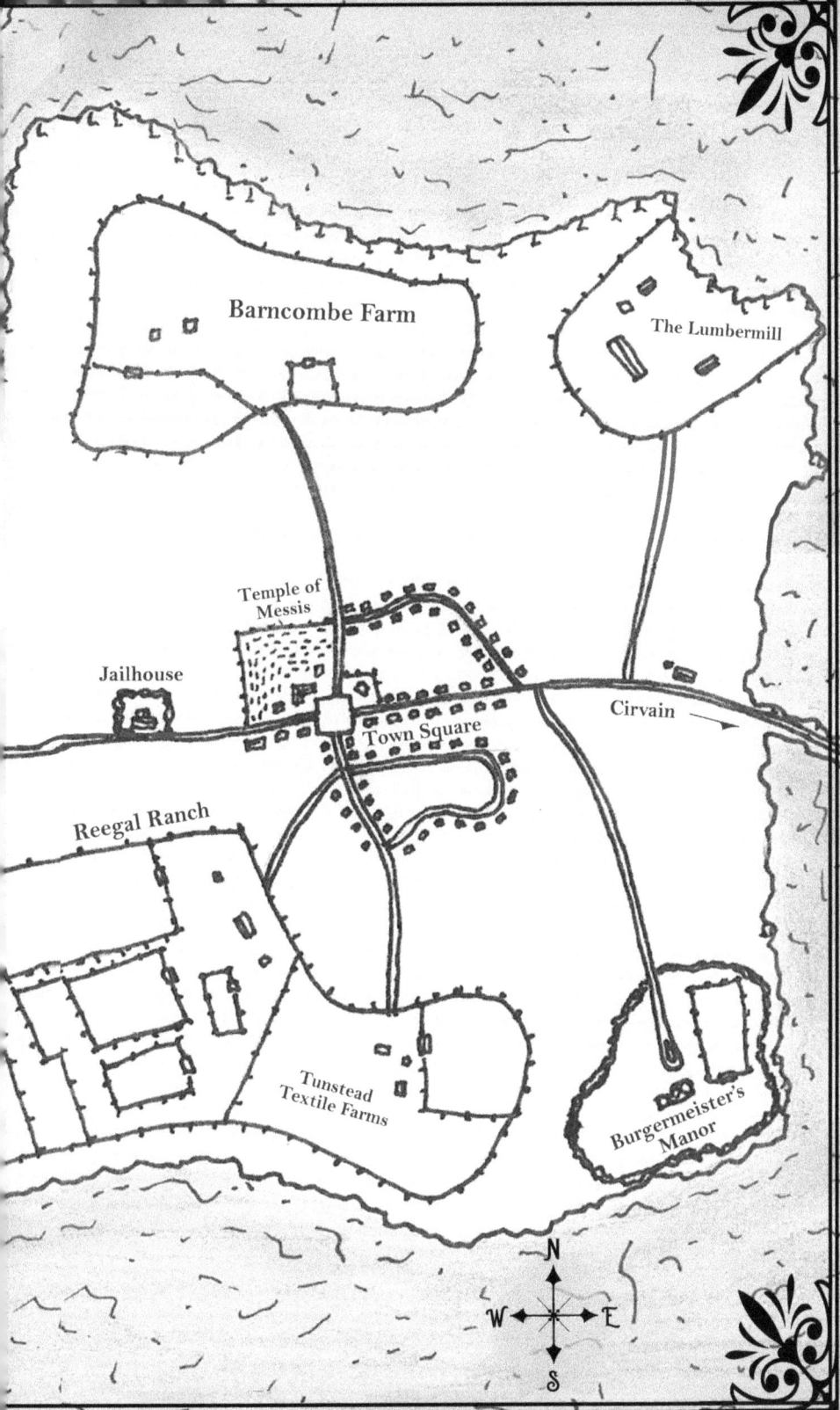

For My Little Gray Cat

May you sleep in every warm sunbeam,
That pours through every window.
And bring peace to those who need it,
Like you so often did for me.

The Scalebearers

THE SCALEBEARERS

BEFORE

In the beginning, there was nothing.
Yet,
What is nothing without something?

The deities of creation built the world to suit their desires.
The deities of destruction carved it apart for theirs.

In their unbridled power, chaos reigned.

So,

To save their creations and satisfy destruction.
The creators gave one last gift to the world.

They left.

Their magicks remained, spreading across the realm, and chaos stilled.

Balance in isolation.

No scalebearers to keep watch.

SWEET

THE SCALEBEARERS

CHAPTER ONE

There are few things worse than waking up hogtied in a locked cell.

Waking up hogtied and daisy-chained to four strangers in a locked cell is one of those things.

Kaj's sleeping body's unsuccessful attempt to stretch against the tight ropes jolted him awake.

"What the hell-" The copper-skinned elvefolk would've remembered being bound; hell, he might have even enjoyed it. Confused, he strained his neck to look around as his nocturnal vision adjusted to the pitch-black room. This wasn't the cell he was thrown into earlier that night.

If it's even night, he thought. He tried to roll over onto his side to get a better view, but stopped short, pulled back down by the clattering of chains.

"Hello?" a soft, frightened voice called, "Is someone there?"

He struggled to angle towards the voice as he tried to get a look at who was speaking.

In the corner of his eye sat a fair-skinned, young human woman in a nightgown, long hair half up and messy from sleep, eyes wide with fear.

At least he wasn't alone.

His gaze followed the chain trailing behind her to find it attached to three other bodies, hopefully asleep on the ground.

"Yes," Kaj grumbled, not thrilled with his situation, "can you see me?"

Her eyes darted around, trying to find some sense of purchase in the darkness.

"No," she said, her voice wobbly with fright, "Y-you're not going to hurt me, are you?"

"I'm a little tied up at the moment," he stated, "but I wasn't planning to."

"What's your name?" she asked.

"Kaj. Yours?"

"Ava."

"What about the others next to you? Are they alive?"

"The others next to me?" Ava's heart was going to burst out of her chest. This had to be the most realistic nightmare she ever had.

"Right," Kaj sighed, "you can't see. There are three

people next to you on the ground. If you shimmy to your right, you should hit one of them."

"B-but what if they're dead?" she stammered. Bile burned in the back of her throat at the thought, "I don't want to touch a dead body."

"And I don't want to be in a shibari session gone wrong right now, but these things happen."

"What's shibari?" she asked.

A dull thud came from the darkness in front of her as something hit the ground.

"I hate small towns," Kaj groaned. "Just scoot over to the right and touch the damn body."

Please don't be a corpse, please don't be a corpse, please don't be a corpse. She took a deep breath to steady her nerves and scooted to the right until she brushed against something soft and body shaped.

"Five more minutes, clock," the body groaned.

Ava squealed, immediately waking the others.

Kaj watched as the form closest to him, a young, muscular, human woman with sleek hair pulled back into a bun, tried to scramble to her feet before promptly falling back on her ass, her balance thrown off by the weight attached to the chain.

Beside her, a young, dark-skinned, half-dwarven

woman with her hair wrapped in a silk scarf sat up as if possessed, pure malcontent on her face.

Then lastly, trying to stretch as if he were leisurely waking up on a weekend morning, the body Ava so warily sat on revealed itself to be a gangly young man sporting a thick mess of curly hair and freckles. As he found his arms manacled behind his back, the boy shot up like a rocket.

Indigestion bubbled his stomach as he, unfortunately, recognized the trio.

"What the hell is going on here?" the muscular woman asked.

"It seems like we're chained up somewhere," Ava answered, "I'm Ava. Who are you?"

"Valma. Member of the townsguard. No need to worry, miss. I'll get us out of here."

"Just my luck," Kaj groaned and figured it better to bite the bullet now than have it shoot him in the ass later.

"You slippery little fuck," Valma called out into the darkness. Kaj snickered as he watched her scowl at empty air, "You're the one who put us in here, didn't you?"

"Unfortunately not," he replied, "But I do have the extreme privilege of being chained to you."

"Why should I believe you?"

"Scooch over to your right. When you hit something bony, covered in fabric, and tied up like a Frosttide goose ready to be stuffed, that'll be me."

19

"Ava?" the sleepy boy she sat on said. Kaj watched a tiny spark of joy cut through her fear as she recognized his voice.

"Gillian!" the tension in her shoulders dropped. His timbre something familiar for her to cling to in this unfamiliar place, "I'm sorry that you're in here, but I'm glad to hear your voice!"

"You know how sometimes you have really bad days," a haughty – and familiar to her in a much less pleasant manner – voice chimed in, "and then you have days that are so bad that even the worst possible thing imaginable could happen to you, and you'd think: why? Why not sink further into the horrific abyss that is your current state of existence?"

"Oh. Hi Ortensia," the sweet lilt in Ava's voice vanished as she wondered what god she pissed off enough to chain her to the town terror.

Ortensia screamed, her frustration boiling over and echoing off the stone walls.

"Shut the hell up!" Kaj hissed.

"Who are you to tell me to shut up, you low-life thief?!" she spat.

"I'm the guy who's going to get your ass out of this cell," he snapped back, "But I can't exactly do that if whoever captured us hears that we're awake and comes in here to murder us."

"I'd like to see them try," Valma said.

"What? You gonna tackle them out of a window too?" he lashed.

"I feel like I'm missing something," Ava interjected.

Gillian leaned over to where he thought she was and whispered, "I'll tell you later."

"Get your hot breath out of my ear," Ortensia snarled. "Can't you cast an illumination spell or something instead of us fumbling around in the dark? Or will you summon the actual sun itself and burn us all into a crisp?"

"Yeah," Gillian mumbled as he shrunk back into himself, "I gotta light spell."

He ignored the guilt upsetting his stomach and murmured an incantation under his breath, "Hend keyadla tenavims." A soft, golden glow spread over his palms and lit up the cell slightly from behind his back.

As their eyes adjusted from pure darkness to sudden, though not blinding, light, the state of the cell around them came into view.

Hundreds of bloody scratch marks covered the floor and walls of the dark stone chamber. Some of them were deeper than others and thickly concentrated around the single barred iron door, changing the color of the dark slate to a soft, bloodstained gray. There was no furniture, no chamber pot, only a pile of hay: wet, rotting, with clusters of mold and dark stains all over it in the far corner.

"Well," Kaj said, "This is worse than I thought."

"We're going to die in here," Ava muttered.

"Like hell we are!" Ortensia snapped, "We've got a member of the townsguard here with us. They'll find us in no time."

"I'm not so sure about that," Valma replied.

Ortensia turned to her, incensed by her rebuttal, "What does that mean?"

"Does it look like I have any of my gear on me?" she said, waving her hand across her body, "I'm in my pajamas. No communication pendant, no Bastion leathers, no way they'll find me."

"Well then, some guard you are," Ortensia scoffed and rolled her eyes at her incompetence, making a mental note to speak to her captain about docking her pay for such a lapse in judgment. "I'm a noblewoman, and even I know to sleep with a weapon at my side."

"And look at how far that got you," she grumbled.

"Can we please stop arguing?" Ava cut off the verbal assault building in Ortensia's throat, "There's got to be some way out of here. Gill, are there any incantations you know that could help us out?"

"Not really," the young mage answered, "if the lock's magical, I could probably figure it out, but at the very least, I'd need my hands to do it."

"You sure you couldn't just, I don't know, split this entire cell apart by summoning a bunch of branches out of the ground?" Ortensia mocked, still furious with the redhead from the night prior.

"The bedrock's too thick," he cast his eyes to the ground, clearly too ashamed to look at her.

"Ah, the bedrock's too thick. How convenient."

"Are we done now?" Kaj spoke up, "I can get us out of here if we're done now."

Valma could help her smile as he shut down Ortensia's childish attitude.

"Yeah, we're done." Valma answered for the group, "What have you got?"

"I can unlock us, but I need you to untie me. You know how to bring your arms in front of you when cuffed, right?"

"Sure do. The tough thing will be doing it with us all chained together, but if we're able to move at the same time-"

"You're actually listening to him?" Ortensia interrupted, "He's a thief!"

"Exactly," she replied, "Who better to pick a lock

than a thief?"

Ortensia looked back at Gillian and Ava in disbelief. The pair shrugged.

"She's got a point," Ava said before turning her attention towards her, "Now, what do we have to do?"

"Right," Valma sat up straighter and deepened her voice with authority, "These chains are pretty short between us, so everybody sit up on your knees."

They followed her instructions, bolstering her pride to bring a small smile to her face.

"Now, sit through your hands. Pinch your wrists between your knees. Then tilt to lay on your right side," she continued and used herself as an example.

After a little bit of shuffling, they all managed to get on their sides, some more gracefully than others.

"Great. Now pull your left leg up and through your arms. Then your right-"

"Gods. I should have gone to circus school," Gillian groaned as he tried his best to stretch his leg through.

"Got it!" Ava cheered with an exasperated huff, her hands now in front of her.

"Ugh," Ortensia grunted as she tried to wriggle her legs through, "easier said than done."

With some struggle and help from those who already

pulled through, they managed to get their hands in front of them; and set to work untying the plethora of knots binding Kaj.

"Man, whoever put us in here really did not want you to get out," Valma said as she struggled with one of the knots.

"Yeah, well, they don't know me very well," he quipped, "I can get out of anything."

"So long as you've got four people helping you," Ortensia said, pulling a chuckle from Ava and Gillian.

"Haha. Very funny. Maybe you should focus more on untying me than your comedy act."

"Oh, I wasn't trying to be funny. Just stating the obvious."

Ortensia finished first, much to Kaj's chagrin, and the others' knots came loose soon after. His arms and legs fell free on the floor, and he let out a sigh of relief.

"Alright, you're free now." Valma said, "Better not try any funny business."

"Wouldn't dream of it." he sat up and stretched, relishing in the ability to move his limbs, "Alright, do one of you ladies got a hairpin on you?"

"I should have one in my hair still," Ava volunteered.

"Great. Then you get to be free first." He walked over to Ava and pulled the hairpin out from the back of her hair, "Wizkid, can you hold your hands over her so I can get a better view?"

"Sure," Gillian turned and held his hands above her manacles as well as he could. Kaj knelt in front of her and got to work picking the lock.

"Excuse me. I'm the nobility here," Ortensia said.

"You're a burgermeister's daughter. Nobility's a bit of a stretch," Kaj replied as Ava's manacles fell off her wrists.

"Alrighty," he turned towards Valma, "If you promise not to choke me out, you want to be next?"

Valma drew a stunted cross over her heart, "Stick's honor."

"Shimmy over then," he waved her over, adjusting Gillian's wrist like the arm of a lamp. Gill looked to Ava for help, but found her ambling around the cell lost in thought, rubbing her wrists.

"Come on, your majesty," Kaj gestured for Ortensia to come forward as Valma stretched her freed arms above her head and walked off.

"You sure you don't want to unlock your work light first?" she spat.

"Would that I could," he replied, "but I'd rather save the hardest lock for last."

Ortensia begrudgingly made her way over and stuck her shackled wrists out. With a quick turn of the pin, the lock came undone.

"That wasn't so bad, was it?" Kaj said. Ortensia rolled her eyes and left to join Valma along the cell wall.

"Your turn, pal," he slapped Gillian on the shoulder, breaking his focus on Ava.

"Uh. Yeah. Great. Thank you," he fumbled before asking, "What do you need from me?"

Kaj pursed his lips at his strange behavior, "Just keep your arms still. All these locks seem to be the same, so with any luck, I won't need your light." He inserted the hairpin, and after a moment of fumbling and a tense look on his face, the manacles clattered on the stone floor.

"Hey," Valma said, the metal pang of the cuffs on the stone floor drawing her attention, "You got the mage free?"

"My name's Gillian."

"Sorry," she apologized, "*Gillian*, would you mind hovering your hands over here? I think we found something."

"I don't mind," Gill stood and walked towards Valma and Ortensia, holding his palms forward to spread the light across the wall in front of them. Their eyes widened as the shadows fled the scratches on the wall and revealed them to be words. Over and over again, overlapping in some places, dried blood filling the divots, forming a single phrase:

RUNDEN RISES

"What the hell?" Ava mumbled under her breath as she came up beside Gill for a closer look.

"Anybody know of a Runden?" Valma asked the group.

Silence.

"So, does that wall have a secret exit to it?" Kaj said from across the room, leaning against the barred door with his arms crossed.

"No?" Valma replied.

"Then let's focus on getting out of here and not on some lunatic's art project," he said, "Wizkid. Light me up?"

Gill headed over, taking a long look back at the wall as he did.

"Oh, so it's okay for him to call you nicknames?" Valma challenged.

"Wizkid's got a better ring to it than 'the mage' at least," he smiled a little, despite how unnerved he was. "I've got two hands. I'll hold my left over the lock while he picks it and the other at you all so you can see if there's any more writing." He stretched his arms apart, one hand over the lock, the other facing the wall, forming an awkward and physically uncomfortable t-pose.

Ava ran her hand over the carvings.

Valma looked over to her and Ortensia, "You two have lived here a while. You sure you've never heard this name before?"

"If it's even a name," Ava said, "could be a thing or a monster of some kind. But I've never heard of such a thing in Elerrï."

"Yeah," she sighed, "The captain mentioned when

I started that you guys don't get much monster trouble here. Something about some ancient magic blessing?"

"The Doe and the Farmer," Ortensia muttered.

"The what?" Valma asked.

"It's this myth. Apparently, a farmer who lived here once helped the goddess, Messis, return to the Plane of Creation, so she blessed these lands as a gift."

"Uh-huh," Ava added, "Any monsters lurking in the Shadowfen Forest won't cross into town because of it. But this could just be what Kaj said," she chewed her bottom lip, "someone probably was just in this cell for a really long time and went crazy."

"Or we're not in Elerrï anymore," Valma added.

"I sure hope not," Ava grew quiet. A dull, aching worry pulled at her heart.

"I got it!" Kaj announced. The ladies turned to see him holding the hairpin up in triumph with the barred door slightly ajar behind him. Gillian sighed in relief as he dropped his shaking arms.

They all crowded around the door.

"Your hairpin," Kaj held the pin out to Ava. The once straight end of it now twisted, "My apologies that it's a bit bent, but I'll buy you a new one to celebrate our freedom once we get back into town."

"No worries," she took the pin and pulled the top half of her hair back with it, "a little bend doesn't bother me."

Kaj's lips wrinkled and nostrils flared as he held back a laugh.

"You want to point those magic hands of yours out so we can see?" Valma asked, drawing Ava's attention away from his confusing reaction.

"Yeah," Gillian grimaced, absentmindedly rubbing his sore biceps, "But as we walk, maybe keep an eye out for a torch or something? My arms are getting tired."

"Will do." She gestured out the door and pointedly looked at Kaj, "After you."

"I'm going first?"

"Dusk elvefolk like yourself can see in the dark, right?" she smirked, "Who better to lead the way down a murky hallway?"

"Fine," Kaj grumbled and stepped through the door without protest.

One by one, the group made their way out of the cell and down the hall after him as Valma waited to be the last to leave.

"I don't mind being in the back," Ortensia said as she watched Gillian's light drift down the hall, leaving the two of them alone in the cell.

"Not to doubt your ability to protect yourself, Miss Ortensia, but I think you'd be much better off if I were behind you."

"Okay." She made no effort to move. Though the ambient light from Gill's spell was fading, Valma could still make out the hesitant look in the half-dwarf's eyes beyond her snooty facade. She felt her chest warm at the sight and placed a hand on her shoulder as she bent down to her level.

"It's okay to be afraid, but don't worry. I'll protect you," she whispered.

Ortensia stiffened as Valma's soft breath brushed against her ear. A frustratingly pleasant sensation during such an unpleasant event.

"I'm not afraid," Ortensia huffed and pulled away, stomping off down the hall.

Valma shook her head, chuckling quietly to herself, and with a deep breath to calm the excitement building in her chest, she shut the door behind her and followed.

CHAPTER TWO

The cramped, subterranean hallway seemed endless. Surrounded by solid stone and darkness, the only sense they moved forward instead of in an infinite loop came from the occasional bloodstain on the wall or sharp turn.

"What a poor design choice for a dungeon," Ortensia wheezed, her lungs heavy from the ceaseless walking, "Having to journey this whole way just to throw some prisoners in a cell? What about every time you have to feed them?"

"I don't think they were feeding them," Valma stated.

"Then what's the use of the cell then? If you just want someone to die, chop their head off and save yourself the walk!"

"Not if you want them to suffer first. Nothing quite says punishment like starving to death."

"You know," Ortensia turned over her shoulder and craned her neck back to look up at the bits of her face barely lit by Gill's light ahead of them, "you're being a bit of wet blanket right now."

Valma scrunched her face in amused disbelief, "I'm the wet blanket? You just suggested that it would be better if the people who captured us cut our heads off instead!"

"Well, I don't think they wanted us to starve!" she rolled her eyes at Valma's ignorance, "They definitely wouldn't want me to starve. I'm an asset."

"And what does that make the rest of us?"

Ortensia furrowed her brow. Her first instinct was to come up with a witty retort, but she found herself coming up short, unable to find an answer as to why they'd all been captured together to turn into an insult.

"Wait. That's a good question," Valma muttered to herself, echoing Ortensia's inner confusion. "Hey," she called ahead to the others, "Why do you think they captured us?"

"I think the more important question is who captured us, Stick," Kaj answered, voice hushed, "and keep your voice down! Didn't they teach you stealth shit at bootlicker base camp? If you want to say something to the group, just pass it down. You never know what could be listening in a place like this."

A few more minutes, or tens of minutes as it was impossible to sense time, passed walking down halls, their footsteps echoing in an infinite tempo. The arches of Ava's feet ached slightly and blisters started to fill on the bottom of her calloused heels. She often walked barefoot for long amounts of time, preferring the feeling of grass and dirt beneath her feet, but the hard bedrock tested her endurance. She could only imagine how much the others hurt, all except for Kaj, who taunted her as he strode ahead in his well-worn boots and black day clothes.

She looked down at her favorite nightgown and picked off a small clump of dirt, jealous that he'd been lucky enough to be captured in sensible clothes.

"Hey, are you feeling alright?" Gillian leaned forward and whispered over her shoulder.

"I mean, as alright as I can be having been kidnapped and imprisoned deep underground," Ava turned to whisper back, "Why?"

She could see his left cheek slightly sunken in, the standard sign of his worry, "You just looked real distant in the cell there, like your mind was a hundred miles away or something."

"Oh," she paused for a moment, recalling where her mind went before deciding it was not something she wanted him to know, and provided another answer, "I didn't even notice. I was just thinking about Marqui. He sleeps on my bed every night with me, so I hope he's alright."

"I'm sure he's alright," he smiled softly to console her, "From what you've told me about all the mice he's caught, I'm sure he can hold his own."

"Definitely," she chuckled lightly to make him feel as though he succeeded and pivoted to one of the hundreds of questions she had about their unfortunate circumstance,

"What about you? Why was Ortensia berating you so hard about burning us all up and summoning branches?"

Kaj laughed ahead of them, apparently overhearing her question.

"Let's just say the dinner last night didn't go as planned," Gill glared at the back of Kaj's head.

"What happened?"

"I'll tell you later." Both cheeks were sunken now and his nostrils flared slightly. Whatever it was, he didn't want to talk about it.

"Fine," she grumbled, "guess I'll add that to the list." She counted on her fingers teasingly to lighten Gillian's sudden shift in mood, "First the comment about being tackled through a window, next crazy dinner party magick things-"

"Oh, the window story is mine to tell," Kaj looked back at them, "Wizkid can fill in the end of it."

Ava cocked an eyebrow and looked between him and Gill, "You know each other?"

"Shhh!" Kaj shushed her as he outstretched his arms and stopped the party in their tracks, "There's a door ahead."

"Oh, thank the gods," Ortensia exasperated.

"I need you all to be very quiet," he explained as he turned around to face them, "I'm going to go up and listen to the door and see if I hear anything behind it."

"Go ahead," Valma said, "We'll hang back."

"Farmer girl," Ortensia added, "You're a hunter, right? You should go up with him too, just to make sure he's telling the truth."

"And how exactly do you expect me to do that?" Ava said.

"You've got to have great hearing to be as good of a hunter as you are. I bet you could hear a pin drop on plush carpet."

"I think Ortensia just gave you a compliment," Gillian said.

"They're very rare," Ortensia scowled at him, "Don't get used to it."

"Then it's settled. Ava and I will go listen at the door while the rest of you stay put." Kaj looked at Ava, "Make sure to hold on to the back of my cloak; that way, you have some clue where we're going in the dark."

"Right," she grabbed onto the black, ratty cloak and followed him deeper down the hall.

The door at the end of the hall was made of plain wood and locked by a padlock. Kaj stopped in front of it and held a hand back to catch Ava before she bumped into him. He turned and grabbed her shoulders, noticing how she jumped slightly at his touch but not commenting on it as he placed her beside the door. With a quick tug on her earlobe, she understood his intention and, together, the two of them pressed their ears against it.

Kaj counted to ten in his head, listening as carefully as he could. Nothing but the faint sound of Ava's breath. He lifted his head off the door and pulled her along with him as he stepped away.

"Hear anything?" he whispered.

"No," Ava whispered back, "You?"

"Nope. There's a padlock on the door though, let's head back and grab the group so I can use Wizkid's magick hands to get a better look."

In his grayscale vision, he watched her doe-eyed stare harden and the resting pleasantness in her cheeks drop.

"His name's Gillian," she said sternly, "You should really call him that."

"But he said he liked Wizkid."

She rolled her eyes so dramatically, Kaj had to stop himself from laughing, "I'm sure he does, but ya know, sometimes you should say a person's real name." Even though he knew she couldn't see him, her eyes still found his in the darkness and stared him down fiercely, "It's a sign of respect."

"Not where I'm from." he scoffed and paused to study her face for a moment. She was cute, no doubt about that in his eyes. The stereotypical farmer's daughter who would invite you in for some lemonade, but her attitude was something else entirely, "What? You jealous I didn't give you a nickname yet?"

"No?"

"Hmmm- sounds like jealousy to me," he teased and wrapped his arm around her shoulder. Ava jumped, her serious demeanor falling apart as she squeaked slightly in surprise. "Come on. I'll lead you back."

A few moments later, they emerged from the shadows, nearly giving the others a heart attack. Ava nearly jumped herself at the questioning look on Gill's face, arching an eyebrow as his eyes flicked between her face and Kaj's arm on her shoulder. Ava rolled her eyes and scowled subtly, noting her disapproval, to which Gill scrunched his nose and pursed his lips in agreement.

"That is truly creepy," Valma remarked, "Like demons rising from the abyss or something."

"Boo," Kaj deadpanned, rolling his eyes as he pulled away from Ava, "There's no sound coming from the door; it's locked, though."

Ava looked down to find Ortensia staring intensely at her.

"He's telling the truth," she took the hairpin out of her hair and handed it to Kaj, "You might as well keep this for now. It seems like you'll be needing it."

He gave a quick nod in thanks as he took the hairpin from her. He brushed his hand against hers, much to her chagrin, before heading back down the hall, waving a hand over his shoulder for the rest of the group to follow.

With Gill's light shining down on the padlock came undone in seconds. Kaj caught the now loose lock in his palm and placed it in his back pocket. He stiffened for a moment as his hand brushed against a soft leather-bound bundle. The books he tucked in his waistband the night prior were still there.

"Alright," Valma said, "Kaj and I will enter first. Gillian and Ava, you follow behind, then Ortensia."

Kaj let out a small exhale of relief as his pause went unnoticed by the townsguard.

"Why am I last?" Ortensia huffed.

"I thought you didn't mind being in the back," Valma shrugged.

"Well, I at least want to be asked."

"Alright then. Cici, do you want to go into the pitch dark room potentially filled with monsters and/or villains first?"

"What did you call me?"

"Cici. Ortensia's way too long and a little pretentious. I think Cici fits you," Valma gestured towards the door, "So, you going in first or…."

"After you," she grimaced, her voice coated in the

venom of unwanted humility.

Kaj watched their little back and forth with a smirk on his face. The Stick wasn't bad at flirting, but unfortunately for her Little Miss Hoity-Toity was too stuck up her own ass to notice.

"Great," Valma turned to Kaj, her tone turning spiteful, "Ready, asshole?"

"Oh, I don't get a cute nickname too?" he retorted.

"Well, there's nothing about you that's cute," she snickered, "So why start now?"

Kaj couldn't help but smile. He hated the Bastions, but he could still appreciate wit, "You know you're one of the only Sticks I've known with a decent sense of humor."

"And you're one of the only thieves I've let live this long. You ready to bash some heads in?" Valma said as she kicked the wooden door open and stepped inside.

The room ahead of them was just another dark void, but as Kaj followed Valma in, he let out a soft and scared behind her, "What the fuck?"

"What do you see?" Valma whispered over her shoulder to him.

"Gillian," he called out, "We're gonna need some light."

Gill entered at his word with Ava and Ortensia

following closely behind. As the mage stepped into the room with his still glowing hands outstretched, small piles of bone emerged as the shadows retreated. The piles grew with every step forward, collecting into one large mass: a mountain of ossein that towered over them. Spines, skulls, rib cages, femurs: bones in every shape and size imaginable littered in mass before them.

"Are these," Ortensia stammered, "real?"

"I don't know I- uh...." Valma stalled. It wasn't often she was caught off-guard, "I've never really seen bones outside of a person before."

"I can tell," Ava chimed in. She swallowed harshly, "I've got to get a closer look, though."

"You know what real bones look like?!" Valma could help the shock in her voice as she looked at the tall and meek farm girl up and down in disbelief.

"It's a good way to track if there are wolves or owls in the area. Plus, I've gutted and skinned my fair share of game," she frowned, her eyes danced over the pile in front of them, "Those were mainly deer and chickens, though."

"Bones are bones," Kaj said, "They just look a little different sometimes, right?"

"Exactly," she grabbed Gillian's arm without a second thought, "Come with me to get a closer look. I'll need the light."

He muttered a barely audible, "Uh-huh," as she tugged him closer to the pile.

Getting closer and with the light of his palms, she could see how truly varied the skeletons were. There were wyrmkith, dwarves, humans, elves, and even more bones she couldn't tell the heritage of. She reached down to grab one out of the pile, a tibia from what she could tell. It was cold and subtly porous to the touch as she wrapped her fingers around it and pulled it free.

The bones around it shifted when she removed it, some sinking in, others falling loose from the pile and clattering to the ground. She froze, startled by the noise, a sense of regret building as she waited for the bones to settle and everything went quiet.

Her sigh of relief stopped short by the sudden illumination of the chamber as unseen torches on the walls lit aflame and the door they entered slammed shut behind them.

"No, no, no!" Ortensia shrieked as she ran to the door and tried to pull it open.

Haunting and hollow, the peal of falling bone reverberated through the room in a deafening cannon as the mass of bones collapsed into itself. Gillian and Ava backed up from the pile as quickly as they could, breaking his focus on his light spell and dissipating the golden glow from his palms.

"Why did you have to touch it?!" Kaj shouted through the noise, backing up against the wall. He patted himself, hoping to find a dagger hidden somewhere, and silently cursed Valma for stripping him of his weapons so thoroughly the night before.

The bones separated, pulled free from the mass by some unseen force, and formed into complete skeletons standing at attention. The tibia in Ava's hand ripped out of her grasp, flying across the room and attaching to one of the creatures.

"Get ready for a fight!" Valma widened her stance and placed her fists up in front of her.

"A fight? Fight with what?!" Ava yelled, "We don't have any weapons!"

Silence returned as suddenly as it had left once the last bone found its home.

In front of them stood twenty-some skeletons; their bones mismatched, some with two heads or four arms, eyeless sockets locked onto the trespassers that awoke them.

"Maybe they won't attack us. Maybe they'll just-" Gillian stammered.

The skeletons let out a piercing wail, like a squall tearing its way down a cobblestone street, and charged.

Kaj, stricken with absolute terror, scrambled across the wall to join Ortensia at the door. He pounded on it as hard as he could, but it didn't even shutter from his blows.

The first skeleton came upon them: a beastly thing

running on six legs that jumped at Valma. Prepared for the onslaught, she grabbed the creature mid-leap, fingers interlocking with its rib cage, and threw it to the ground. The creature shattered, its bones scattering across the floor, some turning to dust as others splintered.

Ava rushed forward on an instinct she didn't know she had and seized a femur that ricocheted from the beast Valma ruptured. She met a skeleton barreling towards her head-on, swiping at the creature like reaping wheat in a field. Debris flew off the monster as her strike connected, sending it wailing in pain and staggering back but leaving it still standing as it launched at her once more.

Time slowed for Gillian as he watched the monster rear back its skeletal claw to swipe at Ava. His already racing heart doubled in time as a sickly familiar and frantic feeling overcame him—an all-consuming fury that coursed through him as something greater than his own emotion.

Protect her, it commanded.

"Leave her alone!" he shouted. The violent power that raved inside him took over, dropped him to his knees, and slammed his palms on the ground.

The stone floor beneath them tremored as eight pillars of stone shot out from it, destroying ten skeletons in their eruption. The ground became unsteady as hills and divots formed from the sudden protrusions and knocked the skeleton lunging at Ava off its footing, allowing it to meet its end as Ava swung her makeshift club through it.

Valma kept charging forward, treating the now uneven battlefield like a training course. She swung around one of the pillars, using it to gain momentum, and kicked another skeleton right through the spine. Like a pinata of bone, the creature burst, joining its shattered brethren across the floor. She looked back at the group behind her and smiled mockingly at the sight of Kaj and Ortensia's fruitless attempts to escape.

"Come on! What kind of criminal are you?" she teased.

"The kind who knows when to run from a fight!" Kaj turned to shout back. His eyes went wide in terror at the sight of a skeletal beast flying right towards him. With agility that often made up for his lack of strength, he dropped to the ground just in the nick of time, sending the creature hurtling into the wall. Dust and fragments rained down upon his head as the beast disintegrated upon impact.

Ortensia cowered beside him as she heard the bones shatter above her, abandoning her attempts to force the door open. She covered her head and hit the ground, hoping to hide from the monsters like a child pulling a blanket over their head to hide from the boogeyman.

One of the creatures that managed to avoid the pillars sprinted towards Gill as he still hunched over the ground. Seeing its trajectory and doubling back, Ava caught the skeleton's fist with the femur before it could crash upon his head. A crack formed in the bone from the force of the skeleton's blow. She gritted her teeth and, using all her might, pushed the creature back and took one last swing. The femur connected, knocking the creature's feet from underneath it but shattering the ossein weapon upon impact.

"Woo!" Valma cheered as she grabbed one of the smaller skeletons and spun it around, "Homestretch baby!" She thrust the skeleton from her hands and sent it hurtling into one of its brethren, their bones exploding off of each other like fireworks.

"Gill, you gotta get up," Ava tugged at Gillian's nightshirt.

He heard her call but could not will himself to move. Instead, the furious force within him drove his fingers deeper into the earth, turning the stone against his fingertips to soft dirt around his touch. The room shook again as the pillars vibrated, and with the shrill sound of shattering rock, pinions pierced out from all sides, branching out through the room. The skeletons that remained were bisected, but Valma, in the middle of the mason forest, was caught in the crossfire.

Quick on her feet, she maneuvered as best as she could. Bobbing, weaving, ducking, and dodging, flourishing the extents of her athletic ability… before being clotheslined by a particularly stealthy pillar that took advantage of her blind spot.

She cried out in pain.

"Gill, that's enough!" Ava shouted as she yanked him off the ground. His grasp on the earth tearing from him left a hollow ache in his chest as she heaved him to his feet.

The room stopped shaking, the pillars moved no more, and their labored breathing was the only sound.

"Stick? You alright?" Kaj called out, knees shaking as he stood. As much as he couldn't stand her meathead heroism, he could admit to himself that getting out of this hell hole would be a lot harder without her muscle around.

"Think I bruised something," Valma groaned as she slowly limped out from the thicket of masonry, "but otherwise, I'm fine." She walked towards the unnerved Gillian and patted his shoulder, "Impressive work. Maybe I'll talk to the captain about having you build an obstacle course near the barracks once we get out of this place."

Gill didn't respond. He stood, withdrawn by the emptiness in his veins, eyes fixated on his granite creations.

Valma looked at Ava, "Nice job to you too. Got one hell of a swing there."

"I'm better with a bow," she replied, the corner of her eyes squinted for a moment as she tried to purse the meaning behind Gill's despondence.

"Alright," Valma clapped, the rush of a good battle invigorating her, "let's search the place. See if there's anything we can use in here before moving forward." She directed, "Cici, you and me on the left. Kaj, you take the right. Ava, try to bring Gill back to reality."

Ortensia's legs wobbled as she rose from her hiding place between the doorjamb and Kaj's cloak. Valma walked over and offered her a hand, but she ignored it.

"What could possibly be of value in here?" Ortensia chided, covering the fear in her voice with conceit.

"Well, these torches for starters. Definitely will give us more light than some glowing fingers," she gestured for them to follow her as she wove her way through the disrupted stones, "plus it'll save his arms from giving out. Though it would be good strength training."

⸻

"Gill," Ava tugged gently on his hand, "Gillian, come on. If you're not gonna move, at least talk to me."

"I'm sorry," he uttered, his voice barely a whisper, his lips hardly moving.

"So you got a little carried away, it happens," she replied, "but you took out most of those monsters and saved all of us."

He turned towards Ava and looked at her blankly.

I saved them, he thought. The empty ache in his chest

started to subside as he focused on her honey brown eyes.

"I didn't even know you could do big magick like that. I thought you only knew how to fix bowstrings and sprout little plants," she smiled softly. He could tell she was trying her best to cheer him up with astonishment, a well-practiced skill of hers he'd bore witness to many times during their school days.

"Yeah, it, uh," he looked back at the pillars, "Hasn't come up much."

"Is this what happened last night?" she asked.

"Something like it."

"Well, it's good you're a part of the Convocation, then. I'm sure Master Gustav will help you learn how to control it better," she patted him on the shoulder. Her tone was overly sweet and consoling, like a mother trying to calm a frightened child.

He studied her face, noticing the subtle contrast between the smile on her face and the uncertainty hidden in the back of her gaze. The hollowness that echoed in his body was barely a memory now, replaced by guilt at making her fuss over him.

"Here's hoping," he let out a big sigh, becoming himself again before calling out, "I'm sorry for my magick going wild… again…."

"At least it wasn't in my house this time!" Ortensia called back, "And don't you think that just because you saved my life that you don't owe me at least a dozen arcane favors for what you did last night!"

"Ah," Ava's toothy false smile closed into a true one, "It's amazing how even in the middle of a terrifying dungeon filled with undead, she is still the worst thing we'll have to put up with."

Gillian laughed.

"Found the way out!" Kaj called out from behind one of the pillars, followed by the sound of stone grinding across stone.

He leaned next to the darkened exit, feigning boredom as they all made their way over to join him, "Took you long enough. I was getting lonely!"

"What else did you find?" Ava asked the group, rolling her eyes and ignoring Kaj's whines, "Any weapons or clues as to what's going on?"

"Well," Valma handed one of the two torches she held to Gill, "Took these off the wall, and Cici found a couple of crates."

"Anything good in them?" Kaj asked.

"Most of it was absolutely disgusting," Ortensia grimaced, "bloody rags and rusty blades."

"The blades will definitely come in handy," he said, "You got them on you?"

"You'd think I touch something like that? Let alone

hold it? Who knows where those things have been!" she scoffed.

While Valma had proven to be of some worth when it came to banter and brawn, and Ava and Gillian provided something easy on his eyes with some serious magick power from the latter, Ortensia's continued pretentiousness was getting under his skin.

Kaj snarled as he leaned down and stared her square in the eye, "I should have left you in that cell."

"Funny," Valma interjected, "I was thinking the same thing about you."

He could feel the Stick looming over him like some snarling guard dog but ignored her. He had to make it known that he wasn't going to let her get away with her shit attitude so easily.

"Where are the crates?" he hissed.

"Over behind the second pillar on the right." Ortensia seethed.

Her better-than-thou stubbornness made his stomach turn as he walked off towards the directions she gave.

"If there's a sword in there, I'll take it!" Valma called after him.

"A bow and some arrows if able," Ava added.

With some shuffling, clattering, and a few curses under his breath, Kaj returned to the group carrying one of the crates and placed it on the ground between them.

51

"We've got a rusty sword, a couple of daggers I didn't want, and a handaxe," he said.

"A couple of daggers you didn't want?" Ortensia asked pointedly.

"I mean," he shrugged and lifted his cloak to reveal two daggers, slightly sharper than the ones in the crate, "finders keepers am I right?"

"I found the box!" she dared to whine, pushing him over the edge.

"And you were too entitled to bring it over! So just try me, rich bitch!" he snapped back.

Awkward silence blanketed the group as they glared at each other.

"I'll take the ax, I guess," trying to move past the tension Ava crouched down and grabbed it from the box as Valma pulled out the sword. She looked up at Ortensia, who seemed to be locked in a psychic brawl with the elvefolk, "Ortensia. Which dagger do you want?"

She looked down her nose at Ava, "Whatever. It doesn't matter. It's not like I'm going to use it."

Ava rolled her eyes, more than used to her venomous nature, and grabbed a dagger with a more ornate handle, "Here. This one seems fancy enough for you."

Ortensia grimaced and took the dagger from her hand, pinching the handle between her fingertips, not wanting to touch it.

Ava grabbed the other dagger and held it out to Gillian, "Here. Just in case."

Gillian grabbed the blade and studied it in his hand. The tip was bent, and the edge had chips in it. *Definitely safer than hurdling magick rocks.*

Valma swiped the sword in the air a few times, testing its balance before turning back to the group, "Ready to move on?"

"I'll say," Ortensia huffed, turning on her heels and stomping out the door.

"Oh! Look who's brave now!" Valma called as she chased after her. Ava followed, and Gill watched her straighten her spine in mental preparation for another famous Ortensia Valborg temper tantrum. He followed closely behind, not wanting to lose sight of her as Kaj took point in the back.

"Thank the gods," Kaj leaned towards Gill and whispered, "Maybe she'll step on a trap, and we won't have to hear her anymore."

Gillian ignored him. *This is your fault, you idiot,* and kept walking.

CHAPTER THREE

Ortensia stormed down the dark hallway, driven by the need to do something, to move of her own accord, of her own choice. She mindlessly dug into her cuticles, a side effect of the pulsing restlessness that left her so unconcerned with the world around her she didn't even notice the torchlight behind her growing closer.

"Hey," Ortensia jumped as Valma's hand grabbed onto her shoulder, "What the matter with you?"

"What's the matter with me?" she snapped as she spun around to face the townsguard. Ortensia stared her down as best as she could as Valma stood a solid three heads taller than her, "I'm stuck in a death trap with people who treat me like garbage! That's what's the matter with me!"

"Oh, come on! So you don't get untied first, and you don't get the shiniest dagger. Is that treating you like garbage?" Valma teased, her playful tone and smiling demeanor further agitating the wake of Ortensia's annoyance, "Because if that's treating somebody like garbage, then every middle child in the entire kingdom must be living in filth."

"You wouldn't understand," she walked away from her. She needed to keep moving.

"You've never been told no before. Is that it?"

Ortensia turned back around and stomped her way back. Her restlessness had a focus now. If Valma wanted to get a reaction out of her, Ortensia was more than glad to oblige.

"I've been told no before. I may have nice clothes and a nice house, but I have definitely been told no before," she spat, poking her in the stomach.

"Well, you sure are acting like it's the end of the world to hear it," That stupid, easy-going smile remained plastered on Valma's face, goading her.

"Because it is!" she threw her arms up in the air, "I have no idea where we are! No clue who kidnapped us. No way to call for help. No guess as to what's lurking around the next corner. No way for me to protect myself because all I can do are stupid fucking parlor tricks!" Ortensia shook her hand, and a few pink glowing butterflies flew from her fingertips, the years of relentlessly practicing her illusion magicks making the gesture second nature, "All I have are no's right now, and I really don't need anymore!"

The shouted statement rattled through her chest, yet Valma still stood there smiling at her unfazed. Unable to stand looking at her a moment longer, she resumed her tirade down the hall, determined that nothing would stop her from getting out of this hellhole.

"Hey, she shouldn't go charging off like that," Kaj shouted at them, "If she's not careful, she could trigger something."

Valma rolled her eyes and jogged to catch up with her. If pointing out the ridiculousness of her tantrum didn't stop her, she was sure stonewalling her with a smile would have, but apparently Miss Ortensia Valborg was more stubborn than she imagined.

Good thing Valma loved a challenge.

"Can you slow down?" she called.

"No!" Ortensia didn't bother to look back at her, "See! Now I'm the one saying no. I'm getting the hell out of here, as fast as I can."

Valma could have sworn she saw her steps falter for a moment, slightly tripping on something under her foot, but Ortensia kept trudging forward.

"Cici!" Valma barked, frustration finally seeping in.

"That's not my name!" she barked back.

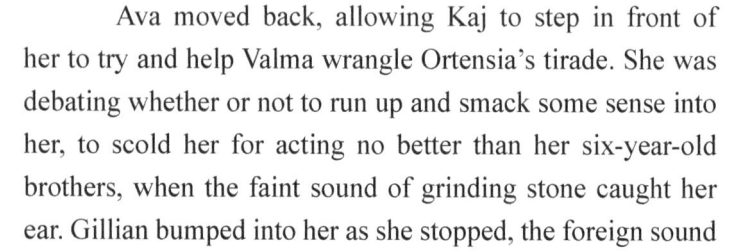

Ava moved back, allowing Kaj to step in front of her to try and help Valma wrangle Ortensia's tirade. She was debating whether or not to run up and smack some sense into her, to scold her for acting no better than her six-year-old brothers, when the faint sound of grinding stone caught her ear. Gillian bumped into her as she stopped, the foreign sound filling her with dread.

"Ava?" Gill asked.

She reached forward and grabbed Kaj's cloak, yanking him back mid-stride, "Do you hear that?"

Kaj stopped and listened past Valma and Ortensia's bickering, catching the tail end of the grinding as it gave way to a vibrating hum.

"Stop!" he shouted ahead.

Valma froze, the urgency in his voice raised the hairs on the back of her neck.

Ortensia kept walking.

"Ortensia!" she screamed, unable to hide her panic.

"I told you! N-" Ortensia's refusal was drowned out by an aching, echoing whine tearing through the tunnel. A chill of fear ran up her spine at its wail and her knees locked in place.

Rocketing out of the void above, jets of water bombarded them, hammering down in a monsoon.

"Run!" Kaj yelled, breaking free of Ava's hold on his cloak and charging forward.

The others followed suit: Gillian grabbed Ava's arm

and pulled her into a run alongside him; Valma took off into a sprint, picking up Ortensia as she passed.

"Dammit, Ortensia!" Ava shouted, holding her arm in front of her face to keep the spray from blinding her, "Why couldn't you just listen for once?!"

Rising water submerged the stones beneath them, cutting their speed. Their muscles and lungs burned as they pushed through the flood, searching for any means of survival. Luckily, the torches they held were made of enchanted flame, lighting their way through the downpour as the water reached up to their waists.

"I see a door!" Valma shouted.

The rising waters pressed heavily against their chests. They pushed past the pain and fatigue that pleaded their muscles to grind to a halt and picked up their pace as the door grew closer and closer.

Valma unceremoniously dropped Ortensia, sinking her under the water as she yanked at the door handle. She tried to push, but it wouldn't budge. She tried to pull, but the force of the water was too strong.

Ortensia swam up to the surface, gasping for air, "At least warn me next time!"

"Just shut the fuck up, will you?" Ava barked at her, "You're the reason this happened, you selfish bitch! Move!"

Her growing frustration with Ortensia and fear of

dying boiled into adrenaline. She shoved the six-foot pillar of muscle known as Valma out of the way as if she were lighter than a curtain. The rage fueled her, and she lifted her ax above her head to swing it at the door with all her might.

It sunk in. The wood splintered as she pulled it out to swing again. Chunks of wood fell away with ease, ripped apart or pushed out from the force of the water as she buried the head of her ax into it over and over again. In under a minute, she carved a hole in the door wide enough for even Valma's broad shoulders to fit through.

"Go!" her glare was fierce and dominating as she commanded, snapping the others to attention and driving them to jump through.

They fell into the room, and the water tumbled in with them, seeking to fill their temporary sanctuary as it poured in through the splintered opening.

"Gillian," Ava called as the force of the water pushed her through the door last. Her focus locked on to the redhead, "that spell you fixed my bow with, can you use it to fix the door?"

"I think so," he stumbled as he forced his way to stand in front of the door. The flow of water turned into a rush as the tunnel continued to fill, knocking him back as he struggled to stand still against it. Ava caught him as he fell back into her, propping him up as best as she could as the waters threatened to sweep their knees out from underneath them.

"Help me hold him!" she ordered.

Kaj and Valma rushed up to grab hold of him, lending their strength to prop up the mage, yet still they slowly slipped, the force of the water just a bit greater than their strength. Ortensia looked on, frozen.

"Come on!" Valma shouted at her, "We need you!"

"How?! I'm not strong!" Ortensia protested. This was all too much for her to handle.

"Ortensia!" Ava growled, the farm girl's wild eyes bore through her, her brown irises looking a daunting black in her anger, "If you don't get over here and help, we will drown! And if we drown, I swear on Messis I will make sure you go first!"

She flinched from the bite in Ava's voice, the sincerity and ferocity behind her threat igniting the few fight instincts Ortensia held. Control of her body returned to her, and she ran to brace herself against Valma's legs.

With Ortensia's added weight against him, Gillian's footing stabilized. He held his hands in front of him, channeling his magick as he muttered an incantation of Wakorin.

"Asavown mothdab knahafee xifirths!" A silver glow spread out from his palms and coated the door allowing the pieces of shattered wood to reverse in time. The splinters and chunks flew back into place, restoring the door to its former state.

The geyser stopped. The door sealed entirely and held the water back. They all let out a collective sigh of relief and slowly let go of Gill.

Ava crouched down, hanging her head between her shoulders to calm her nerves as her arms leaned against her ax handle. Her heart hammered in her chest. The urge to fight that so suddenly overcame her, the need to attack, to tear something apart with her bare hands, was foreign and all-consuming and perhaps even more frightening than the thought of her dying in this dungeon.

"Okay, so," Kaj was the first to speak, "I'm going first from now on."

"Barncombe," Ortensia cut him off, giving her that haughty "how dare you" glare that Ava hated so much, "Don't you ever speak to me like that again."

Her hands gripped the ax handle tightly, knuckles turning white, "Or fucking what?" she snapped back.

"Or I'll have my father tax your family's farm into ruin."

"When are you gonna tell him that, huh? After you die in this dungeon, you miserly bitch?" her long-held hatred of the half-dwarfed flared up, refueling the fear-induced fury she was trying to control. With the slam of her ax head on the granite floor, she jumped to her feet.

"Ava-" Valma moved to intervene, going to place a hand on Ava's shoulder.

"No," Ava knocked her hand away and stalked closer to Ortensia, "You haven't had to see the people you love put up with her and her family's heinous behavior for the past five years!"

Ortensia stood stalwart as Ava closed in on her, her face locked in a vicious scowl.

"Even in a dungeon, potentially miles below the earth, where death is looming around. Every. Fucking. Corner. You can't get through your own thick, narcissistic skull for one moment to save yourself." Ava spat in her face, "I know for a fact you would never do it to save one of us," she pointed to the rest of the group, "but to be so self-obsessed and ignorant that you ignore self-preservation? That's pathetic."

"I am thinking of my self-preservation!" she dared to scream in her face.

"Is that why you wanted to drown yourself?!" Ava roared.

Gillian winced. He never heard Ava raise her voice like this.

"If you were trying to make sure you got out of here alive, you would have been scouring that hallway for traps. You would have stayed in the back and had the rest of us do the dirty work for you. That's what you would have done!"

"I'm not an adventurer; I wouldn't-" Ortensia started.

"Neither am I! Neither is Gill!" she interjected, "We know we aren't, so we let Kaj and Valma take charge! To survive this, we need to work together using each other's strengths!"

"And what are my strengths, huh?" tears welled in Ortensia's eyes. Her voice cracked, "I'm not strong, or cunning, or perceptive... my magick is barely anything worthwhile! What am I supposed to do?"

"Let us help you," the edge in Ava's voice subsided in an instant. Seeing Ortensia cry for the first time, driven by all that self-doubt, poured cold water on her burning aggravation, "you can have strength in learning to let go; that you don't have to control everything all the time. I know that's hard for you, but if you let us take the lead here, you can live to rule the world another day."

"Sure," Ortensia snickered, "like I have control of my life outside of here. I can't even choose what dress I want to wear to dinner."

"Maybe surviving here will change that," Valma piped up, clearly desperate to cut the tension in the room by how she kept shifting her weight, "Escaping being kidnapped and surviving a trapped tomb full of undead sounds pretty powerful to me. The outside world doesn't need to know specifically how it happened."

"Muffy," catching her attempts to cool things down, Kaj leaned over towards Gillian and put on his snobbiest noble impersonation. "Did you hear about how that Valborg girl single-handedly escaped a necromantic crypt and saved four of the local townsfolk? How impressive!"

"Uh-" Gillian stared at him, confused. Kaj elbowed him in the side, urging him to play along.

"Yes? Quite?" he added.

"See?" Valma smiled softly, giving the guys' a quick sidelong glance in gratitude.

The tears in Ortensia's eyes slowed, and her scowl eased. She exhaled and wiped her face, "Alright. I'll follow your lead."

"Thank you," Ava said begrudgingly. She straightened up and looked at the others, "Now. Where are we?"

They looked around the room they blindly entered. Gillian and Valma raised their torches and stepped forward to help illuminate the chamber with soft light.

The room was stone, unsurprising considering every other tunnel and chamber they passed through were stone as well, but instead of the plainly carved rock they'd grown accustomed to, a large geometric pattern was carved into the floor. The deep-set lines led to a stone altar caked in dried blood.

"What the hell?" Valma uttered under her breath as she made her way closer to the altar. The light from her torch spread over onto the wall behind it, revealing a mosaic glittering behind it.

The multicolored tile formed a terrifying landscape: a mob of dark fae ripping people limb from limb danced across barren hills. Some ate the appendages, others paraded around with them like batons, and some used the limbs in depraved acts of self-satisfaction. From the rampage, the spirits of the slaughtered rose into the air, gathering into the nostrils of a giant dark fae warrior's floating head. His eyes spiralled and red with madness as his fanged mouth grinned in rapturous delight.

Gillian, however, did not notice the mosaic. He was too busy running his torch along the outskirts of the room, following the carvings on the ground to get a mental picture of the rune in his head.

"This doesn't make any sense," he muttered.

"A lot of things don't make sense right now, Wizkid," Kaj said from somewhere behind him, "You're gonna have to be more specific."

"This rune isn't for any of the major deities," he clarified.

"What about a minor deity?" Ortensia's voice was small and frightened.

He lifted his attention from the ground and found her with a wide-eyed look of fearful realization that he traced across the room to the demonic mural.

"Mighty Messis," he swore, nearly dropping his torch at the sight.

"Do you know something about this?" Valma asked Ortensia.

She nodded. "Last night at dinner, my father mentioned a book he came across in his library. An old tome written in the ancient language of the fae," she swallowed, "It mentioned that the town was built over the tomb of an ancient dark fae warrior, one who fought and was even worshiped pre-Balance. That's why Elerrï was a barren wasteland before Messis' blessing."

Ava snapped her fingers, "Runden?"

As the name left her lips, the temperature of the room dropped. A chill surged up their spines as their breath billowed out small clouds in the low torchlight. They turned to face each other, the knowing fear that something bad was about to happen in their eyes, and raised their weapons.

Silence. The temperature continued to drop, leaving all but Valma and Gill shivering.

"This is ridiculous. What are we-" Ortensia's complaints cut off as a smokey gray gust rose out from the floor and rushed into her open mouth. She staggered back, choking. Her eyes bulged in panic before suddenly closing—ending her gagging with a swallow as her body relaxed.

"Cici, are you-" Valma met the same fate as another stream of smokey gray wind came up from the floor and forced its way down her throat.

The rest of the group stood there in silence, eyes terrified, mouths shut, watching their companions cautiously.

The girls regained their composure and opened pupilless eyes, utterly white with trails of smoke swirling in them. Twisted smiles curled up their faces.

"This one's strong," Valma said, her voice replaced with that of a raspy, breathless entity.

"Mine's got tricks," Ortensia's head cocked to the side. Her nasal voice darker and deeper. Her hands outstretched to her sides, and in a pink flash of light, five Ortensias appeared beside her, all holding daggers.

Valma cracked her knuckles and stared down Gillian. "Your blood will taste so sweet on my tongue," she hissed as she drew her sword and rushed towards him.

He tried to jump out of the way, but the blade still connected, slashing across his arm. Forcing himself to keep his mouth closed, he let out a muffled groan of pain.

Ortensia and her clones surrounded Kaj and Ava, ready to strike.

Seeing Valma strike Gill, Ava's focus became singular. Unknown instincts kicking in, she sprinted towards the clones, abandoning Kaj as she cut down two illusions with her ax. They turned to pink dust in her wake as she continued forward.

Kaj tried in vain to find the true Ortensia as the doppelgangers closed in. They were identical and terrifying. Kaj thought he hated the pretentious pout she normally sported but found him missing it when faced with four of her most murderous smiles. Not liking his options, he threw a dagger at the one in front of him, hoping that for once, the odds would be on his side.

They weren't. His dagger sailed through the air and pierced right into Ortensia's eye, turning it to dust. The remaining Ortensias chuckled heartily as they rushed in and pierced three blades into Kaj: two in his side, one in his back.

Valma swung at Gillian again, but her blade caught the handle of Ava's ax as she pushed her way between them. She leaned in close to the farm girl, leering at her through clouded eyes, "Now you look like a fun challenge."

Ava's nose wrinkled in aggravation, and she snarled. With a sudden surge of strength, she shoved Valma's blade back and took the opportunity to swing at her ribs. The blunt end of her ax head crashed into her side with a sickening thud, sending the specter who possessed the townsguard flying.

Out of Valma's body and now hovering in the air, a smokey face with hollow eyes and a large gaping mouth loomed over Ava. Its non-corporeal form writhed and roiled, waiting for another host to make itself known.

Gillian, thrown back by Ava, saw Kaj doubled over in pain and covered with Ortensias as he regained his bearings. He scrambled to his feet, rushed over, and reached out to grab the Ortensia clinging to his back. His hands gripped onto solid flesh. He ripped the real Ortensia off of him and pinned her against his chest.

"Let go of me, you bastard!" she shouted. Hearing their master's cries, the illusions pulled their blades out of the elvefolk and moved to encircle Gill.

No longer a shish kebab, Kaj whipped around and cracked Ortensia against the side of her head as she squirmed in Gillian's grasp with the handle of his dagger, hoping that knocking her out would stop her spell. Instead, his strike cast the spirit out, stilling the illusions before they could attack.

Overexerted from his attack and relieved to have avoided being skewered once more, he doubled over in pain and fell to his knees, clutching at his wounds while he held back the litany of swears he desperately wanted to release.

With no mouths open and enraged from being so easily exorcised, the smokey spirits swirled around the chamber, flying faster and faster into a whirlwind that pelted the party with loose stones in its wake.

Valma staggered, grabbing at her side and shaking her head as she regained some sense of self. A spirit swooped down towards her, mouth agape as it released a shrieking wail. She attempted to swipe at the phantom, but her blade phased through the creature without a sign of impact or injury.

Ortensia nearly jumped out of her skin as she came to, finding herself not only grappled by Gillian but staring at two exact copies of herself.

The copies cocked their heads and looked at her expectantly.

Gravel flew at her face as a specter whizzed between them, shaking her out of her stupor. She squirmed her way out of Gill's grasp and glared at her clones.

What the hell are they looking at me for? she thought, *Attack the ghosts, you idiots!*

At her unsaid command, the duplicates leaped at the swirling spirits. One missed, dissipating as its ill-timed leap sent it slamming against the wall, but the other hit its mark. The phantom shrieked as the doppelganger's magick knife embedded deep within it, much to Kaj, Ortensia, and Gillian's surprise as they looked on.

The duplicate continued to hack away at the ghost, shredding it to pieces before turning its sights on the spirit attacking Valma and Ava.

Too busy enjoying taunting its former vessel, the spirit noticed the half-dwarf illusion a moment too late. The clone descended upon it, carving the specter apart like a master butcher, and eviscerated it in seconds.

Ava and Valma's heads snapped back and forth between the illusory Ortensia and the real Ortensia, wearing identical twisted faces of confusion. Ortensia scowled and shrugged at their unspoken questions. The illusion mimicked her.

Gillian held a finger to his mouth, signaling them to remain quiet, and gestured frantically to Kaj, still hunched over on the floor. He would be no help to him now, not without any herbs or potions, but he knew Ava fixed her fair share of wounded cattle and that basic triage was taught to every Berylwood Bastion. His talents would be better suited for finding a way out of this room.

They rushed over to Kaj, and Gill took his torch around the room once more. He closed his eyes and ran his hands along the stone walls. He searched for the familiar hum of a cloaking spell, the same kind his mentor used to hide important rooms from nosy guests at his manor. It was just a hunch given the powerful magicks that bound the spirits to this room, but Master Gustav taught him that hunches should never be ignored.

His fingertips buzzed as he approached the mural. He followed the sensation as it grew, the buzzing turn to the tingle of a thousand ants crawling across his skin as he traced across the mosaic's cool tiles. He stopped and found his resting on the black of Runden's right nostril. He held his flame closer and puffed up in pride as set inside the onyx tiles hid a few that were matte black instead of polished, forming a hidden sigil of concealment. Gillian pulled his dagger out of his belt and dug the point beneath one of them. With the right angle and a hard push, one of the matte tiles came free, and a hidden door materialized in front of him.

Ortensia tapped Valma on the shoulder and gestured to the open door. She and Ava threw Kaj's arms over their shoulders and carried the wounded rogue over, taking care to maintain pressure on the bleeding punctures as they exited.

Gill and the dual Ortensias led the way down yet another dark tunnel, putting as much distance as they could between them and the room until Kaj's weight grew heavy against Valma and Ava's shoulders and his knees started to give out from the blood loss.

"You can make magick clones that can stab people?" he seethed as Ava propped him up and held him steady against the wall while Valma lifted his shirt to get a better look at his wounds.

"Apparently!" Ortensia and her clone said in unison.

She glared at her doppelganger.

"Oh, don't be annoying," it doubled her speech again.

She rolled her eyes and slapped it across the face, turning it to dust.

"That's some real powerful Osla magick," Gillian studied Ortensia with academic curiosity, "Do you remember what it felt like when the ghost triggered it?"

"I think so," she knit her brow and closed her eyes. The memory of smokey trails crawling through her nerves still lingered, and she traced the path it took through her body until she found a familiar pulse of willpower in the back of her brain that sent tingles down her spine as she consciously accessed it.

"Fuck! No!" Kaj shouted.

She opened her eyes and found the five illusions of her resummoned to her side.

"Keep those things away from me!" Kaj winced as he tried to curl into himself, fearing another attack.

"Stop moving!" Valma barked. She pushed her fingers around one of his stab wounds, making the world spin in blinding pain.

"You're bleeding pretty badly," she grimaced, "I'm gonna have to cut off part of your cloak to stop it up." She went to grab a fistful of the ratty black fabric, but he smacked her hand away.

"No fucking way."

"Come on, man. Some shitty piece of wool ain't worth bleeding out for."

If his mind wasn't mush from contestant pulsing agony, he would have taken her comment as an insult and spat back about his cloak having more character than the dime-a-dozen carbon-copy armor she wore. But, his brain was too focused on survival and saving his precious cloak by any means necessary to make a cutting remark.

"Would paper work?" he grunted as Valma pressed a

little harder against the wound.

"Where do you have paper?"

He fumbled as he hurried to pull one of the books out of the back of his pants. With shaking hands, he ripped out a couple of pages and thrust them at Valma.

A collection of confused expressions stared back at him.

"What? Thieves can have hobbies!" he shook the pages in Valma's face, and she took them warily. "Now, can you make those pompous imps of yours disappear? They're giving me agita."

"Really?" Ortensia smiled deviously. The clones all stepped closer to him, bearing the same sickening grin as they did when they stabbed him. Rightfully on edge from their initial attack, Kaj acted on instinct and went to kick one of them but seized in pain when he tried to jerk his knee up. A rush of blood trickled down his stomach.

"Cici," Valma looked back at Ortensia, a false smile on her face as she pleaded, "tease him after I plug up the puncture wounds."

"Fine," she waved her hand, and the clones scattered into dust.

She puffed out her chest and faced Ava, "Guess I'm strong after all, huh, Barncombe?"

"I guess," Ava mumbled.

Of course, she thought, *fate would give you magick murder clones right after that breakdown.*

"What do you mean, you guess?!" she scoffed. Ava bit her tongue and focused on trying to keep her arm from going numb as Kaj's body pinned it against the rock.

Valma stuffed the last bit of paper into his wounds and stood, "Alright. That should do it for a little bit, but it won't hold forever. None of you magick types know how to heal, do you?"

"I can make some healing elixirs, but it takes a lot of ingredients and a lot of time," Gillian replied.

"If we're near the town, we can take him over to Dr. Averye's and get him patched up," Ava said as she helped Kaj stand.

"Let's get going then." His feet underneath him, he let go of Ava, smiling at her in gratitude despite the immense pain he was in, and took a few shaky steps forward.

CHAPTER FOUR

Kaj never thought he'd be so happy to see the ugly mug of a dark fae emerge from the shadows. They could have been walking for minutes or hours through these mind-numbing tunnels, but time was no longer a concept he comprehended. The constant throbbing heat that shot from his stomach seized a bit of his sanity with every step, and if it wasn't for Runden being the direct cause of his torment, he would have sworn his every allegiance to the swirly-eyed fuck at the sight of his visage gracing the symbol of their salvation: a door.

They approached it silently, keeping alert for traps, dreading what lay ahead. Valma held up her hand as she and Kaj inched closer, signalling the others to stop and listen.

"To he who always rises, no matter how time flows," muffled voices chanted beyond the door.

She looked back at the others to confirm they heard it and found their faces stiff with dread, while Kaj continued staring forward, eyes glazed over in pain.

"Laughing in the face of those who rob us of our rights, we offer you a gift..."

Valma locked eyes with Ortensia and smirked. The half-dwarf nodded, understanding her unspoken request, and conjured her clones, daggers at the ready.

"To feed the source of endless life...."

Ava patted Gillian on his shoulder as she readied her ax and stepped past him.

"We harvest the meager shreds the false gods left behind...."

Valma pushed the borderline catatonic Kaj behind her and smiled widely as Ava and Ortensia stepped up by her side.

"...and claim that which they stole from us...."

Knock knock, she thought playfully. Giddy at the promise of the battle ahead, she pulled her leg back and kicked the door down.

A choking, agonizing scream rang out as the door ripped off its hinges and fell to the ground.

Five figures, dressed in dark robes with bronze masks cast in Runden's horrifying image, stood in the room. Three of them guarded a wooden door at the back of the chamber, standing witness as one of their compatriots, tall and opposing, buried a dark, curved blade into the throat of a young, blonde man on his knees before him. Another member knelt beside the sacrifice, catching the dark blood in a bowl that rushed from his neck.

At the crack of the door against the ground, their heads snapped to face the group in eerie synchronization, creating an intimidating visage as the sharp change in angle cast their bronze masks red from the fires that lit the room.

"What is this?" The tall figure seethed, ripping his blade out of the man's throat and dropping his lifeless body to the ground.

Ava and Ortensia stalled, but Valma rushed towards him, unflinching, blade at the ready.

To the right, one of the onlookers drew forth a bow and let loose an arrow that caught Valma in the thigh as she closed in on the tall man. She stumbled as it embedded, and her blade swung wide. He stepped out of the strike's path laughing.

His morbid laugh urged Ava to action. Her eyes followed the arrow's path and locked on to the archer, bringing forth a singular thought.

I need that bow.

Her fear turned to ferocity, and she charged towards them.

"I'll be taking that!" she challenged, the bold words tumbling out of her mouth as if she always said such courageous things.

"I'd like to see you try," he hissed at her. She focused

on the arrowhead, instinctively watching his technique, and as he let go of the string, she shifted her sprint slightly to the left.

Ava couldn't help the smug smile on her face as the arrow breezed past her. The archer swore and reached back into his quiver for another arrow but was too late as she buried the sharp end of her ax into his side.

The kneeling figure threw her bowl to the side and stood, turning to swipe at Valma with a hidden blade she pulled from her robes.

Two of Ortensia's illusions jumped on her before she could connect. One pierced a dagger right through her collarbone, and the figure cried out in pain. The other she managed to slice with her knife as she swung wildly, turning it to pink powder.

Ortensia's mind raced as she sent the other three illusions to back up Valma and rushed to the side of the man bleeding out on the ground, hoping that the face she saw was different than the one she remembered- that his outfit was just a coincidence.

Her small hands pushed the damp and matted hair out of his face, and her stomach turned as her fears were confirmed. She just witnessed the death of Lord Octavian Venzor.

Her potential suitor's blonde hair and pale skin were nearly unrecognizable under all the blood and filth. He still wore the tacky wheat stalk patterned suit from their matchmaking dinner the evening prior. As she ran a hand down his bloodstained lapel, she worried about how disappointed her father would be at this turn of events; he seemed so excited at the thought of his daughter marrying up.

Well, she thought as she wiped his blood off her fingers and onto the handkerchief in his pocket, *this works out for me a bit. He was quite boring.*

⸻

Gillian ran into the room after them, leaving Kaj to hide outside the door frame, and tried to make sense of the cacophony unfolding in front of him.

He readied his chipped dagger and searched for the familiar swish of Ava's wild, long brown hair. He spotted Ava as the other masked figures guarding the door rushed her from the left, her back towards them as she yanked her ax out of the archer's stomach. She didn't notice the assailants incoming, swords drawn and ready to sink into her flesh.

"Ava!" Gill shouted. The dagger clattered on the ground as his arm moved on its own.

Pulled by an unseen force stronger than his will, he ran his arm, palm flattened and turned on its side, parallel to the floor. He felt the earth beneath drawn to him, tracing the motion of his fingertips as he pointed at the space between Ava and her oncoming assailants.

Stop them, his heart pleaded.

A wall of stone erupted from the ground into the middle of their path and knocked the figures back as they ran headfirst into it.

The earth, of its own accord, yanked at the force connecting them and Gillian's wrist flicked back as if it were swatting a fly. The stone slab rocketed across the room, catching the assailants in its wake and flattening them with a gurgling crunch against the wall.

He jumped as the blood splattered out of the sides of his stone barricade, flowing down the wall in a macabre mural of bright crimson streams and flesh turned to plaster. The connection severed from the shock, and his arm fell limp.

A hollow chill ran through him. The will to fight lost in the spatter of his accidental art piece.

"Get off me, you vile little girl!" The masked woman shrieked, yanking the clone attached to her off.

The illusion blew a raspberry as it hit the ground and disappeared in a pink puff of dust. She swiped at one of the illusions nearby as they flanked the tall man, dispelling it before turning around to find the true Ortensia knelt on the ground.

"Cici! Look out!" Kaj shouted. Clearing his mind as best he could, he leaned around the door frame and threw a dagger clear across the room. With well-practiced precision and muscle memory taking the reins, the blade drove into the woman's throat as she snuck behind the half-dwarf.

She let out a gurgling cry as she fell to the floor, clutching at her throat as the blood rushed from it.

Yeah, being stabbed sucks, don't it bitch? he thought as he slumped against the doorway, exhausted from the effort of his throw.

"No!" the tall man bellowed as the woman fell, his attention pulling away from the townsguard for a brief moment.

Valma seized the opportunity and swung at him, cutting into his right arm and nearly severing it from his body. Ortensia's illusions advanced as he staggered back from her blow but turned to dust as his blade swiped through them in an upward arch. The pink dust blocked her sight, hiding the tall man as he changed his blade's trajectory and brought it down, cutting through the cloud to bury the steel into Valma's shoulder.

Defenseless and gravely wounded from the ax blow to his stomach, the archer knelt at Ava's feet. She threw her ax to the side, ripped the bow from his limp grasp, and stole the quiver off his back before shoving him to the ground.

Hands shaking and adrenaline pumping from reaching her quarry, she turned back towards the action to see the tall man looming over Valma, his sword buried in her shoulder. The fear and pain in her newfound friend's eyes centered Ava, and without second thought and with quick precision, she let loose two arrows. Too fast to be seen, they buried into the tall man: one piercing through his skull, the other piercing through his heart.

Valma jolted in surprise as an arrow pierced through to the other side of her attacker's skull, knocking his bronze mask off. His grip on his sword loosened as the light left his pale blue eyes, and he fell to the ground, dead. A ways behind him stood a farm girl with her steady bow arm poised for another strike.

Valma gritted her teeth and pulled his blade out of her shoulder. She smiled through the pain at Ava and nodded, "We should have gotten you a bow sooner."

She said nothing back.

Ava stared at the body, stared at the blood slowly pooling on the stone floor, stared at the unnatural position of his arms as the ferocity that possessed her vanished, replaced by an emotion she didn't quite know how to feel.

Slowly, she lowered her bow as some part of her mind urged her to look for Gill. His eyes drifted to meet hers, pulling away from the carnage around them as if he knew she was searching for him.

They stared at each other blankly, the distance in their eyes fading away as the reality of their actions sunk in. Ava and Gillian had known each other for years. They knew the subtle tells in each other's expression, how each other's posture shifted when they were sad, even though they were not as close as they'd once been in recent years. The emotion that crossed their faces now was something entirely new, so it was only natural that they would share it together. Share in the horrifying realization of how easily they took a human life… and the unenviable terror of being afraid of oneself.

Valma lifted the head of her fallen adversary and studied it. His cheekbones were more sunken than she remembered, his skin only a shade paler than when he was living, but there was no doubt in her mind that Lord Elias Venzor laid slain before her.

"Who are these bastards?" Kaj said as he limped into the room.

"Lord Venzor," she replied.

"What?" The name pulled Gillian out of his head, and he peeled his eyes away from Ava to look for himself.

"It can't be," Ortensia stood.

"It is," he confirmed as he approached the body. He remembered the man's piercing blue gaze as he sat across from him at the Valborgs' dinner table.

"Then he killed his son," Ortensia added. She shifted back and forth between the son at her feet and the father at Gill's, "Why would he kill his son?"

His eyes darted to the body beside her, "That's-"

"Octavian."

Gillian ran his fingers across the nape of his neck and pulled at his hair, "We have to check the other bodies."

Neurosis knotted his stomach with an immediate need for answers. He hurriedly made his way over to the corpse behind Ava and pulled off its mask, "I don't know this one. An older man, balding at the top, tufts of white hair on the sides."

"That sounds like their carriage driver. Which means this must be-" Ortensia's hands shook as she removed the mask from the woman behind her. With Kaj's dagger still embedded in her throat and blue eyes frozen with the fear of death, a dead Lady Driabella Venzor stared back at her.

"-his mother." her voice caught. Confusion and disappointment raked through her heart. She struggled to connect her monstrous actions to the image of the woman so vivacious and kind to her the night prior.

"That is absolutely heartwarming to hear." Lady Venzor's ivory skin glowed gold in the light of the fireplace as she gestured for Ortensia to sit beside her, *"Dedication to one's family is an extremely desirable trait in a wife."*

The memory of her warm words burned the back of her throat with betrayal.

"Well, this is a fucking nightmare then," Kaj stated.

"It wasn't already?" Ava responded. Her voice was distant, almost disembodied, as she watched him hobble over and rip the arrow out of Lord Venzor's chest.

"We weren't the murderers of an entire family of nobles before now."

"Oh, come on now, they were evil," Valma scoffed, "We've got clear evidence of them being super evil," she gestured around the shrine with her good arm.

"People fake evidence and make shit disappear all the time, Stick," he tossed the arrows on top of the archer's body before heading for the door, "so we better make sure that nobody can access this place except us when we get out of here."

"We can't just leave their bodies here!" Ortensia's voice cracked. She tore her gaze away from the dead woman's face and looked to Valma.

The worry and sorrow in Ortensia's eyes tightened the usually unshakable townsguard's chest.

"We can, and we should," Valma replied with a heavy sigh, "None of us are in any condition to be carrying corpses. Plus, as much as I hate to admit it, Kaj is right. We need to leave everything the way we found it, so we don't hurt our case."

She pulled Kaj's dagger out of Lady Venzor's throat and placed a hand on Ortensia's shoulder, "I know it may seem cruel, but it's for the best. You don't want us to be accused of their crimes, do you?"

Ortensia frowned, holding back tears as she took one last look at Lady Venzor's face, then walked away with her to join Kaj. Valma moved her hand to press gently against her shoulders, and Ortensia made no attempts to remove it.

Ava stared at the arrows Kaj so casually discarded onto the torn stomach of the dead archer, and bile burned in the back of her throat. She jumped as a warm weight wrapped around her but calmed when she realized it was Gillian placing an arm on her shoulder to steer her away.

"They were evil people," he whispered to her. She felt his hand trembling as he tried to justify their actions.

"But they were still people," she whispered back, her voice hoarse.

The knots in his stomach pulled even tighter.

"Can you make a stone wall in front of the door after we leave, Wizkid?" Kaj asked.

"Should be able to," he said. Gill dropped his arm from Ava's shoulder and flexed his hands, recalling the sensation of the earth tethered to him.

"Good," Kaj nodded. Valma handed him his dagger back, and he returned it to his belt, "Then let's get the hell out of this hellhole and leave this mess behind."

With Kaj's stilted gait leading the way, they walked out of the chamber and let the heavy wooden door slam behind them.

      The others stood back as Gillian positioned himself before the door and placed his hands against the stone walls of the cavern to cement his connection. Something told him that the earth was ready to move, wanting to move wherever he led it. He tore his hands from the wall with a clap, drawing forth two slabs of stone from either side of the tunnel and sealing the massacre away.

CHAPTER FIVE

Their calves burned as they made their way through another stretch of seemingly infinite tunnel. Though they were weary, the steep incline was a good sign, one of the few good things they could focus on as the ache of their wounds and the questioning of their morals grew heavy on their shoulders. Eventually, the dark of the tunnels lightened, rounding one final corner before the flash of daylight blinded them.

Sunlight melted their worries and dulled their pains with hope as they pushed into a stilted run, with Gillian and Ava helping Kaj and Ortensia keeping pace with Valma. Crossing the illuminated threshold, the suffocating stone gave way to the shaded greens and browns of a vast forest. They slowed, leaves crunching beneath their feet, and looked behind them to find no cave or foreboding entrance warning travelers of the terrors beyond it but a large oak with a shaded hollow at its base.

"An illusion," Gillian panted.

"That's good," Kaj wheezed, "Won't be so easy for others to stumble into."

"Where are we?" Ortensia asked.

"The Shadowfen," Ava chewed at her lip as she took in their surroundings.

"That's a good thing, right?" Valma said, "The forest is only about a mile or so from town."

"Part of the forest is." Ava corrected, "The part kept safe by the blessing but…" She let go of Kaj and made her way towards a tree with decently low branches. She jumped and deftly hoisted herself up on one of the boughs.

"What are you doing?" Gill called up to her.

"I don't hear the river!" she answered and continued to climb. Alarms bells rang in her head, sending her heart racing and tightening her jaw with unease. In the woods near Elerrï, you could always hear the river.

As she crested the canopy, she shielded her eyes from the sun and found herself surrounded by a sea of trees. Behind her, about ten miles south to the west, sat a break in the treeline and the slight glints of sunlit water flashing through the shifting leaves. Ava's heart sank into her stomach, and she found herself hugging the tree's trunk for comfort.

They were miles from home, deep with the Shadowfen, where monsters roamed fueled by wild magicks and unhindered by man.

She highly considered camping here for the night. The canopy would be high enough to keep her safe for a while; but the four exhausted, wounded, and unprepared people below her in what she would consider, before the events of the past few hours, to be one of the most dangerous places in all of Berylwood, changed her mind. She scrambled down the tree as quickly and as carefully as possible, anxiously scanning the forest as she descended for any signs of monstrous movement.

"Well?" Ortensia shouted out as she saw the cream of Ava's nightgown peaking through the branches.

"Shhh!" she hissed.

Ortensia tensed, fighting the urge to bark at her for shushing her but the lingering burn of the smoky poltergeist forcing itself down her throat reminded her not to speak when commanded to be silent.

Ava reached the ground red-faced, hands cut up and raw, with her eyes darting all around the words in fear. "We're deep in the Shadowfen," she warned, too preoccupied with her search to look at them as she spoke, "ten miles from Cedar Lake."

"Shit," Valma swore.

"Hi. For us bleeding city folk back here, what the hell does that mean?" Though his breathing labored in pain, Kaj still seemed to find his wit.

Gillian's grip on Kaj's arm tightened, "It means we'll be walking for hours to reach town... through a forest full of monsters."

91

Ortensia paled and stepped closer to Valma, instantly glad to have a strong woman around that seemed to make a point of sticking by her side.

"Luckily, I didn't see any nearby as I made my way down, and I'll keep an eye out for tracks as we move," Ava looked to Gillian, "The herbs and mushrooms Master Gustav has you collect for the healing droughts, can they still heal someone even if they're not processed?"

"A bit, yeah," he replied, "Not as powerful as the full vigor, though."

"Then keep an eye out for them as we walk. We can use them to treat Kaj and Valma until we can get them to a healer. You could use some on that cut on your arm too."

"Of course."

"Alright then. Follow me," she checked in with Valma, who gave her a curt nod in agreement and readied her bow, "Keep your knees bent and your eyes peeled. These things will smell us miles before we see them."

She faced north and, taking a deep breath, steadied her nerves. *You'll be back home in no time. Just keep moving forward.*

She took her first steps through the brush, setting a slow pace for the injured of the group despite every single inch of her body screaming at her to run.

Following Ava's lead, they wove through the forest, stopping here and there as Gillian gathered medicinal plants and applied them to Kaj and Valma's wounds.

"I'm sorry, book, but I really don't want to die in some hicktown's woods," Kaj lamented as he tore more pages out and handed them to Gill.

The mage ran a sprig of ikiwort over it, smearing it with sap, and his academic curiosity couldn't help but read the page as he did so.

17 – Vesin – 887 AB, scratchy handwriting dated at the top of the page. **The King's builders have been working in the woods for three weeks now.**

"Hey, you gonna hurry up and apply that thing, or do you secretly want me to bleed out?" Kaj snapped.

"You know that book is a diary, a really old one too," Gill crumpled the paper sap side out and plunged it into the gash, "Where'd you find it?"

"Where do you think I found it?" he winced. His eyes darted towards Ortensia, checking to make sure she was out of earshot, "Don't say another word, alright? I already got enough holes in me from those psycho clones of hers."

"What if it's some family heirloom?" he slathered more sap over his skin, "Or was that what you were sent there to steal?"

"What I was sent to steal is none of your business," Kaj warned.

"What are you two mumbling about?" Ortensia glared at them as she finished tying her headscarf back around Valma's wounded shoulder.

"Whispering!" Ava hissed down, not taking her eyes off the horizon as she took watch in the canopy above.

"We good to go?" Valma whispered to the boys. Gillian wiped the sap and Kaj's blood off on his knees as he stood and nodded.

"All clear," she called up in a hush. Ava gave a stern nod in acknowledgment and made her way down.

"How are you all doing?" she asked as her bare feet softly landed on the forest floor.

"Still terrible," Kaj pulled down his shirt and took two steps on his own. He limped slighter now, "but feeling less close to death."

"The wrap is a bit tight," Valma moved her arm stiffly.

"You told me to apply pressure!" Ortensia hissed.

"Yeah, but I didn't think you'd try to cut off circulation," she snickered, playfully glancing at Ortensia's puckered face.

"Do you need me to loosen it?" she grumbled.

"No, no," she flexed her good arm, "My muscles will do it over time." Valma stared at Ortensia with a smug smile as she watched her eyes drift over her bicep before turning away with a huff.

"Let's keep moving," Ava, despite her tense demeanor, couldn't help but roll her eyes at the exchange, "We've only got an hour or two left of daylight, and I want to get as close to Elerrï as possible before we have to make camp." She took the lead again, resuming their trek.

"Make camp?" Ortensia followed behind her, Valma at her side, and Kaj and Gillian trailed in the back.

"Unfortunately," Ava replied, "that's not going to be a problem, is it?" her tone dropped in a warning.

"Nope," Ortensia bit her tongue. As much as she wanted to tell the farm girl off, the argument wasn't worth summoning a giant monstrosity to slaughter them, "What noblewoman wouldn't want to sleep in the middle of monster-infested woods?"

Gillian whispered into Kaj's ear, "It wasn't just jewelry, was it?"

Kaj mumbled back out of the corner of his mouth, "Not telling."

"Come on, who am I going to tell? I'm just a dopey mage's apprentice who makes a mess out of everything. What harm could I possibly bring?"

"Well, you turned two of those Runden cult freaks into people paste. So I would say a lot of harm."

The mirth Gill enjoyed while teasing Kaj vanished.

He suppressed the shiver that ran through him at the memory of their spines crunching beneath the stone slab.

"You think she has something to do with this?" Kaj asked.

"Who?" Gill swallowed, shoving the image to the back of his mind.

"Cici. She's the one who invited the Venzors to town for that dinner last night."

"Sure, but it was her dad who wanted her to marry Octavian. In fact, it was practically a done deal that they would be betrothed." he said, "After the meal, Lord Venzor said he would need to speak to his wife first, but otherwise, an official proposal would be made in the morning."

"Does she know that?" Kaj pointed a finger at Ortensia.

"I don't think so," Gillian answered, "Otherwise, I'd think she'd be more upset."

"Betrothed or not, she still should be more upset." he remarked, "In fact, she seemed more distraught about the mother than the son." He arched his eyebrow and gave a side glance to Gillian. Gill shook his head.

"Ortensia's cruel," he said, "but in the entitled brat kind of way, not the murderer kind of way."

"Well, anybody can be a murderer. Doesn't really matter if they're cruel." Kaj looked forward, eyes burning into the back of Ortensia's head.

Gillian bit the inside of his cheek. He looked at Ava with her bow at the ready and her movements much more predatory than he was accustomed too, and glanced down at his own hands.

"Alright. We'll camp here." Ava stopped at a small clearing as the forest sank deeper into the soft blue bath of dusk, "Kaj and Valma, gather some leaves and brush nearby for bedding. Gill and Ortensia go with them and look for wood for a fire. Make sure to keep your eyes open and ears perked."

"And what will you be doing?" Ortensia challenged. She looked up at her with that narrowed eye glare of entitlement that once made Ava feel inferior. Coupled with an upturned nose and puckered lips, Ortensia's highbrow prejudice was the bane of the townsfolk of Elerrï, scorning the efforts of their labor at the town festivals and belittling their simple lifestyle, and was only eclipsed by her father's indignation.

Ava pulled her release arm away, holding the arrow between her fingers, and placed her hand against her chest. They weren't in Elerrï, this wasn't a festival, and Burgermeister Valborg was nowhere to be found. Ava thrived in the forest, and she'd rather send an arrow through her foot than let Ortensia make her feel small here.

She thumped her palm against her chest slowly as her vision grazed across the lower branches of the canopy. Her drumming picked up its pace, a soft but fast beat that she rolled off with a flourish as her eyes locked on an unseen target. Ava twirled the arrow in her fingers, nocked it against the string as she lifted her bow, and fired. Small branches cracked overhead as a large grouse fell to the ground about twenty feet in front of her, and she smiled.

"Making dinner," Ava's face fell back to serious as she addressed Ortensia, "Don't wander too far off. I've got a decent range on this thing, but the nightstalkers are quick."

"N-nightstalkers?" she stuttered, her haughty expression slipped.

"Nasty panther-like motherfuckers created by the Goddess of Shadows herself," Valma said, kicking a rock in annoyance, "Let's get moving. The darker it gets, the more likely it is we'll bump into one, and as much as I'd love to brag to the guys back home that I took one on, my shoulder's too busted." She walked off pouting, and Ortensia hurried to follow behind.

They spread out, following her orders and leaving Ava alone. She exhaled for what felt like the first time since she woke up this morning. Though they were far from the woods she knew so well, the endless rows of tall trees and the smell of decaying earth still brought her comfort.

I wonder if Kieran is looking for me, slipped from the back of her mind and shot through her chest. Ava swallowed, pushing the thought aside to focus on anything else before the pain behind it brought tears.

She focused on dinner, readying her bow and shooting down two more birds, and set them on the ground to prepare them to roast. Her eyes coasted across the forest, checking for the familiar faces of her fellow captives among the trees one last time.

Ortensia seemed to be whining about the work as Valma listened, shaking her head softly with a smile on her face. Kaj and Gillian muttered closely to each other as they dutifully gathered supplies; Kaj wore a wry look on his face while ignoring Gill's despondent posture.

She looked away to the game resting in front of her. She grabbed one of the birds and turned it onto its back, splaying its wings open. She placed her feet on each wing, pinning its chest to the ground as she pulled the grouse up by its legs. It had been years since she'd seen Gillian look so sad, but it still made her want to go over and hug him. They weren't in primary school anymore; hugs wouldn't solve every problem. The grouse's spine followed its legs a damp snap, separating from the breast.

She repeated the process with the other two birds then found a flat rock to dress their legs on. It was difficult to slice the birds with an arrowhead, drawing all her conscious focus away from keeping her unconscious mind from wandering.

Kieran probably doesn't even notice I'm gone, which is probably for the best. Who would want to be with a cold-blooded murderer?

Lord Venzor's body seizing and falling limp as her arrows skewered him. The masked archer staggering to hold in his organs after she raked that ax across his stomach. The bloodied corpses scattered across the stone cavern floor. The scenes played over and over again, and she agonized over every gory detail.

She lost control of her body as the pounding of her heartbeat boomed in her ears, shaking out the tears she tried to keep at bay. Obsession threatened to drown her in its vortex with the unfiltered repetition of her actions, but her hands kept moving, kept butchering her prey: the practiced motions tethering her to reality like twine.

Guilt, sorrow, and horror consumed her.

So Ava couldn't have noticed the scattering of leaves behind her on this windless night.

But she could feel the searing pain of the nightstalker's claws tearing across her back.

Ripped from consumption straight into survival, Ava whipped around and swung her blood-soaked arrow into the cat that loomed over her. It screeched as the arrowhead pierced it and stumbled back.

The beast steadied itself, dug its paws into the forest floor, and snarled. Its slitted red eyes glowed through the shadows that rolled off of its pitch-colored body like smoke as it bared its long jagged teeth. It reared back, opening its mouth wide, and lunged.

Her mind went quiet when faced with the void of the cat's throat closing in, preparing itself for the empty fields of death to claim her.

But the Goddess Laeth's domain would be left waiting as charging forward, swinging her sword with her good arm, Valma slashed into the nightstalker's side. The beast flew back, letting loose a painful screech that shook the trees.

"You alright?" Valma asked as she positioned herself in front of Ava, blade at the ready.

Before she could answer, a dozen ear-splitting shrieks rang out around them, answering the nightstalker's cry. The hard thudding of wings drew their focus to the barely lit canopy and the dark shifting mass of a flock of birds heading their way.

"Skrills!" Ava shouted. Instinct took over, and she drew her bow, firing a flurry of arrows at the avian fiends. Frazzled, she only shot down two before they descended upon them. Razor-sharp talons tore at their skin, leaving stinging scrapes that oozed a soft green glow from the caustic poison that coated them.

Valma swiped wildly at the flock, cutting a few of them down as the nightstalker used the distraction to make another attack. The cat leaped through the birds, claws outstretched, and landed on Valma's chest. Its paws retracted, sinking its claws into her flesh, tearing out a painful cry from Valma's throat as it pinned her to the ground.

"Get off of her!" Ortensia shouted.

Her illusory clones dog-piled on top of the creature, daggers stabbing with reckless abandon into its shade hide. The nightstalker released the townsguard, bucking and swiping at the swarm of Ortensias that plagued it.

Two daggers whistled through the air, skewering the

birds that tore at Ava's hair as Kaj and Gillian ran to her side. Gill's palms glowed brightly, and the flashing rays of daylight scattered the remaining skrills. He offered Ava his gold-drenched hand as Kaj held his daggers at the ready, watching the birds as they flew off.

"You okay?" Ortensia hovered above Valma, concerned. The townsguard's lips curled into a snarl. She let out a furious grunt and jumped to her feet.

"I'm gonna neuter that cocksucker," she swore and charged towards the severely wounded nightstalker.

The last illusory clone of Ortensia clung to the beast's face, stabbing at its eyes. The cat raked its claws across its muzzle, ridding itself of the nuisance only to be met with the unfortunate sight of Valma's sword coming down upon its head.

Pushing past the pain in her shoulder for a two-handed strike, her fury-fueled strength drove the blade through the nightstalker's skull, splitting it in two. Its body dispersed into pure shade, joining the dark shadows of encroaching night as its limp form hit the ground.

"Everyone alright?" Gillian asked as the last of the skrills disappeared in the canopy.

"Yeah," Ava said half-heartedly, scratching at her arm as he helped her up.

He glanced down to see hives spreading across her skin—an unfortunate side effect of the skrills' acid.

"Shit," he dug around in his pockets, "I don't think I have the right ingredients to treat this."

"It's alright. I can rub mud on it for now to help the itching," she said. She pulled her hand out of Gill's and let out a heavy sigh, "I'm sorry, everyone."

"Sorry for what?" Kaj replied, "That big cat was sure to come eventually. I don't know what you could have done to stop it."

A lot of things, Ava grimaced.

"Did you all find enough brush to make camp?" Maybe if she focused on something else, her disappointment in herself would go away.

"Yeah," Ortensia added, "Valma had to drop hers to save your ass from being cat food."

But of course, Ortensia wouldn't let that happen.

"It's alright," Valma winced as she hobbled over, "it's not too far away. I can go grab it."

"No, I'll go get it." Gill insisted, holding up his luminous hands, "these bad boys will keep any nasty shadow beast far away."

"That's not the only thing they'll keep away," Ortensia remarked. Kaj and Valma chuckled under their breath.

"Haha. Very funny," Gill mocked. "Watch me as I walk just in case, alright?"

"Sure thing," Kaj answered, following him as

he walked off, "I don't know shit about setting up a camp anyways."

Ava picked up the remnants of their dinner. Her arms and back burned as she bent over, and tears blurred her sight. The fight stole their final minutes of daylight, and with the clearing still unprepared, the grouses halfway prepped, and her body screaming in agony at herself for being so careless, she came to an unfortunate realization.

"Ortensia, could you maybe conjure your clones again to help us prep the camp?" Ava hesitated to ask, "I wasn't going to ask but with Valma even more wounded than before and my back and arms all torn up-"

"Ugh," Ortensia rolled her eyes, "Just because I'm super powerful now doesn't mean you guys get to use my magicks all the time."

"Look, I was gonna do it all myself, but-"

"But now you're an inconvenience," she interrupted, and suddenly, Ava felt smaller than a bug.

"Cici-" Valma warned.

"You know what? I'm feeling fine all of a sudden," Ava limped away, shoulders stiff as she leaned down to pick up sticks to roast the birds on, "I'll do it myself."

"As you should. Make sure not to bleed in my bed." Ortensia boasted, a sick smirk on her face. It was good for the farm girl to learn not to be so cocky.

After Ava left earshot, Valma spoke up, "I don't know who hurt you, Cici, but you're not gonna get back at them by hurting others."

Ortensia whipped around to face her, armed with a cutting comment as her temper blistered in offense but came face to face with Valma's back as the townsguard hobbled away to rest.

CHAPTER SIX

The campfire was not the brightest ever built. Their meal was not the most delicious meal ever eaten. And the brush and leaf bedding was far from comfortable. But when compared to the onslaught of horrors they faced in just one very long day; the camp was a well-wanted respite.

"We should keep watch in pairs," Valma suggested as they sat around the fire finishing their meal, "and one of us will have to keep watch alone."

"I'll do it," Gillian volunteered, "I'm the least beat up out of all of us, so I don't mind. Plus, if anything gets close, I can just turn on the lights and send them scurrying." He held up his hands and wiggled his fingers.

"Okay then, you'll take first watch. Kaj and I are the most torn up, so we should probably go last so we can get some sleep. Which leaves Ortensia and Ava for the middle shift."

"What?" Ortensia squawked.

"Great," Ava grumbled as she pulled the last bits of

meat off of a drumstick.

"Why should I have to sacrifice my beauty sleep to keep watch?" Ortensia whined, "Despite her blunder earlier this evening, Ava is perfectly capable of keeping watching on her own."

"Ava's pretty scraped up," Valma stated coldly, "and other than a sore throat from that phantom jumping in you and some bruises, you seem to be in pretty good shape to me."

"That's so unfair," Ortensia pouted.

"This whole thing is unfair," Kaj chided. "You should be swimming in your frilly bed in that fancy manor yours. Stick should be snuggled in her bunk bed. Wizkid and Ava should be-" he paused for a moment, furrowing his brow in thought as his eyes darted between the two of them, "-wherever they should be. And I should be staying at a lovely brothel lounging on a bed of bodies a hundred miles away from here. So suck it up for tonight, Princess Pain-in-the-ass, and hopefully tomorrow you'll be back in your manor of mundanity."

"Well then," Ortensia stood with a huff, nostrils flared and fists clenched, "guess I should get a head start on my beauty sleep." She stomped away to the small pile of foliage Ava had made up for her.

Ava watched her walk over to the bed out of the corner of her eye. Ortensia pawed at the pile in vain to make it comfortable before laying on her side with her back to the group. A slight, wicked smirk crawled up Ava's face.

"What did you do?" Gill leaned over and whispered, catching her smile.

"Oh nothing," she glanced up at him, a spiteful glimmer in her eye, "it's just that I'm not sure if those leaves I saw were weeds or poison sumac."

He chuckled, "You know she's gonna be a nightmare during your watch because of that."

"When is she ever not a nightmare?" Ava rolled her eyes, "You'd think she'd be a little less of a brat after that screaming match her and I had down there."

"Yeah, that was intense." Gill ran an anxious hand through his curls, "You had your fair share of fights in school, but I've never seen you that angry before."

"I just couldn't stand it anymore!" her voice came out sharper than expected, and Gill flinched. His reaction sparked a flash of shame at her outburst, and she took a deep breath to calm herself, "The stress of the whole situation probably didn't help, either."

"Definitely not."

He chewed at the inside of his cheek and his eyes fell from her face to the fire, "This is a lot, Ava."

Her breath caught in her lungs. "I know."

The silence between them was stifling. She found herself longing for Kaj or Valma to interject, but Kaj was too engrossed in one of his books, and Valma busied herself by studying the sharpness of her blade.

"I don't-" Ava scraped her thumbnail across the long cleaned bones of her meal, "I don't know how I feel."

"I'm scared," he admitted, quiet enough for only her to hear, "I'm worried but like... it's all pushed in the back. Like hearing music from rooms away."

His words hung in the air between them. The archer's red blood staining his gray skin as he laid dead at her feet taunted her.

"I wonder if the music will ever stop playing," she mumbled, so soft she thought he missed it.

Ava couldn't wait for Gill to respond. The long-forgotten yet still familiar expectation for him to react to her crept up and dried her throat. Growing up, Gill always said the right thing by accident, but never when she sought it. Never on purpose. Ava learned that lesson a long time ago, and she was too tired and too tense to bear any more instruction.

Plus, the idea of burdening anyone with the emotions she failed to keep in check made her skin crawl.

She threw the bone into the woods behind them, taking her frustration with herself out on the drumstick and drawing Gill's attention back towards her, "I should try to get some rest too. I'm gonna need all the sleep I can get to put up with her tonight."

She paused as she stood, taking a brief count of his freckles as his pale blue eyes scanned her face in confusion.

"Listening is more important than seeing in the woods," she pulled her focus from him to address Valma and Kaj, "Keep alert."

Kaj placed a finger in his book and smirked at her.

"Heading to bed already?" he asked.

"You should, too," she responded.

He cocked an eyebrow, "Well, I didn't expect you to be so forward. How bout I take a rain check? I wouldn't be able to give you my best with these stab wounds."

"And you're about to get another if you don't behave yourself," Valma remarked idly as she played with the firelight glinting off her sword.

"Huh," Kaj snickered, "Didn't expect you'd be a prude."

"Not a prude," Valma corrected, "Friends don't let friends sleep with criminals."

"Oh, they do. And sometimes, they even pay double for it."

"Okay," Ava interjected, not wanting the light blush creeping across her cheeks to get worse, "Just make sure we don't get mauled in our sleep, alright?"

"Will do," Gill replied. The redness that flushed his entire face subsided as he tried to hide his disappointment as Ava walked away. Part of him hoped that tonight would be the start of something different. That she wouldn't end the conversation before it started as she did ever since he left their secondary school.

中

Soon, all but Gillian headed to sleep. The campfire's flames dwindled, but the coals still burned red. He held his hands over the fire pit as he looked out into the dark woods and listened to the forest.

A soft, chilled wind of early spring flitted through the trees, rustling their leaves as it carried the nocturnal calls of hidden creatures along with it. Some of them familiar, and others hauntingly unknown.

The thick canopy absorbed any splashes of moonlight. So much so that if it weren't for the soft glow of the fire illuminating the few trees that surrounded their campsite, he would have sworn they were floating in space—five poor souls drifting in the dark.

As he listened, his curiosity pulled him away from the vast darkness to the dirt beneath him. The dark umber he knew would be warmed from the fire called to him, and he touched his fingertips to the dry, loose soil. His heart beat faster as the pull in his body returned, terrifying and exhilarating him. He slowly lowered his palm to lay flat against the earth, chasing the sensation.

He couldn't take the time to study it before. The urgency of their escape and the sudden possession of his body by this unseen force pushed back the analytical nature of his mind. Still, while lost in those moments, he could tell he felt the earth moving in a way he'd never felt before. And he certainly never read about any other mage of Messis experiencing such a connection. Although it came to him naturally, the Convocation recommended that he refrain from using the earth goddess's magicks, stating that to control his raw power, he should start with the enchantments of other deities... that things would be safer that way.

He wondered if the Convocation was mistaken as his nerves bonded with the currents of the nature around him. Against his scalp, he felt the wind tug the roots that surrounded them, from the grass that struggled in its path to the roots of trees that barely quivered. His skin stretched as the plants grew slowly. Up and down, side to side, the dirt that tumbled as they pushed through sent goosebumps up his arms. Each grain of earth ran across his spine. Small rocks shifted their way towards the surface, hoping to get a glimpse of the sun at the base of his skull. Deep beneath the earth, the large ones strained against his tailbone under the immense pressure of the world above them.

He felt them all, nature's children, and they, in turn, felt him. They called to him, begged for him to know them, to play.

A sudden hunger tempted him—*teased him*—to continue his journey, to dive deeper and see just how much of the earth he could feel. Would he feel the heat of the world's core in his blood? The chill of the snow-capped mountains of The Arid Frosts on his tongue? His fingers flexed to dig in at the behest of his subconscious urges but stopped at the memory of Ava struggling to break his connection as his stone pillars surged. Followed by the crunch of the cultists' bones against the wall echoing through his mind as blood poured from the seams of the stone slab he summoned.

His breath hitched as he tore his hand from the ground.

Stay.

A soft, warm voice whispered in the back of Gillian's mind.

Drowned out by the haunting harmonies of his actions, he thought it just another gust of wind blowing through the trees.

"Ava," Gill whispered, gently shaking her shoulder, "Ava...."

"You came?" she grumbled back, eyes still closed.

"It's time for your watch," he continued, ignoring her dream talk, "I wanted to wake you before Ortensia."

She groaned, Ortensia's name waking her up better than any alarm, and lumbered her way up to a sitting position. She rubbed her eyes and glared at Gillian drowsily.

"Do I have to wake her?" Ava asked, her voice hoarse from sleep.

"I can do it," Gill answered.

"But do you have to?"

"I mean, I could stay up with you, but-"

"No, no. You need to sleep," she groaned, "Go wake the nightmare. I'll add a few more sticks to the fire and post up."

Gill walked away to wake the thorn in her side.

Ava stood, stretched, and tried to gather her wits as she fought against the soreness that seized her muscles.

A few moments later, after Ava added more brush and stoked the flames, the cranky primadonna stomped her way over to the campfire.

"You can handle this yourself, right? I can go back to bed?" irritation oozed off of her.

"Nope." Ava put the last of the sticks she gathered onto the glowing coals, "Just take a seat, and keep your ears open for anything strange. It'll be over quick."

"Oh, come on-"

"Do you want me to wake up Valma?" Ava shot her a tired glare, "I barely know the girl, but I have the feeling she won't be too happy to hear you wanna back out."

Ortensia scowled and sat down, arms folded across her chest like a toddler in time out.

They sat in silence. Ava listened to the forest and watched the fire's embers pirouette in the air while Ortensia restlessly tried to find something to entertain her idle mind.

Silence always unnerved Ortensia. When she was

a baby, if her nursemaid didn't consistently keep a music box wound, she would wake up immediately and scream to fill the air with sound. Fortunately for the waitstaff and her family members, Ortensia's talent for Osla magicks presented immediately after birth, turning the shrill cries of a newborn to a melodious trilling so beautiful her nurses often hesitated to soothe her.

She racked her brain for something to talk with the peasant girl about. Talking about the events of the past twenty-four hours was completely out of the question, as she would much rather shove the whole ordeal into the back of her mind and forget about the entire thing. They were from such different stations too. Ava would know nothing of the latest trends among the high society of Moreacor, and discussing the latest gossip from Cirvain's Gala Season would be a more fruitful conversation if she had it with a wall.

Ortensia supposed she could ask her about the things happening in town, but the thought of hearing a story about how some horse gave birth on the side of the road or whatever else excited farmers and commoners bored her immensely. Ortensia excelled at pretending to be interested in a boring conversation. Her governess, Ms. Sabar, taught her well. However, she was tired, and her feet hurt, and honestly, she watched Ava kill two people without a second thought. They were far past the pleasantries of playing pretend.

So, Ortensia drew inspiration from yet another lesson on conversation from Ms. Sabar and focused on the one thing that most women shared in common.

"So, how long have you and Gillian been courting?"

she asked.

"What?" Ava sputtered, looking utterly baffled. Her question apparently caught her off guard.

"Look, I'm trying to have some girl talk with you or whatever," Ortensia rolled her eyes, "If I don't do something, I might fall asleep of boredom. And I'm afraid you'll drop a lump of hot coal in my hair in retaliation."

"Don't give me any ideas," she mumbled.

"So, you and the mage. How often has he been calling on you? Any signs of a proposal on the horizon?"

"One, that's not how relationships work for us lowly peasants. And two, Gill and I are just friends."

"Just friends, my ass." Ortensia scoffed, "Have you seen the way he looks at you? Gods, we were surrounded by death at every turn, and he still couldn't take his eyes off of your face."

"Gill likes to study things. Maybe I had some dirt or something on me," she defended.

Ortensia raised an eyebrow in disbelief.

"But even if he was looking at me like that, he can look all he likes," Ava said with a tinge of bitterness, "I've got someone else waiting for me back home."

"Who?"

"You wouldn't know him."

"Yes, I would. I know lots of people."

"What's the name of the man who runs the general store in town?"

Ortensia paused for a moment. "This town has a general store?"

"See, just like I said. You wouldn't know him."

The fire popped between them, sending a burst of sparks twirling into the air.

"But," Ava pursed her lips. Ortensia caught a mischievous glint beneath the innocence she suddenly donned, "if staring at someone means you like them. What does it mean when you can barely look at someone without getting flustered?"

"What do you mean by that?"

"Well, even though you and Valma seem to have become fast friends during this whole disaster- which, not for nothing, surprises me greatly- every time she makes eye contact with you, you look away...." she dramatically pondered, "....as if you can't bear it for some reason."

Ava glanced at Ortensia, and her feigned naivete shifted to something more devious. Ortensia

Flashes of Valma walking alongside her, smiling down at her so warmly, rushing in without hesitation against her adversaries, flooded her thoughts.

Ortensia swallowed, trying to ease her inexplicably dry throat, "In high society, it's rude to make prolonged eye contact with someone."

Ava smirked. "It's okay if you like her, ya know. She seems to like you back for some reason."

"What do you mean for some reason?" she bristled, "I'm very likable!"

"You have the likability of a screaming toddler. You're rude, pretentious, entitled, and emotionally immature," Ava stated, having the audacity to keep that sly smile on her face as she casually insulted her. "But despite all that, that very strong woman seems to enjoy interacting with you. I don't get why, but maybe having her around to keep you in check is a good thing."

Ortensia's eyes darted over to look where Valma slept.

"Well, after this whole incident, I was thinking of mentioning to my father that we should hire our own private guard," she considered. She did her best to keep her face neutral as she remembered how safe she felt as Valma carried her through the flooded tunnel. Ortensia hated when people tried to pick her up without permission. But given the circumstances and Valma's innate skill at holding her like a precious object, she figured that if anyone were to do it, she wouldn't mind it being her.

"Valma's athleticism is impressive," Ortensia continued, "and her gaze can be intimidating when necessary. The perfect muscle to fend off criminals… even if it does lead to her destroying the manor again."

"She destroyed the manor?" The smirk fell from Ava's face, replaced by confusion.

"Oh yes. You weren't at the dinner last night." The chaos of her matchmaking dinner felt as though it happened weeks ago. The reminder that she would be returning to a manor half-splinted soured her mood.

Ava looked at her expectantly, and Ortensia sighed, figuring now was as good a time as any to fill the poor farm girl in on what she had missed.

Ortensia pointed to Kaj sprawled out on his brush bed like a starfish, "That bastard broke into my home to steal our valuables while my family, the Venzors, and Master Gustav and his ward were distracted with the festivities." Ortensia moved her hand across the campsite to gesture towards the townsguard sleeping stiffly on her side. "Valma was on patrol thankfully and confronted him, but somehow the two of them came smashing through our drawing-room window, right in the middle of my piano-forte solo. Kaj fled, Valma followed, then the redheaded rampage over there-" she moved to point at Gillian sleeping on his stomach and snoring deeply, "-summoned hundreds of tree roots from the earth, tearing our manor asunder while apprehending the both of them at the same time."

"That's-"

"But you know, it's all well and good," Ortensia held her hand up to stop whatever cutting remark Ava was sure to have. "Now that the Venzors have unfortunately passed, it's not like anyone from the nobility will know of our little faux pas." A forlorn look settled on her face from the weight behind that statement. Lady Venzor's eyes turned from kind and glowing in the firelight of her drawing-room to terrified and lifeless as she laid on the cavern floor.

The silence she hated so much took over once more, but Ortensia was too caught up in her grief to end it.

"I'm sorry," Ava said after a moment.

"Why?" Ortensia grumbled.

"Because clearly they meant something to you," Ava said, "I mean when ma and I dropped off your produce order yesterday, you were so stressed and anxious about getting everything perfect. Then not only does all that work get torn apart, but then the Venzors turn out to be-" she sighed, "-you know."

Ortensia pulled at her hangnails, irked by their roughness compared to the rest of her hands, while her mind scrutinized every interaction she shared with the Lord and Lady of the Sparis Ward over the past few weeks.

"They must have been using me," she remarked.

"You think so?"

"It's too much coincidence," Ortensia admitted. "My father finds that dumb old book, sends it to Cirvain to have it translated, and not a few days later, we get a letter from the Venzors' estate saying that they wish to visit my father to discuss my prospects?"

"Fate is good, but she's not that good," Ava conceded after a moment.

"Exactly."

"Well, hopefully, that'll help our case when we get to town then." Ava paused, "Do you think they've noticed we're gone?"

"What type of stupid question is that?" A pinprick of blood beaded on the cuticle of her thumb, "Of course they have. I know my father has the entire town searching for me. It's only a matter of time before they find us."

"I hope you're right." Ava drifted back to the fire, getting lost in the flickering flames and withdrawing into herself as Ortensia seemed too focused on her manicure to continue talking. Her mind wandered to last night, sitting alone and watching the moonlight dance across the lake while she waited for Kieran to show up.

She traced her finger over her knee, drawing their initials in the same pattern they had scratched into the boulder that marked their secret meeting place, and wondered if he was out there searching for her too.

Ava and Ortensia's eyes were heavy by the time their watch came to an end. Ava stoked the fire one last time while Ortensia took it upon herself to wake Valma, saving Ava the pleasure of waking up Kaj.

Kaj blinked his eyes open slowly as she shook his shoulder and a no-good smirk crawled on his face.

"Good morning, gorgeous," Kaj croaked, "I thought the most beautiful thing I'd see this morning is the sunrise, yet here you are."

Kaj was handsome on top of being a rakish scamp, a combination that usually meant trouble for her, but Ava was tired and taken, and the last thing she needed was Ortensia thinking she was courting a criminal.

"Sun will start to rise in about three hours, so there probably won't be too many beasts roaming around," Ava yawned as she headed towards her makeshift bed, "Still though, keep an ear out."

"Will do, Sharpshooter," Kaj saluted behind her. She tensed a bit at the nickname but chose to ignore it and nestled herself into the pile of gathered brush.

Kaj walked over to the fire. His movements were stiff, and the muscles in his stomach burned as his scabbed over wounds stretched by the smallest movements, but he thankfully didn't feel like death's side piece anymore. He made his way over and stood opposite of Valma as she warmed her hands over the flame.

"How's the shoulder, Stick?" he greeted.

"A little sore, but better than before. Ribs hurt like hell after the one-two punch of taking Gill's pillar to the side and Ava's ax swing," she answered. "How's the stomach?"

"The bleeding stopped, so, you know, death is a little less imminent."

"Pity," Valma's voice went cold, and an accusatory

glare replaced her playful charisma.

Kaj let his friendly demeanor vanish as well and sat down.

"I was wondering when you were gonna drop the enemy of my enemy act," he said.

"Your people have something to do with all this?" Valma didn't waste any time. She folded her brawny arms across her chest and stared down at him stalwart and disapproving.

"What do you mean, my people?" Kaj glared back at her. He'd never let a Stick intimidate him before, and he certainly wasn't going to start now.

"The fur traders from Krosten," she flexed her fingers in air quotes.

Kaj sat pinched in the corner of the tavern booth, pressed to the side by Talwar's hulking mass, and casually picked at the fries that sat in the middle of the table.

"This town may not have anything exciting going on, but man, they sure know how to make a sandwich," Bolo relished through a full mouth, crumbs and mustard smeared in the corners of his thin lip.

"For a skinny fucker you sure do eat a lot," Seax remarked, taking a sip of her ale as she kept her gaze locked onto the tavern's dancefloor.

"Not my fault I'm always hungry," Bolo wiped his

hand across his hollow cheeks and licked the mustard and crumbs off the back of it, "it runs in the family."

"I still can't believe you ate all of my pastries without asking," Talwar slumped, his pock-marked face pouted and arms crossed.

"I didn't eat all of them," Bolo rolled his eyes.

"I had one eclair!" Talwar slammed his fist on the table. The fries jumped on the plate. "Kaj barely had half of a cinnamon roll, and by the time Seax showed up, you were licking the crumbs off the bottom of the last box!"

"Yes, and you've just proved my point. I didn't eat all of them. I ate the rest." An eat-shit grin peeled his lip, and Talwar slowly turned red with frustration. Seax placed a hand on his shaking fist.

"Save it for the fighting grounds. That rage will make you some coin." She pulled her attention away from the dance floor and looked at Kaj, "So. You ready for your first solo mission?"

"Yup. I scouted the place out last night. Looks like the daughter's bedroom balcony is gonna be my best bet. No windows underneath, covered in shadow at night." Kaj replied, "Unlocked more importantly. Our contact said Valborg's office is on the third floor, right?"

"Yeah, big dark door covered in carvings," Seax looked back out at the crowd, "He keeps things locked in his left-hand drawer."

"Left-hand drawer. Got it." Kaj popped another fry

in his mouth, "Anything specific I'm looking for? All Keris told me was that I was looking for something to use for blackmail."

"Yeah," Seax's eyes locked onto someone in the crowd and trailed them. Her voice grew a bit distant in tone, "Valborg's not a well-liked character for some of those upper crust Moreacor folks, apparently. Just look for something a noble might want to hold over someone's head. Pictures of a mistress, sex toys, records of a bastard kid, something like that."

"You got something, Seax?" Bolo asked.

"That townsguard newbie's at the bar." Seax turned back to look at them and snickered, "That's how you know it's a small town. The Stick can have a drink at the local tavern without worrying about what goes on at night."

Kaj's hackles raised as he snuck a glimpse at the raven-haired townsguard chatting cheerfully with the bartender.

"Need me to do something about her?" Kaj asked.

"No, no." Seax ran a hand through her dark, curly hair and turned back to continue her scan of the crowd, "She's only been here a week. Even if she did give us trouble, it wouldn't be much of a fight."

"Plus, this is a stealth mission, Kaj," Talwar said, "Nothing will get a thief noticed faster than a missing guard."

"I told them you were trouble," he chuckled half-heartedly, recalling his last meal with his guildmates. "They said not worry about some rookie townsguard."

"You all stuck out like sore thumbs in the tavern that night." Valma noted, "Let me guess, you were trying to build up an alibi?"

"You could say that."

Valma narrowed her eyes and ran her tongue across her teeth in contemplation.

"What about that vanishing trick of yours?" she asked

"Benefit of my bloodline," Kaj held his hand up against the dark sky and breathed in deeply. He relaxed the tension in his body and focused on the cool air against his skin. The night coated his deep copper skin in its shade, and his hand vanished, becoming part of the evening itself.

"Very handy." Valma uncrossed her arms and sat down carefully, minding her bruises, "So what are y'all really here for? Surely four people wouldn't come here just for one of them to pull off a minor burglary."

"You gonna let me off the hook if I tell you?" he asked. Her guard may have been coming down, but Kaj still kept on his toes. Cracking jokes and witty banter with a Stick one thing, but trusting one? He'd rather cut the tips of his ears off than make a mistake like that.

"Not my decision," she answered.

"Then I have no idea who those people were," he shrugged, "They just offered me a bit of drink and conversation."

"Really? Is that all you're gonna give me?" Valma scoffed as she leaned forward, resting her elbows on her knees, "After all of this?"

"After all of this, are you still gonna throw me in prison?" he leaned forward as well and stared her down with a smile on his face and disdain in his eyes.

The two glared at each other, waiting for the other to break, searching for any signs of a secret on the other's face.

"You have no clue what's going on here, do you?" Valma ended their staring contest with a roll of her eyes and a heavy sigh. Her forte was apprehending suspects, not interrogating them.

"Took you this long to figure it out?" Kaj snickered.

"No, I had a feeling that was the case considering you were tied tighter than a Frosttide Roast down in that dungeon. I just needed to make sure." She reached her arms up to stretch but stopped short as searing pain shot through her shoulder.

"I think it's Cici," Kaj stated.

"What?" Valma barked out a laugh as her nose scrunched up in disbelief.

"Think about it. She knew those people in there, let us do all the fighting, all of a sudden unlocked her magick stabby clones," he said. "And she honestly looked more hurt to see that woman dead than the guy she was supposed to be hitched to."

"You can't base anything off that." Valma shook her head, refusing to let the seeds of doubt he tried to plant take root.

"What do you mean?" Kaj's eyes bugged out, and he threw his arms in the air, "All of that points to her being super evil and crazy! Plus, how many times have her goddamn temper tantrums gotten us into harm's way?"

"Only one specifically."

He pulled at his hair, "That's one too many!"

Valma looked across the camp at Ortensia, snoring gently. Her face softened, no longer tensed by the impertinent mask she wore, and Valma wondered what it would take to make her face look that serene when awake.

"People handle stress in different ways," she offered. "You give snarky comments and outlandish anecdotes. She keeps shouting to drown out-"

Kaj barked a laugh, "Pretty wise words for someone whose best plan of action was to tackle a thief out of a window thirty feet from the ground."

"I was excited, alright!" Valma threw her arms up in the air instinctively and yelped.

She lowered her arms down slowly, letting out a steady hiss to breathe through the pain.

"I've been in this town for a whole week, and the only crime I stopped was a raccoon in some old guy's backyard," she admitted. "I signed up for the Bastions to make a name for myself through kicking some ass and saving people, not pest control."

"Gods. You're loving all this psycho undead cult shit right now, aren't you?" Kaj rebuked, "I knew all you Sticks had some sort of bullshit, adrenaline-fueled, savior complex."

"Is there something wrong with that?" she spat defensively.

"I don't know," he teased, "guess people handle stress in different ways."

"That's it," Valma grumbled, miffed by Kaj using her words against her, "You're only getting plain oatmeal when we lock you back up. I was gonna treat you to some cinnamon raisin toast for helping get us out, but not anymore."

Kaj smiled. "I saved the burgermeister's daughter. You know there's no way in hell I'm not getting off scot-free."

"We'll see about that."

CHAPTER SEVEN

The golden beams of the rising sun split through the trees, blinding Gill as he sleepily walked over to join Kaj and Valma by the dying campfire.

"Here," he dug into his pockets and pulled out some clumps of dandelions and oyster mushrooms as he approached, "I grabbed these just in case Ava had a hard time catching something for dinner last night." He laughed at himself for even considering the notion, "Foolish, I know, but at least we can take breakfast off her mind."

"You sure these aren't poison?" Kaj questioned as he took a small handful out of Gill's palm.

"Very sure," Gill took a bite out of one of the mushrooms, and an amusing idea came to mind. He swallowed his bite dramatically and waited a moment before crossing his eyes and falling back onto the ground as stiff as a board.

"Gillian!" Valma shouted.

Gill felt her heavy footsteps shake the ground as she ran over to his side and couldn't keep a straight face, breaking out into a fit of giggles as Valma's shadow fell over him.

"What's going on?!" Ava gasped as she jolted awake.

"Wizkid is trying to be a comedian," Kaj rolled his eyes, unable to keep a smirk off his face as he munched on one of the dandelion leaves.

"Sorry Ava, didn't mean to wake you," Gill's laughter subsided as he sat up, "They looked so nervous when I took a bite I couldn't help but pull their leg a bit."

Valma offered him a hand to stand, and he took it, only to be met with a playful slap to the back of his head as he rose.

"Ow!" he over-exaggerated and rubbed the sore spot she left.

"Keep crying wolf like that, and one day you'll actually poison yourself, and I won't help you," she said and snatched the foraged goods from Gill's fist.

"Oh, please. Like you'd do any good if you actually did help," Kaj mumbled through a mouthful of mushroom, "Last time I checked, you trained to be one of the crown's cronies, not a doctor."

Kaj and Valma's bickering became background noise as Ava walked over to him.

Gill dug into his pocket, "Care for some dandelion and mushroom salad?"

Ava pouted, "I would have gotten us something, you know."

"I know," he held a handful out to her, "The mushrooms are just ripe enough."

He smiled brightly as Ava took his offering.

"You're awfully chipper," a soft smile tugged up at the corner of her lips, "I thought you weren't a morning person."

Gill's heart skipped a beat at the sight of her subtle grin. He always liked Ava's warm and welcoming smile, and while this one wasn't as brilliant as the ones she used to share with him, it was still a smile, and it still belonged to her. A lot of things made Gill happy, but making Ava smile was definitely one of the best.

"Oh, I'm not," Gill chewed on a dandelion, "There's just a lot to be excited about."

"Like what?" Valma teased, "Because my stiff shoulder and the blisters on my feet say otherwise."

"Well, we're alive for one," he explained, "We're not stuck in a cult's dungeon anymore; that's two. And three, I had a breakthrough with my magick last night."

"You messed around with your magick last night?" Kaj asked.

"I wouldn't call it messing around. Experimenting is more accurate."

"So, your experiment was that your magick didn't kill us in our sleep?"

"Kaj!" Ava scolded.

"It's a fair fucking question!" Kaj shrugged, "Look, Wizkid, that earth magick ya do is outstanding but also incredibly terrifying."

Gill's heart sank a little, but he kept smiling. Kaj had a point. His inherent abilities were terrifying, especially with what little control he had over them. After last night, however, feeling the movements and will of nature so vibrantly, Gill hoped that lack of control wouldn't be an issue much longer.

"I wouldn't call it terrifying," Valma picked at a piece of dandelion stuck in her teeth, "Badass is more like it."

"Things can be badass and terrifying at the same time, ya know," Kaj stated.

"Oh, I am well aware," Valma smirked and slowly flexed her biceps, "Left one's badass. Right one's terrifying."

The wry expression on Kaj's face dropped. "Please tell me you don't actually call them that."

"I don't. I just wanted to see you die a little inside." Valma lowered her arms and turned her focus towards Ava, "So, how much more do we have to go?"

Ava walked over and took a seat beside her, "Should be about four hours of walking left, then we'll be back in town. We'll know for sure when we reach Cedar Lake."

"That's good to hear," Kaj added, "I'm not sure I could take anymore walking."

"At least you're wearing shoes," Ava noted before

continuing, "We'll be coming out by my family's farm, luckily. We'll stop there, and I'll be able to saddle up some horses to help take some of the stress off of Kaj and Valma as we head to the Doc's. Plus, having my parents see us arrive might be good for when we have to tell everyone what happened."

"Sounds like a plan." Gill popped one last mushroom into his mouth and sat down next to Kaj. He patted his hand against Kaj's knee, "Kaj. Wake up Ortensia."

"No way in hell!" he protested, shoving Gill lightly. "You do it! I told you I don't want to get stabbed again!"

"I've got it," Valma sighed. She finished the last of her meal and stood.

Gill, Ava, and Kaj intently watched as she walked over to where Ortensia slept, waiting to see if Valma would be skewered with bated breath.

Valma crouched beside her and stifled a laugh at how deep of a sleeper Ortensia was. She paused, taking a moment to admire the serene look on her face before gently shaking her shoulder.

"It's too early, Cordelia," the sleepy Ortensia murmured.

Valma winced. *Who the hell is Cordelia?*

"Come on," Valma shook her again, "It's morning. We have to start walking to town."

Ortensia's eyes slowly opened, and the serenity on

her face shattered as she cinched her eyebrows and let out a growl of frustration.

"Sorry," Valma patted her shoulder and stood. Ortensia, stiff from the hard night's sleep, sat up and rubbed the sleep from her eyes.

"What time is it?" she asked.

"Time to go," Ava answered.

Valma looked over to find Gill kicking dirt over the fire as Kaj and Ava walked over.

Ava nocked an arrow and drew her bowstring taught, "Same deal as before: keep quiet and stay alert. There'll be fewer monsters the closer we get to town, but you can never be too careful."

"Aren't we going to have breakfast first?" Ortensia whined.

Gillian ran over to join them and held out a fistful of the wild veggies he collected towards her, "Here, dandelions and oyster mushrooms."

Ortensia looked up at Valma in utter disbelief, willing with her eyes for Valma to tell her he was joking.

Valma shrugged and seized the opportunity to participate in her newly acquired hobby, teasing Ortensia.

"They're not half bad," Valma said, "I only found one or two bugs in them while I ate."

Ortensia paled.

"On second thought, I'll starve," she scowled.

"Oh well," Gill shrugged, passing a sidelong glance at Valma before popping a piece of mushroom in his mouth, "more for me."

<hr />

The final trek through the depths of the Shadowfen was easy on the weary wanderers. The terrain evened out, with moss and clover padding cushioning their steps, and soon the sharp pricks of fallen twigs and spreading brambles fell away, bound to stay in their unkempt domain. Shimmering patterns projected against the tree trunks and glinting off the undersides of maple leaves brought a little bit of spirit back to their aching bodies as the water of Cedar Lake came into view.

<hr />

Now on the blessed lands of Messis, Ava's worry washed away. She fought the urge to run ahead, to leave the group behind, and burst through her farmhouse's doors into the waiting arms of her surely frantic mother.

The same hopeful energy coursed through those beside her, causing even Ortensia to smile and their pace to pick up. Through the thinning trees, the steeple of the Temple of Messis arose, and they broke out into a jog, their joy overcoming the pain of their blistered feet and the aches from their lingering wounds as the fenced-in pastures of Barncombe Farm appeared.

"We did it!" Gillian jumped on the bottom rung of

the wooden fence and cheered, raising his arms in the air in jubilation.

Ava giggled and tugged him down by the back of his pajama shirt, "Come on, Gill, let's help Kaj and Valma over the fence."

As the others caught up with the Ava and Gill lent a hand to their wounded members. Valma politely refused their help, opting to vault over the fence using her good arm, while Kaj welcomed the help with a cheeky comment that made the pair blush.

"Need me to give you a lift?" Ava asked Ortensia.

The half-dwarf gave her a withering glare and simply ducked under the bottom rung of the fence, using her diminutive height to her advantage.

Ava went to climb over and found Gill on the other side, arms outstretched and ready to help.

"I'm fine, Gill," she said and tried to keep herself from wincing as she leaned her weight on her arms to throw her legs over.

"Uh-huh," Gill grabbed onto her waist firmly, taking some of the pressure off of her torn-up shoulder blades and eliciting a reactionary exhale of relief from her. "Did you forget I got a first-hand look at those claw marks when I patched you up last night?"

He helped her down but kept his hands on her waist even after her feet firmly planted on the ground. She felt the warmth of his palms through the thin cotton of her nightgown, and though it was Gill's freckled cheeks and pale blue eyes in front of her, she could only think about how Kieran would have gripped her tighter.

"And it's a testament to your knowledge of medicinal plants that I feel good enough to try," she patted him on the shoulder and ripped out of his grasp, running towards the farmhouse as she called, "Mom! Dad! Tate! Tallon! I'm home!"

There was no response as Ava ran up the back steps, still shouting, "I'm back! It's Ava! I'm back!"

"Meerrrooowww!" a howl bellowed from inside, underscored by frantic scratching at the back door.

"Marqui!" Ava cried and threw open the unlocked front door.

Marqui, a gray cat with bright yellow eyes, tumbled out of the house as Ava opened the door. Yowling excessively in greeting, he rammed his head into her legs and whacked her shins with his tail as he rubbed his body against her. Ava scooped him up in her arms and covered his head in kisses.

"Oh, Qui! I missed you so much!" Tears of joy gathered in her eyes as Marqui's purrs rattled against her chest. Ava stepped into the house and called out again, "Mom? Dad? I'm home!"

Her voice echoed through the silent house.

"They must be out in the fields," she told herself and Marqui, "or the barn..."

"You can go in and make yourselves at home!" Ava called to the others as she stepped back outside and dashed down the steps, "I'm gonna go check the fields and the barn to see if my folks are there."

"Is she holding a cat?" Kaj asked the others as he watched the feline's head bob in time with its owner's hurried steps.

"Yeah. That's Marqui! He's a very good boy." Gillian answered.

Kaj flexed his eyebrows in resignation, "I'll take your word for it."

Following Ava's suggestion, they made their way up the back steps and into the Barncombe's home.

The worn back door opened into their kitchen with a creak. The kitchen was humble in size and quaintly decorated. A handmade gingham tablecloth covered the round wooden kitchen table in the center of the room, matching the drawn curtains that dampened the midday sunlight. Crocheted hand towels in a faded shade of cornflower blue tied the scene together, highlighting the dark knotted wood of the cabinetry, floors, and staircase that sat against the back wall.

"Gods, it's so rural," Kaj groaned as he entered and made a beeline for the icebox.

"What are you doing?" Valma asked.

"She said to make ourselves at home, right? I'm

starving." Kaj opened the icebox door and peered inside, "Oooh! Mincemeat pies!"

Ortensia ran up beside him, "Hand them over!"

"Hey! I found them first!" he protested as he tried to block her reaching arms.

"I'm going to make some tea," Valma sighed to Gillian and walked over to the stove.

He stifled a laugh as he watched Ortensia slap Kaj in the stomach, right against one of his wounds. The elvefolk doubled over, dropping one of the pies into Ortensia's waiting hands. Gill caught the deadly glare in Kaj's eye and quickly made his way out of the kitchen and into the sitting room, wanting to avoid getting caught up in whatever petty fight was about to occur.

Gill knew the familiar gingham print continued throughout the home, upholstering the sofa and chairs, adorning the windows. He was there when Mrs. Barncombe brought the bolts of fabric home, interrupting he and Ava's study session as she excitedly regaled how she negotiated the price with a traveling salesman. The gingham was a deeper blue the last time he saw it, but that was a little over five years ago.

He ran his hand over the small fireplace that sat nestled in the wall, tracing his fingers around the few ceramic trinkets decorated the mantle like he did when he was younger. There was a dull ache in his heart. Though his visits grew rarer and rarer as his instruction with Master Gustav became more rigorous, the Barncombe's house still held a fond place in his heart. When he came to Elerrï it was the first place in a long while that fit his definition of home.

As he took in the room, he imagined the Barncombe family sitting by the fire, sharing stories of their day, and tried to ignore the emptiness that weighed on his heart. It had been fifteen years since his parents passed, but the hole they left in his life remained.

As he took a moment to mire in his melancholy, he noticed something glinting in the sunlight, a sparkle on the rug in the center of the room. His curiosity piqued—and being more willing to explore a new mystery than dwell on the past—Gill stepped closer. Between the coffee table and the sofa, two large, dark brown splashes stained the carpet underneath the shards of a pair of shattered sherry glasses.

"That's odd," he muttered to himself. *The Barncombes weren't neat freaks, but to leave such a mess-*

A horrifying notion popped into his head, and a chill ran up his spine. Gillian headed back into the kitchen quickly.

Kaj and Ortensia sat at the table, their feud apparently having ended in a truce as they furiously ate their handpies. Valma was in the middle of filling up four mismatched mugs when Gill approached her.

"Valma, can you come upstairs with me real quick?" he asked as he came up to her side, keeping his voice hushed to try and hide the worry in his voice from the others.

She stopped pouring, and her posture stiffened.

"Is something wrong?" Valma asked quietly in return.

"Not immediately, but," he swallowed, "I just have a bad feeling."

"Okay," she nodded curtly and set down the kettle.

"Our tea!" Ortensia whined from behind them at the sight of Valma placing the kettle to the side.

Gillian headed towards the stairs as Valma wordlessly grabbed the two mugs she filled and dropped them off on the table wordlessly before following him.

"And where are you two going in such a hurry?" Kaj asked.

"Wizkid's showing me where the bathroom is," Valma lied, "Ain't that right?"

"Right!" Gill's voice cracked, and both he and Valma winced.

Kaj shook his head, ashamed, "You're terrible liars."

He turned back to his pie, "Luckily for you, I'm too tired and hungry to care. Just make sure to scream if shit hits the fan so Princess Persnickety and I can get the hell out of here, alright?"

They both nodded and resumed their path upstairs.

"What's going on?" Valma asked as they climbed,

keeping her voice low, unsure if they were out of earshot.

"Two drinks were spilled in the other room: broken glass and everything. If the Barncombes were home, they wouldn't have just left it like that," Gill replied before stopping suddenly at the top of the stairs. He paled at whatever he saw down the hallway next to him.

Valma brushed past him and peeked around the corner to find all of the doors down the hall thrown open. She steeled herself. The Berylwood Bastions were trained to stay calm and collected to the best of their ability no matter the circumstance, and while disturbed by the implications of the scene before them, standing here wouldn't give them the answers they needed.

Valma tapped Gill's shoulder, and he jumped. She placed a hand on his shoulder and jerked her chin forward, urging him to move. With a shaky inhale, Gill took the first step forward. The two of them crept their way down the hall. Valma's hand rested on the hilt of her sword as they glanced into each room they passed.

The first room containing a large bed for two was untouched.

The second was crowded with toys. A bunk bed sat against the far wall across from the door. Sheets poured off the bed in a set of twin waterfalls, one off the top bunk and one off the bottom, cascading into a path parting the messy sea of children's clothes and toys that covered the floor.

The third was the bathroom, and, except for the open door, it showed no signs of tumult.

Pressed flowers hung up all over the walls of the fourth and final room. A small desk covered with sewing supplies sat nestled in the corner, and the small bed across from it had its own waterfall of sheets, just like the bunk beds in the other room. The folding door of the room's closet was pushed open just a crack.

Gillian and Valma stepped into the room cautiously and walked over to the closet to find hundreds of fine scratch marks across the frame and door.

Gill whispered the truth that Valma anticipated from the moment he walked back into the kitchen, "They took all of them."

The restless calls of the animals inside trickled through the barn's doors as Ava approached. With another kiss on the head, she placed Marqui down beside her and stepped inside.

Daylight poured into the barn as she heaved open the doors. The livestock oinked, mooed, whinnied, clucked, and bleated in discomfort and frustration at her entrance. Jasper, Ava's dapple-gray horse, leaned his head out of his stable and stuck his muzzle into his empty feed cage, nudging it back and forth so the metal rang to stand out in the cacophony.

"Whoa boy," she walked over to him and stroked his nose, "Did they forget to feed you?"

Ava looked across all the stables. None of the stables were cleaned, and there was no feed in any of their troughs.

"Did they forget to feed all of you?" she murmured.

The small pit in her stomach that she tried her best to ignore grew. Afraid of the thoughts it pulled her mind towards, she sought to fill it.

"Maybe they're still out in the woods somewhere searching for me," she whispered to Jasper, attempting to speak her hopes into existence.

She addressed the rest of the barn, "Sorry that I caused y'all to worry! Imma get ya fed and out to the pasture now."

Ava grabbed a pitchfork off the wall and heaved a scoopful of hay into Jasper's feed cage, "I can't let you out yet, bud. We're gonna need to take some folks into town in a bit."

Jasper whinnied a sassy thank you and dug into his late breakfast.

Ava's thoughts were slipping. The creeping panic that seeped in her stomach sought a way to crawl into her brain, so she set to work opening up the barn. There was no point in her worrying. Worrying would only distract from the task at hand. Taking care of her animals eclipsed letting baseless worries monopolize her focus.

So she filled up the slop and seed for the pigs and chickens while trying not to remember the songs her father used to sing to his favorite sow. The sheep and goats headbutted her softly in retaliation as she let them loose, and she tried not to think about the late spring days she'd spend with her mother spinning their fleece. The cows and horses were much gentler, simply holding their heads high and ignoring her as they walked out into the pasture, and she tried not to picture how Tate and Tallon would ride on Ol' Annabelle's back, pretending they were bandits on the run as the cow lazily grazed in the fields.

"Ava."

Startled, Ava dropped her shovel.

When did Gill get here? Why did he sound so serious?

She turned around and smiled, looking everywhere but at Gillian's silhouette standing in the barn door.

"Can you believe this? The animals have been in here all morning! Must be one hell of a search party they've got going for us." Her words were too cheerful, practically drowning in fabricated positivity. But maybe, just maybe, if she kept at it, the somber look on Gillian's face would go away. "I'll have to come back and clean their pens once we drop Kaj and Valma off at Doc's. They haven't made a mess of the house, have they?"

"Ava," he stressed, "They're gone."

"I know, Gill," Ava chuckled hollowly, ignoring the sudden spike in her heart rate and the tingling in her fingertips, "I just said they must be out searching still."

"Ava, look at me," Gill insisted and stepped into the barn.

Ava didn't want to look at him, but his voice was so sad. An old part of her, the part of her that still recognized him as her best friend, hated it. She'd sworn to him once that she'd never let anyone make him cry, that she'd never let anyone hurt him. It was a playground promise, only bound by a pinky swear, but still, she felt bound by it. Her younger self screamed at her, cutting through all the worries and wishful thinking, and demanded her to make it right. To stop whatever upset him no matter what.

So Ava looked, and the black hole of dread she tried to fill with wishes and flimsy excuses swallowed her whole.

Her eyes fell not on his face but on one of her mother's sherry glasses, a gift her father had given her for their tenth wedding anniversary, broken in his hand.

"I'm so sorry," Gill rasped.

CHAPTER EIGHT

The fake smile fell from Ava's face as her eyes locked onto the broken glass in Gillian's hand. He braced himself for her tears, biting down on the inside of his cheek to help calm his nerves. It was hard to tell her about her parents, but he was the best person for the task. And if he was honest with himself, he wanted to be the one. He didn't have to imagine what her grief felt like. He would be there for her, hold her while she cried, and talk her through the next steps. Gill would be there for her, just like all the times she was there for him when they were kids.

Marqui must have sensed the shift in her mood as he ran over to her and smoothed his head across Ava's legs. Ava remained transfixed onto the broken, her face void of emotion.

Did she not recognize it?

Gill opened his mouth to explain.

"I have to go and get them," Ava went from frozen to frantic faster than Gill could blink.

She rushed past him.

"W-what?" he faltered, turning around to find her heading towards her saddle.

"I left them in that goddamn dungeon!" she shouted.

Gill foundered for control of the situation as Ava slung the saddle over her shoulder and reached to grab her reins, "Valma should know a thing or two about horses. Gentle Paul will be easy enough to hitch up to take you all to town."

She moved faster than Gill's thoughts. She was clearly panicking, still barefoot in her nightgown and preparing to head back into the Shadowfen as if it were as easy as riding into town. Ava wasn't thinking rationally, but he was.

"You're not going anywhere!" Gill protested.

"Like hell, I'm not," she spat and ripped the reins off their hook.

He stepped between her and Jasper's stable as she stomped towards it.

"Get out of my way, Gill." she hissed. Tears welled in her eyes.

"You running off alone into monster-infested woods isn't gonna solve anything," he reasoned, trying to keep his voice as calm as possible. Calm and rational, that's what would stop this. He was sure of it.

"My family, *my six-year-old brothers*, are sitting in that bloody crypt being tortured right now!"

The last time he saw her brothers was when they were barely a year old, but the image still hurt.

"You don't know that," he stated, reining in his emotions.

"I don't know a lot of things!" The tears she held back finally broke through. Sobbing, she shouted, "All I know is that my family is missing and that somehow it's my fault!"

Ava's words sucked the air out of his lungs.

"How was it your fault?" he asked, completely confused.

"I don't know- I-" she struggled to get the words out through her hiccups, "I-I was the one who caught the meal for Ortensia's stupid dinner!" she concluded. "If I had said no to that rich bitch in there, m-maybe none of this would have happened!" Ava fell deeper into despair. Her sobs shook her whole body, dropping the saddle and reigns out of her hands as she folded into herself.

Gill dropped the sherry glass from his hand and moved to hug her, but his rational mind stopped him. There was too much risk in the action, too many unknowns that could come from putting his arms around her. She pushed away from him so quickly when he helped her down from the fence that he was certain she would run away the second he touched her.

"It's not your fault, Ava. It's none of our faults," his inner turmoil slipped out in a hoarse whisper as his throat tightened. A high-pitch wail seethed through her clenched teeth in response.

Calm and rational.

Gillian took a deep breath and regained his composure,

"I know you're hurting right now, but we need you to come inside to work out a plan."

"But they are still-" she heaved.

"They're not back there." he asserted, "That tomb was a one-way street. The exits we found were the only way out."

With a heart-wrenching keen, Ava's knees gave out, and she dropped to the ground, curling into herself.

She closed herself off from him completely. Each heaving cry that burst from her trembling body slammed the door shut in Gillian's face. He stood beside her, unable to step away but too disappointed in himself to act. Rationality had failed her. He had failed her.

It was useless for him to cry too. He knew that. But he was useless anyway, so what did it matter if he let a few tears fall.

Ava's heartbeat filled her ears as her mind raced, its increasing rhythm threatening to stop her heart at any moment. Guilt, crushing and constant, twisted her stomach. She pulled at her hair, trying to tear the image of her family being slaughtered like Octavian, throats slit as they groveled on the ground from her mind. She was drowning, dying, her body torn between the urge to run, the urge to hide, and the urge to fight. Something was hitting her back.

Something was purring and hitting her back.

The action brought her a brief moment of clarity as Marqui headbutted her side, purring like crazy. He forced his way through the small gap between her legs to sniff her face. His purr's percussion changed tempo with each inhale before he set to work licking the tears off her cheeks.

His sandpaper tongue tickling her was a wave of fresh water, clearing a path in the sludge of her sorrow. She couldn't help but focus on it, the pleasant feeling a welcome respite in the middle of her hysteria. It was tangible, real, unlike the intrusive scenarios she kept picturing.

"They're not back there."

Gill's confidence in that statement grounded her. He was right. She knew he was right the moment he said it, but the implications behind it pushed her over the edge.

Her tears subsided as Marqui continued to brush his tongue against her; his fussing soothed her as she caught her breath.

She rubbed her thumb across the side of his head and kissed him on the temple.

Ava was scared; scared of all the terrible outcomes that could have befallen her family, but tears would only further her agonizing.

"They're not back there."

Children cry when their parents go missing, she scolded herself. *Adults go out and find them.*

"Thanks, Qui," she croaked, her voice wispy and raw,

"I'll bring them back."

"Arow," he clipped in response.

"Yes," she laughed and wiped the tears off her face, "I'll feed you first."

Ava's sobs turned to laughter. Gillian tensed at the sound. She started to untangle herself, and Gill rubbed his eyes to hide his tears as Ava stood.

"Sorry, Gill," her eyes were still red and watery, her breath shaky, but her expression was calm.

"Don't be." His jaw hung slack in confusion.

"The others are working on a plan, right?"

Gill nodded, too dumbfounded by her quick turnaround to speak.

"Okay then," she wiped the last few tears from her eyes, "let's go plan."

She walked past him, Marqui by her side, and left the barn.

He grabbed the saddle, the reins, and the broken glass from the floor. Collecting the objects as well as his thoughts, he returned them to their rightful places before following after her.

"Why should I go with you?!" Ortensia's shrill protest

broke through the front door, "We're back in town now! Let me go home!"

Ava opened the door and stepped into the kitchen. Valma, Kaj, and Ortensia froze, huddled around her kitchen table in the middle of an argument.

"Ava!" Ortensia cried, "You hate me! Wouldn't it be better if I just went home and left you all to solve the mystery of the mysterious kidnappings?"

Ava walked past them and headed to the icebox.

"I don't hate you," she said as she opened it and pulled out some leftover chicken for Marqui. Making sure to keep her promise. "I hate your sense of superiority."

Ortensia knotted her brow and sat down. Confusion and disappointment puckered her face.

A few moments later, Gillian came into the kitchen and sat down at the table, joining the others as they watched Ava intently.

Marqui danced around her feet, eagerly meowing as she pulled apart the chicken and placed it on a plate.

"You can keep talking," Ava said and kept her focus on prepping Marqui's meal, "I'd like to know this plan Gillian was telling me about."

Valma cleared her throat, "Well, there are two things we need to do: patch up me, Kaj, and you, Ava. You still got those hives from the skrills, right? And I bet where that nightstalker tore ya up aches like hell still."

"Yes, but I'm managing," she replied.

"Still. They should be treated," Valma said. "We also need to check and see if anybody else from town is missing. Considering whoever took us took your family too-"

Gill caught Ava's flinch as she placed the plate on the ground in front of Marqui.

"- it wouldn't be surprising if they took people from the jailhouse, the Burgermeister's Manor, and Verdeer Manor."

"So, should we split up?" Kaj asked.

"Yes!" Ortensia piped up.

"No," Gillian retorted.

"Why not?" she whined.

"Because you just want to run away and hide." Ava made her way over to the table and sat next to Valma, "It'll be better to stick together. Strength in numbers and all that."

"I can get some vials of vigor from Verdeer," Gill offered. "So that'll check two things off the list."

"And as much as I never want to set foot in the place again, we should definitely head to jailhouse so you and I can get our weapons," Kaj said to Valma.

"Let's go to the jailhouse first then," Ava said, "it's the middle point between the Burgermeister's and Verdeer."

"From there, can we split up?" Ortensia asked, "Two of you with me, one of you with Gillian."

"Cici-" Valma started.

"Please," she interrupted.

The word shocked them into silence.

"Did she just say please?" Kaj muttered under his breath to Gill.

"I'll go with you," Ava said.

"You will?" Ortensia scoffed.

"Oh uh-" Gill stammered

Ava looked at him, "What?"

"I was gonna ask you to go with me, but if you really want to go with Ortensia-"

"Actually, I want Valma and Kaj to accompany me," Ortensia spoke over him.

"Okay! That settles it then," Valma clapped her hands together to cut through the awkward exchange. "Jailhouse together then split up. Gillian and Ava, you'll meet us at the Burgermeister's once you grab the fix-it juice."

Ava nodded, "We'll take my horse, Jasper. The rest of you can ride on Gentle Paul."

"I have to ride a horse?" Kaj judged, "Named Gentle Paul?"

"You want to walk another 4 miles with those wounds

of yours?" she challenged.

"I mean, couldn't the horse be named something cool? Like Falcon?"

"Why would someone name a horse after a bird?" Gillian questioned.

"Because it's a cool name!" He crossed his arms, "Whatever. Let's get going."

Laughter filled the kitchen as Kaj's childish frustration gave them their first genuine chuckle in a while.

"I have to grab a few things from my room and saddle up the horses, then we can go," Ava said as her laughter subsided. She stood and headed towards the stairs.

"Ava?" Valma called. The edge in her voice caused Ava to pause, foot resting on the first step.

She looked at her sternly, "It's rough up there."

Ava gave a soft, sad smile.

"Thanks for the heads up," she said and continued upstairs.

"She's handling this well," Kaj remarked once she was out of earshot.

༺༻

Ava kept her eyes locked on her bedroom doorway as she walked down the hall, consciously ignoring the flung open doors that taunted her from both sides. Her fingers tingled with numbness, and her heartbeat filled her ears. She picked up her pace as she struggled to ignore her morbid curiosity but made sure to keep her steps light to keep those downstairs from panicking at the sound of her frantic footfalls.

Her breathing was shallow by the time she crossed the threshold into her bedroom. She closed the door and held the doorknob tightly. She pressed her forehead against the door and steadied her breathing, fighting against the tightness that gripped her chest before turning around.

Nausea rolled through her as she took in the disheveled space. The trail of sheets left on the ground from her unconscious body being dragged out of bed and the claw marks from Marqui trying to fight back and get out of the closet caused the room to spin.

We have to grab our bow and get going, she reminded herself. *There's no time to get emotional.*

Ava walked over to the closet and pushed the door fully open. The small burst of relief from seeing her hunting gear sitting untouched on its shelf withdrew as next to it lay the straw hat she'd meant to give to Kieran the night of the dinner party.

Seeing the blue velvet ribbon she so carefully sewed on by hand, stung her already raw throat.

"Well, I've never seen a magpie as stunning as you," a smooth voice purred from the rafters of the Burgermeister's stables. *"Let alone a magpie that could ride a horse."*

Ava couldn't help her smile as she looked up to

glinting moss-green eyes shaded by soft, brown waves. Kieran rested his chin on his forearms and looked down at her with a playful smirk.

"And I've never seen a barn cat with such a roguish smile," she replied.

In one fluid motion, Kieran swung himself down from the rafters and landed gracefully in front of her as she climbed down off of Jasper's back giddily and hitched the horse to one of the stalls.

As she tied the final knot, Kieran wrapped around her waist. She twisted around in his arms as he pulled her in close. His hand made its way to the back of her hair, tangling his fingers in it as he pressed his hungry lips against hers.

"Couldn't wait for tonight, huh?" she teased between kisses.

"Nope," A smile crept on his lips as he stole one final kiss, "I'll meet you at eight, right?"

"Yes, indeedy," she smiled, "aaaannnd I'll have a special gift for you!"

"A present? For me? Why?"

"To celebrate!"

"Did something good happen?"

"'Did something good happen?'" she mimicked, "It's been three months!"

"Three months since…" he stared at her, bewildered.

"Three months since we.. ya know… started seeing each other..." she blushed. Embarrassed and bashful for being so sentimental, she looked away from him.

"Really? Three whole months?"

"Since the Frosttide Feast."

"Oh yeah," Kieran pulled her attention back to him by peppering kisses on her neck, "You looked so hot with that holly braided in your hair."

Her giggles of delight from the compliment stopped short at the sound of heavy boots crunching just outside the stable door. Kieran spun Ava out of his arms, sending her stumbling a few feet away from him.

"I'm sorry, miss, but I can't spare any hay for your horse," he said as the stablemaster entered.

"Not even a small handful? Jasper here has been an awfully good boy today, helping lug veggies all the way up here for the dinner tonight," Ava pleaded. "I could pay you a couple of bister if that would help?"

"Boy," the stablemaster's voice rumbled like thunder, "Give the girl some hay and let her be on her way."

"Of course, sir." Kieran bowed his head and went to grab the hay. The stablemaster walked up next to Jasper and rubbed his hand over his saddle.

"I see you've been using the saddle conditioner I recommended," he said.

"I have been! Thank you so much for telling me about

it." Ava stroked Jasper's nose as she spoke, "I haven't had a problem with mold since I've started using it."

"Good," he grunted.

Feeling the stablemaster's hands inspecting the leather, Marqui popped his head out of the saddlebag he'd been napping in. The gruff man jumped in surprise but recovered quickly and scratched the gray kitty cat under his chin.

Kieran jogged back and handed the hay to Ava, "Here you go. A handful of hay, miss."

Their hands brushed against each other for a moment, and goosebumps crawled up her arm.

"Thank you!" she bowed her head and set her sights towards untying Jasper's reins, "Now Jasper, you'll get this once we meet Ma back by the kitchen. Good to see you both!"

"You too, miss. Have a good day." The stablemaster called after her as she made her way out of the stables.

She turned over her shoulder to steal one last look at Kieran before she left and caught him winking at her just in the nick of time.

※

The memory of the last time she saw him brought the horrifying image of some psychotic cultist dragging his unconscious body into a dank cell. Her nausea subsided, and her dizziness cleared as hatred coursed through her veins. Ava wasn't afraid at the thought of Kieran suffering. She was enraged.

I'll kill them if they hurt you.

She grabbed her sheathed bow and added the remaining arrows from Rundren's temple to its quiver. She threw the rest of her pilfered gear in the bottom of the closet. The man she killed for them's entrails, slowly slipping out, popped into her mind, but the guilt that plagued her yesterday didn't follow.

She slammed the closet door shut.

༺ ༻

"Shall we head to the barn?" Ava asked as she came back downstairs, dressed in her hunting leathers and well-armed. Marqui met her at the bottom with a squeaky mew.

She looked down at him, "Yes, you can come too."

"You're bringing the cat?" Kaj questioned.

"Of course," She scooped Marqui up in her arms and scratched at the star-shaped patch of white fur on his belly.

Kaj looked back at the rest of the group for context, "Am I missing something here?"

"I'm just as lost as you," Valma added.

"Let me guess. It's some kind of magic cat that will solve all our problems," Ortensia rolled her eyes.

"Nope, he's just a cat. A very smart and handsome cat, but a normal cat nonetheless." Ava kissed him on the head.

"Lock the door behind us, will you?" she added as she walked outside.

Gillian followed, patting the flummoxed Kaj on the shoulder, "Come on. I can't wait to see you struggle to mount a horse."

Kaj scowled at his comment and trudged along, unwilling.

"So she can bring a cat, but I can't go home by myself?" Ortensia looked up at Valma.

"Well, one could get you killed," Valma replied, "The other is a cat."

Valma stood by the door and held it open for her, "Come on, my lady. We've got a mystery to solve."

Ortensia exited with a huff, and Valma followed, making sure to turn to lock the door as she left.

CHAPTER NINE

"I hate every part of this," Kaj grumbled as he sat sandwiched between Valma and Ortensia. Valma's muscular arms surrounded them both as she led Gentle Paul down the winding dirt road from Barncombe Farm to the town square.

"Me too," Ortensia commiserated, thoroughly discomforted by Kaj's grip around her waist.

"Doesn't your family keep horses, Cici?" Ava asked as she kept pace beside them. Gillian sat behind her, idly petting Marqui as the cat sat in his custom saddlebag.

"Ugh, now you're calling me that?" Ortensia groaned. "Yes, we keep horses. But I never went near the things. They're mainly used to pull our carriages."

"Well, perhaps after all this is over, I could give you a lesson," Valma offered.

Ortensia looked over her shoulder at her, dumbfounded. "W-why would I want that?" she stammered.

"You never know when it could come in handy," she shrugged, "The Bastions trained us pretty thoroughly at boot camp, so you'd be learning from a professional."

"I'd like to see you and Ava go toe to toe then, Valma." Gillian looked away from the cat to playfully challenge her, "From what I've been told, Ava learned how to ride a horse before she learned how to walk."

"Is that so?"

"Gill's exaggerating a bit," Ava gave him a sidelong glance in disapproval, but his attention was conveniently back on Marqui, "I'm okay. Jasper and I have been together for years now, so it's his trust in me that makes me look better than I am."

Ava scratched the side of Jasper's neck, and he whinnied happily in response.

Kaj leaned forward and whispered in Ortensia's ear, "She downplayed her archery skills too. Next thing you know, she'll be having that horse do somersaults or something."

Ortensia squirmed, "Don't get close to me like that. I don't want to feel you breathe."

He frowned, then blew hard in her ear. She slapped the side of his face in retaliation.

"Quit it, you two," Valma scolded. Her tone turned stern as the quaint country buildings of Elerrï's town square came into view, "We're here."

At this point in the afternoon, the square usually bustled with children leaving the schoolhouse and heading home, folks finishing up their errands, and laborers pushing through the last few hours of their work. One would hear their voices trickling in as the building grew closer, a soft and cheerful murmur accented with bursts of children shrieking and people laughing.

Yet they heard nothing and saw no one.

The clopping of their horses' hooves on the cobblestones echoed across the vacant square, searching for ears to fall on to no avail. Valma and Ava slowed their horses' trot, taking caution in the unease of the emptiness caused. The silence smothered any lingering want to talk. Their hackles raised, and their hearts sank into their stomachs as the worst-case scenario became the only scenario.

The entire town of Elerrï was gone.

They dismounted when they reached the jailhouse and hitched the horses in the covered stable following Valma's lead. The townsguard's somber expression twisted with bitter anger as she pushed the heavy wooden door to the jailhouse open with ease, finding it unlocked, and led them into the empty reception area.

"Hello?" she called out only to have her voice echoed back at her.

"Are they all out looking for us?" Ortensia's voice wavered.

"You know they're not," Ava answered coldly. Marqui's ears perked, and pupils went wide, checking out their surroundings from atop her shoulder.

"Let's grab what we need and go. Quickly," Valma

said. "Kaj, follow me."

"Yes, ma'am," he followed her to the back rooms of the jail, leaving the others behind.

"What the fuck is happening, Stick?" he asked when they went out of earshot, "A whole town kidnapped in one night?"

She stopped abruptly and turned around to face him.

Her eyes threatened to burn holes through him, "If you've got something to do with this-"

"I told you already. I don't!" Kaj cut her off before she finished the thought.

She studied his face, looking for any sign of a lie, before stomping down the hall.

"Your shit is on this shelf," Valma threw open the door to evidence storage.

"Are you mad at me for something?" he walked into the room and followed where she pointed.

"I'm just mad."

Kaj grabbed his lock picks, daggers, and grappling hook off of the shelf and dispersed them between his belt and the inside of his cloak.

"Is- Is there anything else in here that might be useful?" he hesitated to ask.

"No," Valma stated. "You can head back out front. Tell the others I'll be out in a minute."

Kaj scowled and stepped past her out of the room.

"Go punch something while you're back there, will ya?" he said as he walked down the hall, "I know shit sucks, but having a bad attitude about it isn't going to make it any better."

She remained silent as she shut the door and waited until he left to head to the barracks.

Although she'd only been assigned there a week, Valma had grown accustomed to the daily routine of the Elerrï Townsguard. By this time of the day, she would have just been woken up by Deputy Knox to get ready for the night shift. Halfway through their daily game of King's Kith, Tobin and Porter would be laughing to themselves in the corner as she scrambled out of bed, and once she dressed, she'd wander out into the mess and find Captain Reids having her afternoon tea. They'd sit and go over what she needed to be aware of during her patrol that evening before switching to light small talk.

As she entered the mess now, with the familiar golden glow of the afternoon sun illuminating the room, it was as if someone had ripped a hole in her favorite painting.

"The Valborgs are hosting Lord Venzor and his family from Cirvain at a dinner party this evening," Captain Reids said as she brought over two mugs of tea, "You may want to add another pass or two down that way to your patrol tonight."

"You think there's something going down?" Valma's voice tinged with excitement.

"Not particularly. Those noble types just love knowing that guards are a shout away. Gives them a sense of power."

Valma slumped back in her chair, "Great."

"What? Were you hoping for something to go down?"

"No," she lied, "no. It's good that everything's relatively calm here."

"Yes, it is," Reids arched an eyebrow, "It means the townsfolk are safe and free of worry."

"Absolutely." Valma took a long sip of her tea.

"You're bored, aren't you?"

"Bored? I'm not bored," she lied again. "To be honest, I made off easy with my assignment. I've got three years of herding stray goats and booking kids for cow-tipping in my future. Way better than those poor suckers in Moreacor who have to track down the Hilt."

"This town gots its problems," Captain Reids said, "Last year Tom Reegal's prized dairy cow Petunia got killed by wolves. He got absolutely tanked at TOTS the night after. Went around in a drunken rage, pounding on everybody's doors, demanding they bring their dogs out so they can 'pay for the crimes of their ancestors.' It took four of us to hold him down and drag him to the jailhouse to sober up."

"Really? The old man from the ranch?"

"Don't judge a person by their looks, Chan," Captain Reids shook her head. "Tom Reegal could topple a charging bull in his prime, and his son Samuel? If I ever need to put him in a cell for the night, I may need to call the Kyresore Garrison in for reinforcements."

"He got a mean side to him?" Valma was on the edge of her seat.

"No, thank the gods," Captain Reids finished her cup of tea and took her mug to the sink, "That's how you know the world revolves around balance. A man who could crush an ogre's skull with his bare hands has the temperament of a kitten."

Balance, huh? Valma reflected bitterly. Captain Reids empty chair irked her. *What good equals a whole town being abducted?*

She continued to the bunk room, digging into the ground with her heels.

The state of the bunk room mirrored the scenes in Ava's home. Blankets and belongings hung off the punk or sat crumpled to the side by the bodies that were dragged through them.

Valma stepped over the mess and opened her locker, taking out her leather armor and standard-issue longsword. She ran her hands over the Berylwood Crest stamped into the center of her chestnut brown breastplate, tracing the new and deep scratch marks that marred it.

Valma chewed at her fingernails to try and circumvent the unending urge to get up and patrol the western half of the town as she sat waiting in the captain's office.

When the office door finally opened, she hopped to her feet at Captain Reids's entrance.

"I was getting real worried. I didn't know if I should check on you or go ahead and finish up my shift..." Valma drifted off.

"No need to worry about that," Captain Reids walked past her and sat behind her desk, "I've sent word to Annice. She'll be covering the rest of your shift tonight."

"What? Why!" Valma stared at her superior, shocked and confused.

"Why?" Captain Reids spat back, "You broke into the Burgermeister's Manor without letting any of your fellow guards know and destroyed the place!"

"How was I supposed to know that lanky ginger kid was gonna send a bunch of roots through the floorboards?"

"You couldn't have! That's the point!" Captain Reids slammed her fist against the desk, "You could have told us about that thief with the touch of your fingers! It's right there on your wrist!" The captain held up her arm and pointed to the communication pendant embedded in her bracer, "And I know they taught you how to use it at boot camp."

Valma looked down at her own pale yellow pendant, a soft glow slowly pulsing against the leather bracer it rested in.

"Look, I get it," the captain continued. "You're young, you got settled with a slowpoke town for your training, and you're just busting at the seams for some action; but rushing head-on into dangerous situations blindly and without backup is not only going to get you killed but will get a shit ton of other people killed."

"But what if there's not enough time? What if you just have to act?" *Valma stood tall and defiant.*

"There is always enough time to think," *Captain Reids was unfazed, her gaze damning and severe,* "The more you do it, the faster you'll get."

The two stared at each other for a moment; Valma stalwart, Captain Reids studying. The captain shook her head and looked down at the paperwork in front of her.

"Take the night, get some sleep, and take a vigor for your injuries. You still have the day off tomorrow, and we'll start you on day shift next week. You're dismissed."

Valma gripped her breastplate tightly. She was so angry, so sad, and so unable to do anything about it.

What do I do now, Capt.? Is there enough time to think?

"Ah! There's that signature shit brown suit!" Kaj cheered as Valma walked back out into the main lobby, donned in her uniform with her proper sword sheathed on her side.

"You ready to go?" Ava asked.

"Just one second," Valma placed two fingers on the communication pendant on her bracer.

"Captain Reids, can you hear me?" She said, "We're safe and at the jailhouse."

To the others, she spoke without sound.

"Oh, that's so smart!" Gillian gushed. "Gods, I can't wait to learn how to make those."

A light bulb went off in Kaj's head, and he slyly ran his fingers over the palm of his left glove, searching for the hidden pendant.

I should check in with Seax and the others. If they got taken-

His train of thought stopped short as his fingers brushed against an empty socket.

"Something wrong with your hand?" Ava asked, noticing him staring at his hand in awe.

"Valma has magick?!" He pulled away from his hand and played off his panic with cartoonish bewilderment.

"Oh, come on," Ortensia scoffed, "You really don't know what that thing is?"

"Nah, I do." Kaj smiled fiendishly, "I was just trying

to lighten up the mood."

Ortensia rolled her eyes. Ava's eyes narrowed in suspicion.

"No response," Valma reported as she removed her fingers from the pendant, "Either none of the guards are wearing theirs, or they're out of range. There were a few people on duty last night, so I have a feeling it's the latter."

"What's the range for those?" Ava asked.

"Five miles," she replied.

"But there could be other things causing interference," Gill added.

"True. Gods, I hate how much we don't know." Valma rubbed her palm over her face and sighed, "Alright. Let's split up, grab us some vigors, and get you two some regular clothes." She looked at Gill and Ortensia's blood-stained and dirtied pajamas.

"And perhaps a bath as well while we're at it?" Ortensia asked.

"No," they all replied.

CHAPTER TEN

They parted ways. Gillian and Ava headed west to Verdeer Manor while Valma, Kaj, and Ortensia headed towards the burgermeister's in the east.

Nerves knotted up Gill's stomach as he and Ava traveled further from the others, accentuating the vastness of the empty town much to his unease.

"Do you think he'll be there?" Ava asked. Her full focus was on the road in front of them.

"I don't know," he replied to the back of her head. He couldn't help but notice how even though her hair was matted, with dried splashes of blood and leaves scattered throughout, it somehow still shined.

"Master Gustav's pretty strong," she said, "I'm sure that with whatever happened to everyone last night, he made it out."

"I hope so," he mumbled. His master was an extremely capable wizard, and Verdeer Manor was extremely well warded, yet somehow Gillian wound up in the cell at the bottom of an underground tomb.

"You're pretty strong too, ya know," she added, "Was that the first time you used heavy-duty spells like that?"

A pang of an old and familiar guilt pulled at his chest. He looked down at Marqui, his tiny head just peeking out of the saddlebag, sniffing the air softly, and reached down to rub his little gray nose with his finger. The cat purred contently.

"No," he admitted quietly.

"Oh."

He spoke a little louder, "You were right though- what you said in the skeleton room- the Convocation sent me here to learn how to control it." He cleared his throat, "If it's any consolation, I haven't done anything like that in years."

"You were sent to the Convocation? I thought you joined." Ava turned to look at him. Her brows furrowed with concern.

He looked up at her and half-smiled.

"I'll tell you about it later," he pointed ahead, "We're almost there." He didn't want her to worry about him, not when she had so many other things to fret over.

She scowled for a brief moment, turned back around, and snapped the reigns, quickening their pace as they approached the domed roofs of Gillian's temporary home.

"So why'd you pick the Stick and me to go with ya?"

Kaj asked.

The trio turned down the fork in the road that led to the uphill residence of Burgermeister Delvin Valborg and his family.

"Because you two are obviously the most capable," Ortensia stated, "The mage is too much of a risk. He already destroyed my house enough for one lifetime."

"Yeah, but we destroyed your house too," he replied.

"You broke a window and interrupted a dinner party where now half of the attendees are dead," she said, "that's a minor offense comparatively."

"Right," he doubted, "But what about Ava?"

"What about Ava?" she spat back.

"She's still upset that she told her off," Valma answered. "And here I thought your little watch together patched things up. I was surprised when I woke up to see you both in one piece."

"Ladies of high society can be cordial with someone and still hate their guts," she bragged, "Otherwise, nothing would ever get done."

"So not only do you have five clones, but you also have two faces," Kaj remarked.

"Would you like another hole in your stomach?"

"Look, I've got my stuff back now, so good luck getting one of those freaks near me," he boasted.

"You never know," Ortensia teased, "I could be one right now."

"Don't joke about that!"

Valma's hearty laugh interrupted their petty argument.

"What are you laughing at?!" Kaj exclaimed.

"It's funny watching you two become friends," she answered.

"We're not friends!" they shouted in tandem.

Verdeer Manor sprouted no gardens, only a long green lawn with a stone paver path that led from the tall wrought iron gate to the red brick manor. The brass domes atop the cylindrical tower that framed the building shown brightly in the midday sun, looking as unweathered as the day they were erected.

"Walk right behind me, and make sure to hold on tightly to Marqui," Gill cautioned. "Master Gustav loves his booby traps."

"Well, it looks as though none of them have been triggered," Ava lifted her cat from his saddlebag and laid him around her shoulders as she glanced over the spacious yard, "That could be a good sign."

"No," he sighed. "Master made the traps clean and reset automatically so he wouldn't have to." Gillian made his way down the path, footsteps landing directly on the center crack that split the two columns of pavers. Ava followed close behind.

"Now the steps aren't trapped on the way up, but they are on the way down," he instructed as they got closer, "If you have to leave, skip the fifth step, then stay on the right of the path. Does that make sense?"

"Yup. Skip the fifth, stay to the right."

They made their way up the steps without issue. Gillian approached the door cautiously and held his hand over the simple brass doorknob. He searched for the thrumming of Gustav's ward and found nothing.

"Shit," he swore.

"What is it?" Ava asked.

"Someone removed this trap."

"That's a good thing, right?"

"No, it's not," Gillian chewed at his bottom lip, "Master and I only disarm the traps. If it's been removed, then someone else has been here."

Ava grabbed Marqui off her shoulder and placed him on the ground beside her, "Stay close," she instructed the cat as she readied her bow.

Gill watched her intently as she nocked her arrow and pulled her bowstring back slightly. She gave him a curt nod.

He opened the door.

The large foyer of Verdeer Manor resembled a high-end antique shop more than a home. Decorated with a varied collection of art pieces, large paintings, sculptures, and intricately carved and upholstered furniture pieces cluttered the path surrounding the main staircase and the hallways on either side of it. The upper portion of the stairs blossomed into a balcony that oversaw the hodgepodge gallery and led to the upper rooms.

"We should head upstairs first," Gill whispered, "There's a communication curio in my room. If Master is here, we'll be able to speak with him that way."

"Okay."

"Now, we don't know what traps have been removed, so you'll need to pay close attention to how I move through the house, alright?" He paused as the reality of what he was about to do in front of Ava set in. "And promise not to laugh."

"Why would I laugh?"

Gillian pleaded with his eyes as his face turned a soft shade of red, "Just promise me."

"I promise?" Ava questioned. She looked down at Marqui and instructed him, "Copycat."

Marqui's ears perked up, and he moved behind her. The little gray cat sat on his hind legs and lifted his front paws, stretching one forward and bending the other to mirror her stance.

"Good boy," she turned back to Gill, "Let's go."

Gill inhaled a deep, shaky breath, trying to forget that Ava was there to cool the heat of embarrassment that burned his face and coax the butterflies in his stomach to rest their wings.

He took his first step into the foyer and began to sing.

"The robin got fat on the first spring day-"

His singing voice trickled out less like the strong bravado of a musical troupe's lead and more the timid mutterings of someone with stage fright.

"- and lost his nest to the old blue jay-"

He hopped across the parquet pattern of the foyer's wooden floor to the melody, weaving around the statues and furniture with well-practiced grace from the hundreds of times he had traversed the foyer since he came to live here at the age of six.

"-So on the ground he had to stay-" on the elongated note of "stay" he reached the bottom step of the staircase.

"-and became the kingsnake's prey!" he tapped his hand on the wooden blue jay that sat on top of the left banister's newel post.

The step creaked as Ava and Marqui landed on the bottom step next to him.

Every muscle in Gill's body stiffened at the sound. He'd forgotten for a fleeting moment that Ava was following him, watching him. Mortified, he continued to face the blue jay a little longer than needed, looking to the wooden bird for some way out of the awkward situation.

"Is something wrong with the blue jay?" Ava

whispered over his shoulder.

"N-no," he stammered. His cheeks burned, and his palms went clammy.

A heavy silence hung in the air.

"You're a decent dancer-"

"The staircase is disabled," he interrupted her. If he focused on the task ahead of them, maybe this moment would pass. "Once we get up, we'll make a left and head down the hall towards my room. Make sure to skip every fourteenth floorboard."

His words were met with silence, and he sheepishly turned to look at her.

Ava's face was knotted up and turning red from holding in her laughter.

"You promised not to laugh!"

"I'm really trying not to, but you're being so ridiculous that it's hard!" she choked out, "I'm serious! One night out at TOTS, and you'll have the ladies lining up to dance with you!"

"Now you're just teasing me," he groaned and started to trudge up the stairs. Ava chased after him.

"No, I'm not!" she protested and looked to the cat keeping pace beside her, "Marqui even liked your singing, didn't you Qui?"

"Aerw," he gave a clipped meow, mirroring the

hushed tone of Ava's and Gill's whispers.

"Don't bring Qui into this," Gill chided, stepping over the first fourteenth floorboard, "I don't need to know that cats can lie."

Ava and Marqui skipped over the same board.

"He's not lying! Marqui never lies. Right bud?" Marqui's wide yellow eyes stared up at her, "Yeah, you're right. You did try to hide that you ate all of the bacon Pa cooked up for Ma's birthday breakfast last year."

Gillian skipped over another board, "Just don't tell the others, alright? It's one thing if you tease me, but you know Kaj will never let me live it down."

He stopped in front of his bedroom and turned to face the door. Ava skipped the last step, just as he did, and stood beside him.

"Look, if I were teasing you, you'd know it, alright?" she said.

Gillian turned to look at her, cocking his eyebrow in disbelief only for the expression to quickly vanish. He didn't expect her to be so close to him. Her big, brown eyes were playful and bright as she smiled coyly at him. It had been a while since she last looked at him like that. He missed seeing her like this, at ease and sprightly, especially when it was because of something he did, even if it was at the expense of her teasing him.

A sudden realization of the possible implications behind her words caused a different kind of blush to heat his freckled face.

"This is my room," Gill mumbled.

The spark in her eyes snuffed out as her smile dropped, pulled down as her jaw clenched.

Gillian blanched as quickly as he blushed.

Did I say something wrong?

"Right. I'll keep watch out here," Ava said. "You go ahead and see if you can reach Master Gustav."

Her eyes flitted between his body and his face, "And get changed while you're at it."

His remorse was immediate. He rebuked himself for forgetting the purpose of their visit so easily. How many times had Master Gustav scolded him for feeling his emotions too deeply? For being too caught up in the moment that all rationality went out the window.

Gillian drew his attention away from her and focused on the door in front of him.

"Be careful. Shout if you need me." His fingertips glowed red as he tapped them against his bedroom door, hitting the invisible arcane protection sigils imbued into it. A red shimmer of magick flashed across it as he turned the doorknob and entered.

༺ ༻

A gothic monstrosity of gray stone and ebony, the Burgermeister's Manor sat upon a high hill looming over the verdant countryside of Elerrï like the shadow of a hawk over prey. For Kaj and Valma, the manor seemed even more haunting, knowing that the town below it was empty, but to Ortensia, it was just as villainous as it always was.

"Don't bother stabling the horse, Valma," she said as they approached the main entrance, "It's beneath us. I'll have one of the stewards take care of it once we get in the household."

"And if there are no stewards?" Valma asked.

"All of my servants are extremely loyal and would never leave my family in their time of need," she reasoned, "and besides, this horse is an outside creature. The fresh air will be good for it."

Ortensia didn't know exactly when she started to pick at her cuticles on the ride up, but the sharp sting as she peeled off a long strip of skin drew her attention down to find blood trickling down the side of her thumb.

"Ortensia!" Her maid, Cordelia, pulled her out of her frenzied mind by her hands. Ortensia's vision cleared, the fog lifting as she focused on her worried gray eyes, "Your hands. They're bleeding."

Ortensia looked down to find her russet palms stained red. Her cuticles picked apart and left raw from her fit.

"Oh dear..." she shuddered, her panic picking up again as she realized the severity of the damage.

"Come. Sit." Cordelia led her to the chair in front of her vanity and seated her. She rushed to pull a rag out of the drawer and wrapped Ortensia's fingers in it, applying pressure to stop the flow of blood. "You must be more careful when you go into your fits. If I wasn't here to stop you, you would have picked your fingers to the bone, and it'd be too painful for you to play."

"Well, it won't matter for tonight," Ortensia fretted, "No sonata or jig will save me from the grave error I have made."

"Grave error?" Cordelia questioned, "What? Lord Octavian's allergy?"

"I should have known. I should have asked when I wrote my missives to father's contacts in the city."

"You asked what their preferred foods were, correct? Perhaps the ladies did not know. Nobles tend to be very secretive about any possible invalid tendencies within their families," Cordelia removed the rag and pulled a vial of astringent out of one of the drawers. "There. It's a little better. I'm going to apply this just to keep them from getting inflamed. It will sting for a moment."

Ortensia flinched as she dropped the astringent on her cuticles but didn't pull away.

"The evening is far from ruined," Cordelia continued. "You learned about the lord's predicament just in time and addressed it accordingly. If anything, it was very fortunate that Ava was with her mother."

"Ava?" Ortensia asked. Cordelia stood, putting the bottle away and tossing the rag in a hamper.

"The Barncombe's daughter. She's quite the accomplished hunter. Remember that large buck that was delivered as a gift for the Frosttide Feast last year?"

"I think so."

"That was her work."

"I guess fate doesn't hate me too much then," Ortensia sighed. "In my frenzied state, I would have said yes to any hick who said they hunted," she pulled at her skirt, "So stupid!"

"Shhh…" Cordelia smoothed her hand over Ortensia's thick, curly hair, "You're stressed. Beating yourself up will only make it worse."

"I have to learn these things, or I'll never survive in proper society."

"Well, then add learning to forgive yourself to the list." Cordelia placed her hands on Ortensia's shoulders and turned her towards the mirror, "The world is already harsh enough. We don't need to help it hurt us."

Ortensia grimaced and looked at Cordelia through the mirror, admiring how stunningly the streaks of blonde hair that hung loose from her bun framed her pale face as the maid's reflection smiled at her.

How can a person as beautiful as you be so kind? Ortensia thought.

"Now, let's start getting you ready for this evening." Cordelia gently pulled the pins out of Ortensia's hair, "I hear the women in Moraecor like to take at least ten hours getting ready during courting season."

Ortensia wrapped her thumb up in her grimy nightgown and applied pressure.

With Gentle Paul hitched to the railing, they walked up the porch steps and found the doors to the manor locked.

"Well, that's a good sign," Kaj remarked and set to work picking the lock. The tumblers clicked in place easily, and in a few seconds, he held open the door for them, playing gentleman.

"My lady," he bowed.

"Now that is the treatment I should have been receiving this entire time," Ortensia held her chin high in the air as she walked past.

"Should I let the door hit her in the ass?" Kaj grumbled to Valma after Ortensia entered.

"I don't know," Valma replied as she walked through the door, "Are you looking to become a saint?"

"What?" Kaj stepped in behind her.

"Because she'd make you even more holey," she smiled a smug, eat shit grin.

Kaj grimaced and groaned, "Kill me."

A large portrait of the Valborg family looked down upon them as they entered the sparsely decorated main foyer of the Burgermeister's Manor. Burgermeister Valborg's fat, balding head and pale skin marred with rosacea looked garish compared to the warm browns of his family. He loomed over the shoulders of his wife, daughter, and son, clearly standing upon a stool hidden from view by the Burgermistress' billowing skit. Their stoic, painted faces seemed filled with disgust as they looked upon the wreckage of the other night's escapades.

The once sturdy staircase with a beautifully carved banister was shredded, splintered, and consumed by a tangle of thick roots. Piercing through the foundation of the manor, some of the roots were a foot wide and reached well up into the second story, while others had their jagged ends chopped off by the servants tasked with removing Kaj and Valma from the wreckage.

"What a disaster," Ortensia muttered to herself at the sight.

"Cordelia! Baretta! Wilfred!" her shrill calls echoed off the walls.

"Shit, that feels like a lifetime ago now," Kaj remarked as he studied the thicket. "It seemed smaller inside of it."

"I guess we're lucky it was roots and not rocks," Valma added, running a hand over one of the thicker branches.

His eyes grew wide, "I didn't even think about that. Fuck."

"Yeah," she sympathized.

"This is unacceptable!" Ortensia huffed, "Why haven't they come yet?"

"Because cultists kidnapped them," Kaj answered honestly.

Kaj and Valma continued to stare at the root-bound monolith while Ortensia pushed down the feeling of sadness that trickled down her spine as the silence of manor became oppressive.

"Well, fine then. Let me get out of this filthy nightgown, and we'll go look for them," she spat.

"How are you going to get to your room? Isn't it upstairs?" Kaj asked.

"How do you know where my room is?"

He hesitated for a moment, "Because most noble people have their bedrooms upstairs?"

"That's how he snuck into the house last night," Valma said, giving Kaj a sidelong glare. "You need to start locking your balcony doors."

"So you're a thief and a pervert!" Ortensia shrieked.

"I am not a pervert!" he shouted back, "And if I were, I certainly wouldn't be rooting through your bedroom!"

"What? Are my undergarments not good enough for a pervert?"

"Alright, I'm ending this squabble right now because

it's not leading anywhere good," Valma interjected. "Cici, do you need help getting upstairs?"

"No, there is a stairwell that the servants use towards the back of the house," she replied.

"Good. Then you go get changed while Kaj and I look around to see if there are any clues telling us where they've been taken," she said, "Sound like a plan?"

"Works for me," he grumbled.

"Just keep him away from my bedroom." Ortensia stormed off towards the back of the house.

"I'll go left. You go right?" Valma asked as the patter of Ortensia's footsteps faded.

"Actually," Kaj said, "there was something I noticed the other night that I wanted to check out."

Valma looked him over curiously and let out a wary, "Lead the way."

The red glow of the communication curio sat on Gillian's desk, taunting him as it pulsed softly with magick.

So Gill decided to get dressed first.

He took off his ruined pajamas slowly, blaming his sore muscles on his procrastination. The thin cotton peeled off of him painfully. The minor wounds he sustained from the night prior bound themselves to his clothes, ripping off scabs as he undressed. The reopened wounds burned no matter how careful he was.

If this is painful for me, I can't imagine how it must be for Valma and Kaj, he thought. The nightstalker's shriek ran through the back of his mind, or Ava, for that matter.

His gaze lingered on the back of his bedroom door for a moment.

He threw his clothes into the laundry basket and headed over to the dresser to grab something clean. It was comforting to slip on an unbloodied pair of pants, their cleanliness a stark contrast to the sullied state of his skin. Ortensia's want to take a bath made all the more sense now. He opened the top drawer to retrieve a clean shirt and found his Cerulean Mage's vestment folded just the way he left it.

"Are you almost finished?" Master Gustav's voice echoed from the hall outside of the laboratory.

"I'm filling the last bottles now!" Gillian shouted back. He gently tipped the bubbling beaker. His hands grasped the tongues tightly, trying to keep the flow of piping hot ooze steady as he filled each vial.

"My boy, you are so very lucky you are the apprentice to a master mage," Gustav said, tone dripping with sass, "otherwise your ass would be filling vigors in the back of a rickety carriage."

"True. But you are a kind and powerful master who knows how important it is for a student to finish their work," he topped off the last vial and placed the beaker and tongs off to the side.

Master Gustav dipped his head under the door frame, the tips of his long, elven ears brushing against it, and entered the room, donned in his formal robe and obsidian vest. He handed Gillian's cerulean vest to him with a thrust, "Save me the flattery. I can teleport us there, and you knowingly took advantage of that."

"Knowingly?" Gill scoffed as he took off his gloves and apron, "I told you I got lost! Your ability to teleport is more like a godsend for my incompetence."

"A mage is never incompetent, merely misguided," Gustav took the gloves and apron from Gill and hung them on the wall, "And we'll craft you a returning rod tomorrow to help with that."

Gillian buttoned the final button on his vest, "How do I look?"

"Like you in a blue vest." Gustav rolled his eyes, "You ready?"

"I suppose," he sighed.

He slid the vest over his shirt and buttoned it shut. He looked in the mirror and smoothed his hands down his sides, tracing its quilted swirls as he exhaled heavily. He glanced back over at his desk and the red beacon of unknowing that taunted him.

He chided his hesitation. Mages of the Arcane Convocation protected all of the Kingdom of Berylwood's citizens. How could he ever call himself one of them if he was too scared of his master being captured to touch a damn gemstone?

He forced himself to approach it. The communication curio was a clear beryl gem, rounded and smooth, attached to a small wooden base carved to resemble a bird's nest. The signature red glow of Master Gustav's inherent Prakari magicks, pulsed inside it, giving it color.

Gillian appeared alone in his bedroom.

"Master?" he asked the air, confused.

There was no response.

Usually, when they teleported back to Verdeer, Master Gustav would have them arrive in the foyer.

Gill walked over to his desk and touched his curio, "Master Gustav? Is everything alright?"

There was a moment of silence before the gem returned an answer.

"Go to sleep, Gillian," Gustav's voice rang in his head. "We'll talk in the morning."

The disappointment in his master's voice weighed heavily on his already guilty conscience.

Gillian sat on his bed and stared at his hands for a

long while. That overwhelming magick swirled beneath his skin, calmer than when it manifested, but still pacing like a tupping ram locked in its pen.

Those roots... he called them, and they answered even though he didn't say a word.

Is this what happened back then?

He shuddered and wrung his hands together.

"I must practice more," he mumbled under his breath, "I must have greater discipline. I can't save people if every time I come to their rescue, I destroy their home."

He kept kneading his thumb across the palm of his hand.

Gillian placed his hand on the curio, determined to stall no longer.

"Master," he spoke, and the curio's magick swallowed his voice, "I'm back and have so much to talk to you about. Something terrible has happened. Are you here? Are you in the manor?"

There was no response.

Calm and rational.

He took a deep, though shaky breath.

"I'll be heading to the laboratory. Ava is with me. We'll be heading to the Valborgs' manor after," he removed his hand from the gem and wiped away the tears that rolled down his cheeks.

He took another deep breath, grabbed his satchel, and headed out.

―――

The door opened behind Ava, and she nearly jumped out of her skin. She whipped around, bowstring pulled taught, and the tip of her arrowhead brushed against Gill's throat.

"It's me!" he yelped.

"Sorry," Ava loosened her grip on the bowstring and lowered her weapon, "sorry, I'm just-"

"It's okay," he consoled her, "We're all a little jumpy." He stepped out of the room and closed the door behind him.

"Any word?"

"No. That doesn't mean he didn't hear me, though. I let him know where we're heading. Come on." Gill led the way, making sure to skip the same floorboards as before, "The potions are in the laboratory. Same deal as before, just follow what I do exactly, alright?"

"Alright," Ava confirmed.

"Arow," Marqui added.

―――

After a cursory search on the bottom floor, Kaj and Valma found the servants' stairwell and made their way to the third floor. Though they were there briefly the other evening, the third floor of the Burgermeister's Manor seemed like a different world in the daylight.

"Man, it's a lot less creepy when it's not the dead of night," Valma remarked as they walked down the hall. "A lot easier to see too."

"Speak for yourself," Kaj said. "All this sunlight is starting to give me a headache."

"You sure it's the sunlight and not all the blood you've lost?"

"Probably a combination of the two." They turned a corner and found themselves just down the hall from Ortensia's bedroom.

"Brings back memories, doesn't it?" she clapped a hand on his shoulder.

"Come on," he shrugged her hand off, "better move quickly, or she'll think we're both peeping Toms."

They moved past her bedroom, not daring to look at her door, and turned down the hall to their left.

"Good gods," Valma stopped in front of Burgermeister Valborg's study, "someone actually has a door like that in their *home*?"

"Valborg definitely makes some strong design choices," Kaj said.

The door to the burgermeister's study was quite unlike that lined the halls of his manor. Made of thick ebony, the door was carved with swirling vines entangled around a plethora of incredibly detailed magical beasts. All the beasts called out with open mouths, frantic as the vines wrapped tightly around their necks.

"I'm surprised you didn't notice how garish it was last night," Kaj continued.

"Well, one of us is a dusk elvefolk who can see in the dark, and the other is not, so...."

"Right," Kaj gripped the doorknob, but it wouldn't turn. He thumped his head against the door and groaned before reaching for his lock picks. Valma grabbed his wrist as he pulled the picks out of his cloak.

"What are you doing?" she warned.

"The door is locked. I'm picking it," he looked over his shoulder, "Remember, 'who better to pick a lock than a thief.'"

Her grip on his wrist tightened, "I can't just let you break into someone's private office."

"An entire town is missing, and you're worried about the legalities of a minor B and E?" he scoffed. "I promise I'll lock it when I leave."

"Just," Valma warred with herself, "tell me. What does the burgermeister's study have to do with all this?"

Under the cover of night, Kaj stepped into Delvin Valborg's study slowly. He scanned for traps and people lurking in the shadows and, finding nothing, shut the garish door behind him.

Everything in the study sat low to the ground to suit its dwarven owner, save for the bookshelves that stretched to the ceiling. Kaj walked alongside them, running his hand across the books, reading some of the spines whose language he understood. He pulled his hand away to find his fingertips covered in dust.

"I am so sorry," he whispered to the books, "I'll take some of you out of here."

He stood on his toes and grabbed two books off the highest shelf and them into the back of his pants, held snugly against him by his belt, lest Seax and Bolo teased him when he showed them his haul.

He made his way over to Valborg's dark wooden desk, lock picks in hand, and went to work on the left-hand drawer noted in his briefing. The lock came undone in a matter of seconds, and the drawer slid open in welcome as the last pin nestled into place.

There, sat snugly in the drawer, rested a neat stack of letters. He removed the stack and leafed through the pile before pulling out a random letter to read. A giddy smile crept up his face at the extremely dirty words written in the very neat cursive of Carran Bay's Archduchess, Alarice.

"You really ought to get better at hiding things, Valborg," Kaj scolded as he folded up the letter and stuffed the entire stack into one of the hidden pockets in the inner lining of his cloak.

"Now," he twirled his lock picks across his fingers, "let's see what you've got in the other drawer."

He placed the picks inside the right drawer's lock. It looked nearly identical to the one on the left drawer, and Kaj expected it to have just as little resistance as its counterpart but met a different set of tumblers. Baffled, he got onto knees and pressed his ear against the wood to listen for the clicks of success as he worked.

"Shit," he cursed after a few minutes. Frustration took over, and he stood, rattling the lock picks inside it, begging for it to just unlock.

"His desk has two different locks on its drawers," Kaj said honestly, making use to look Valma in the eye as he did, "I was tasked to take whatever was in the left drawer and leave."

He laughed softly, "And let me tell you, a toddler could have picked that lock. So, I got a little greedy and went to check out the right drawer as well, and…" Kaj glowered, "it was like the type of lock they'd use to keep criminal masterminds chained up or something."

"Then clearly there's something important in there," Valma stated. She narrowed her eyes, "Why should I let you have it?"

"That's why I asked you to come with me," he admitted. Kaj sighed heavily and rubbed his face. He tired of her constantly questioning his motives.

"I'm not trying to pull any tricks with this one. If it's something important like town documents or something, I'll just close the drawer and relock it. But if it's something to do with this craziness-" he rolled his eyes in disgust, "Well, I guess someone of *the law* should bear witness."

Valma's tense demeanor eased, and that irritating, cocky smirk of hers crept onto her face, "So you've decided to give up your life of crime and become a law-abiding citizen then?"

"Nope," he gave an eat shit grin back. He found himself happy to see Valma loosen up, "Just trying to get out of prison on good behavior."

"Alright then, pick the lock to your heart's content. But first, you got to tell me one thing." She asked, "What did your mysterious employer want you to steal from Valborg in the first place?"

He reached into the hidden pocket of his cloak and felt for the folded letter. He held it out. Valma reached out to grab it, and he pulled it back.

"Don't tell anyone I showed you this."

"Is it dangerous?"

"Not particularly," Kaj snickered as he handed it over. "Depends on how innocent you are."

A blush came over Valma's face as she read. She lasted only a few seconds before she shoved the letter back at him.

"So," she cleared her throat and looked at the door behind him instead of his face, "blackmail then?"

"Yup." He tucked the letter back into his hidden pocket, "You'd think he'd have something as incriminating as this locked uptight. Makes you wonder what he's got in the other one then, doesn't it?"

Out of nowhere, Valma's eyes widened.

"What?" Kaj asked, his voice wary.

"I kicked this door open when I was chasing after you," she stated. "The doorjamb isn't even splintered, and the lock is fixed..."

She locked eyes with him, her expression fierce, "Open this door. Now."

Gillian and Ava stood in front of the door to Gustav's laboratory. Gill tapped his fingers across it, touching the hidden runes engraved in the wood in the proper pattern. As he touched the last sigil, a red shimmer of magick cascaded over the doorway.

He looked at Ava and nodded, silently questioning if she was ready to proceed.

She raised her bow in response, and Gillian opened the door.

As the door swung open, the light from the hallway poured into the dark laboratory. Its beam illuminated a portion of the brown, stone tiles and a tan, unconscious elven man, bald with long pointed ears, too tall for the chair he was heavily chained to.

"Master!" Gillian cried and rushed into the room. His hands reached to pull the chains off of Gustav, but as he touched the cool metal, his body seized.

A guttural scream tore through his throat.

"G-gill?!" Ava choked out.

"They're lead," he forced through the muscles locking up his jaw, "I can't move."

She sheathed her bow and rushed into the room, "What's wrong?"

"Lead," the pain grew unbearable as the metal slowly cemented his magicks, stopping their proper circulation through his body. "Blocks magicks. Hurts."

"Okay," Ava swallowed, "D-do you have bolt cutters down here? A-any tools that we-"

The door slammed shut, swallowing them in darkness.

Marqui let out a low rumbling growl, and a deep, gravelly laugh echoed through the laboratory in response.

"You have a cute little kitty," a menacing voice said.

A lantern ignited near the door, illuminating the large, meaty hand that held it, and the pock-marked face of the man connected that hand.

"But you're not supposed to be here."

Ortensia laid naked on her bed, staring at the ceiling.

The weight of a sadness she could not name sank her deeper into her mattress.

She woke to the sound of Cordelia placing her breakfast on the bedside table.

"Good morning, miss," she greeted as she noticed Ortensia's eyes flutter open.

"Could you be a little quieter, Cordelia?" She sat up in her bed, "The clattering of the silverware woke me, and you know how much I need my beauty sleep with Lord Venzor arriving today."

"Of course, miss. However, you would like to make sure you have the proper time to prepare, would you not?"

"I do suppose," Ortensia held out her hands for a teacup. Cordelia obliged. "What time is it anyway?"

"A little past ten, miss."

She sipped her tea, "Wonderful. And things are well underway downstairs?"

"Everything has been tidied and decorated as per your instructions. The main courses are marinating, and the produce from Barncombe Farm will be delivered at noon."

"Good. Any word on the Venzors' carriage?"

"Nothing yet, miss. But the garrison stationed on Kryesore Road has been instructed to send word once they've been spotted."

Ortensia held her hand out, and Cordelia passed a plate of scones over to her, "Thank you."

She took a bite and slightly smiled, a rare shift from her usual, nonplussed expression. "Did you make these?"

"Yes, I did, miss," *Cordelia smiled back,* "How did you know?"

"You're the only one who knows how much I love cinnamon."

"Well, I figured you might want to start the day off on the right foot."

Ortensia met Cordelia's bright gray eyes, admiring them for a moment, before turning to look towards her wardrobe. She sighed.

"What color gown should I wear for this evening then? Since you know me better than most."

"Well, miss, I've always thought the lavender gown with the embroidered vines looked stunning on you."

"The lavender one. What about the dark blue one with the lace trim?"

"That one is pretty, but the lavender one," *Cordelia's hand brushed Ortensia's as she took the empty teacup from her,* "looks so lovely against your skin."

"Lord Venzor's favorite color is blue." *Ortensia said, her voice metered,* "Father told me I should wear the dark blue one."

"I've never known a man to know much about women's dresses," Cordelia replied. "But if that is what the burgermeister wants, then that is what the burgermeister gets. Perhaps later this evening, you have a costume change."

Ortensia chuckled and turned her attention back to her maid, "Perhaps I will."

"Finished with your plate, miss?"

"Yes, I am."

Cordelia bent down and picked the plate off of Ortensia's lap.

"One moment, Cordelia," she said.

Cordelia stilled as Ortensia took her hand up to her face and smoothed a loose strand of hair back behind her ear.

"It was bothering me."

"Thank you, miss," Cordelia grabbed the plate, her cheeks slightly rosy, "Will that be all?"

"Yes, I suppose." Ortensia's chilled demeanor returned, "I'll be down in a moment to check on the arrangements. Please make sure that mother is out of my way."

"Of course, miss." Cordelia bowed her head and headed out the door with the breakfast tray in hand.

Ortensia pulled herself off of her bed and walked over to the wardrobe. The lavender dress with embroidered vines hung where she left it. She ran a hand down its sleeve, tracing the delicate stitches under her fingertips, before grabbing it off its hook and putting it on.

She looked in the mirror of her vanity as she buttoned up the last few buttons of the bodice. She flattened her hands over the dress and studied herself. As she picked a few stray leaves out of her tight curls, she scowled, regretting having given Valma her headscarf to use as a bandage, and twisted her hair up to secure it with one of her jeweled hair combs.

Ortensia ran her hand over her haphazard up-do and frowned, "It would look better if Cordelia were here to do it."

She yanked the comb back out, placed it on top of the vanity, and left the room.

"I thought you were an expert at this," Valma grumbled as she hovered over Kaj's shoulder.

"I told you this lock is fucking tricky as hell- but I almost-" the final pin clicked. Kaj grinned from ear to ear, "-got it!"

He stood back and opened the drawer slowly.

Inside was a folded letter addressed to Delvin Valborg, its wax seal broken, and a small black leather folder. The seal and the folder shared the same sigil: an hourglass on its side with sand resting equally in each half.

A piercing scream from beneath them shattered the silence.

"Shit!" Valma bolted out of the room.

Kaj palmed the letter, folder, and a few loose documents he felt underneath them, stuffed them down his pants, and ran after her.

They sprinted through the halls and tore down the servants' stairwell.

"Cici!" Valma screamed, "Ortensia!"

Another shriek rang out, louder and more precise, from the foyer.

Valma made a hard left and ran down the hall towards her screams, Kaj right at her heels. The passageway led to the familiar staircase covered in roots and the unexpected sight of an elven woman with short black hair and a hard face holding a curved blade against Ortensia's throat.

They skidded to a stop.

The elf cocked her head to the side in surprise at Kaj and Valma's frantic entrance, and a sickening, pleasant smile curled up her face.

Kaj's blood ran cold.

"Well, Kaj," she said, "I didn't know you hung out with spoiled rich kids. Did you know that, Bolo?"

A bony hand rested on each of their shoulders, and their knees buckled, suddenly fatigued as if they had eaten in days.

"No, I didn't, Seax." Bolo leaned in close to Kaj, his

breath hot against his cheek and reeking of rot, "You should have stayed in your cage, newbie."

CHAPTER ELEVEN

In a panic, Ava tore her bow from its sheath and fired. Too startled to aim, the shot flew wide and shattered the lantern, snuffing out the flame and sinking the room into darkness once more.

The man's deep and taunting laugh swallowed her, "Silly girl. I lit that lantern just for you."

Ava dropped to the ground as she felt his heavy footsteps shake the room. She scrambled across the floor, blind as her eyes adjusted to the darkness, searching for a place to hide as he charged towards her.

Tiny teeth sunk into her right forearm and tugged. She rolled towards them, taking cover under an unseen table, as something crashed against the floor where she'd been. Sparks flew off the stone tiles, glinting off the metal of the man's terrifying morning star.

"Ah! She's a quick one!" he said.

Marqui flicked his tail against Ava's arm, signaling her to keep moving.

Her eyes adjusted to the slight glow emanating from some of the components in the room, defining the shadows of the large stacks of shelves that housed them. Ava moved quickly, staying low to the ground, and followed Marqui as he disappeared into the stacks. A sickening crack rang out as the man demolished the table she left behind. Her steps covered by its splintering, she dove onto one of the lower shelves and laid flat on her back, hopefully hidden.

"Come on, girlie," the man growled. "You're making me wreck the place!"

The glass vials on the shelves above her shook, letting out a vibrating ring as his massive footfalls grew closer. His boots smacked the ground beside her, each boot twice the size of her head, and Ava held her breath.

The man continued walking past.

She tilted her neck as much as she could, without revealing herself, to follow his steps, and exhaled slowly as she caught the outline of hulking mass lumbering down the next shelf over.

I have to get out of here. I have to save Gill. I have to save Gustav. I have to save Qui.

The man prowled through the stacks, hunting for his prey.

If I run, he'll catch me, and if I do get away, he'll hurt Gill.

She trembled from the force of her pounding heart, and silent tears streamed down her face.

What do I do?

Gillian burned. The wild magicks that grew with his emotions abandoned him, paralyzed by the lead in his hands siphoning their power. He willed his body to move, to push through the pain of his locked muscles, and save Ava with every ounce of his spirit, but his body didn't even twitch. His heart climbed up his throat, threatening to choke him with every hammering step the man took. The glass ringing out as he stalked the shelves hunting her taunted him—their tinkling chimes delighting in his helplessness.

His magick surged at their conduit's anger, only to seize once again from the lead's effects. The rapid constriction pulsed through his entire body, knocking the breath out of him.

Come after me, not her, his soul pleaded, *please just come after me.*

He tried to cry out, to call the man's attention to him, but the constant agony of his magick's struggle paralyzed his jaw and locked his throat. The only movement to his body was the tears rolling down his face.

I am useless. I am nothing.

"You like playing cat and mouse, don't you, little girl?"

I can't save anybody. Not then, not now, not ever.

Marqui pawed at Ava's cheek, pulling her attention away from her tormentor to face him.

The cat stood on her chest, watching the goliath lumbering through the shadows intently. He pressed his paw deeper into her cheek and rhythmically extended and retracted his claws.

"Do you want to get him?" she whispered.

His paw stopped. Marqui's slitted yellow eyes focused on her, and he let out a low growl.

"I don't want you to get hurt."

He sunk his claws into her cheek again, piercing a little deeper.

"Alright," she conceded, "you distract him. Turn his attention away while I ready my shot."

Ava rubbed her thumb over his paw, "Be careful."

Marqui licked her nose before jumping off her chest and running off of the shelf. His tiny paws moved swiftly and silently as he disappeared into the shadows. Ava's stomach twisted as she imagined the man's morning star catching Marqui in its spikes. She swallowed the thought and waited for his distraction.

A bottle fell from the shelves on the man's left and shattered on the ground. His head snapped towards the noise.

Ava rolled out the other side of the shelf quickly and stood, hiding behind the shelf's joints.

She peered around the joint and caught a blur of glinting silver crashing down through the stack the bottle fell from, splitting the shelving unit in two with a single swipe. Her heart stopped as it crumbled to the ground. Despite her shaking hands, she pulled an arrow from the side quiver of her bowsheath and nocked it against her bowstring.

A small shadow jumped up on the stack to the right of the wrecked one, kick-starting her heart. She stilled herself and stepped out from behind the joint with her bow raised.

Marqui knocked another bottle down, and the man looked up at him, centering her shot and opening up his face. He raised his morning star high in the air, poised to swipe down at the cat, but Ava's arrow flew faster.

The man howled as her arrow shot through his left eye and out of the side of his skull. His strike swung low, hitting the shelves just below Marqui. The broken wood hissed filled as the liquids from the bottles his stray morning star shattered fizzled. The shelf ignited with a brilliant, blue flame and Marqui leaped from it, disappearing into the shadows once more.

The fire lit the writhing behemoth, and Ava sunk two more arrows into his chest. He barely flinched.

"You rotten bitch!" the man roared as he reared back and shoved the burning shelf into the stacks behind it. The stacks fell onto one another, spreading the flames as they toppled like dominoes. Ava ran before the blazing timber could crush her, shooting arrows fruitlessly into his body.

"You take something of mine?!" he challenged.

Blood gushed from the arrow wedged in his eye socket. "I take something of yours!"

He barreled forward, not towards Ava, but Gillian, kneeling paralyzed at Gustav's feet.

"No!" she shrieked.

The spikes of his morning star glistened in the blue firelight as he raised it in the air, preparing to bury it in Gillian's skull...

...when a flurry of gray fur descended upon him.

Launching out of the shadows from atop one of the few shelves left standing, Marqui latched onto the back of the man's head. He buried his front claws deep into his face as his back claws dug into his neck, cementing him to the man as he sunk his fangs into his ear.

The man unleashed a gargled scream and dropped his weapon as he grabbed for the cat.

"Get off of me, you damn-" The man tightened his fist around Marqui's throat, ripping the cat off his face. Marqui took his ear along with him, "- cat!"

Ava's fear dissipated. The sight of his meaty fist tightening around her best friend's throat filled her with an emotion more primal than fear: bloodlust. An eerie calm took over her, and she focused on the plethora of vulnerabilities he offered her. Face forward and screaming in rage as Marqui taunted him, his severed ear in his jaws, made him primed and practically begging for his death.

And Ava gladly delivered.

His scream stopped short as she sent her arrow through his mouth and out the nape of his neck. She wondered idly if her aim was sharp enough to pierce through his uvula.

His grasp loosened, dropping Marqui as he grasped helplessly at his throat. The man's eyes bulged as he choked on his blood, gurgling and squelching as he struggled for breath. He collapsed onto his knees and looked up at Ava. The menacing bravado he boasted gone, his good eye pleaded her for mercy before it glassed over. The entire room shook as his body hit the floor.

Ava smiled at the sight.

Marqui ran to her side and rubbed against her leg. She wanted nothing more than to collapse onto the floor beneath her and hold him, bask in their victory, but the rising heat and smoke from the spreading flames had other plans. She ran over to Gill and Gustav and found the former bound by pain, tears streaming down his face. She wrapped her arms under his and tried to pull him to his feet.

A stunted squeal squeaked through his rigid throat and his body spasmed in her grasp. She let go, and his hands remained pressed against the chains.

She looked the chains over, afraid to touch them in fear of whatever unknown curse bound both wizards, and found a large padlock holding the chains together on the back of the chair.

"Fuck! Where's Kaj when you need him?" she

coughed, the smoke stinging her lungs. She looked across the laboratory, hoping to find something to cut them free. She glanced over the hulking mass of a dead man lying next to them and caught a blue glint off a ring of keys attached to his pants.

She tore the ring off of the corpse's pant loop and knelt in front of the padlock. Smoke and sweat burned her eyes as she fumbled through the keys, skipping some and trying others twice until the padlock unlatched and fell to the ground, pulling the chains down with it.

The chains fell from beneath Gillian's palms, and the nerve-wrenching pain disappeared.

"Ava," he managed to croak out. His vocal cords loosened as control of his trembling body came back to him, and he forced himself to stand, legs wobbling beneath him.

"Careful," Ava grabbed his elbow and helped him up.

"I'll handle the fire," he rasped, looking over the spreading flames. "The vigors are on that table over there. Smell them first, the first one that smells like mint give to Master."

"Gill, are you sure? I could-"

He couldn't look her in the eye.

"Please," he begged. "Let me do this."

She let go of his arm.

He hobbled closer to the blaze and placed his palms flat together. Gill pointed his fingertips at the fire, reciting an incantation of Ves.

"Wryom-fee prifft-ling mv-oss-" Cough broke up the words as the smoke coated his already sore throat, but the incantation took. A weak blue glow covered his hands, conjuring forth a dribbling stream of water. He forced his will into the spell to try and increase the water pressure, but his taxed magicks could only go so far.

Ava sniffed the vials, holding them close to her nose to try and cut through the smoke. The bright smell of mint hit her nostrils, and she hurried over to pour it into the unconscious mage's mouth.

The potion ran down his throat, causing the bruises and cuts on Gustav's face to fade slightly, and his eyelids fluttered.

"Gillian!" The rousing Gustav whined, "Did you burn breakfast again?"

"Something like that, sir," Gill answered with a hoarse chuckle.

"Wait, how are you-" the elf's head lolled to the side to face his apprentice.

His half-lidded eyes shot open wide, "What did you do to my lab?!"

Gustav jumped out of the chair and rushed to his

side. He waved his palm through the air, "Daamar anthdines djinns shoon," and shouted out a harried incantation, "hifade mornstily opttons!"

A glowing cloud of pale and dark blue magicks appeared above the fire and, with a crack of thunder, let loose a downpour that snuffed out the flames.

"Sorry, Master," Gillian wheezed, dropping his spell. He folded in half, resting his hands on his knees to catch his breath.

"What the hell happened?" he asked.

"Does this guy look familiar?" Ava called.

Gustav turned around to face her. She stood next to the felled goliath, pointing down at his pockmarked mug.

Master Gustav scowled.

"Unfortunately," he said, "That brute snuck in here somehow and got the better of me with those damn lead chains."

Gustav turned back to his apprentice, "Is that why you look like shit?"

He glared at his master.

"I'll take that as yes." Gustav walked over and picked up two of the vials. He sniffed them quickly before handing one to Gill, "Here. Drink."

He threw his head back and chugged the vigor.

"You too, Ava."

She grabbed the vial from his outstretched arm and drank. The minty green liquid coated and cooled her throat as she swallowed. Her aching muscles, the shooting pain of her nightstalker wounds, and the itching from the skrill's scratches subsided, not entirely, but enough to keep her moving forward.

"This stuff is fantastic," she remarked.

"In small doses, yes," Gustav replied, "but if you drink too many and keep pushing yourself, you'll wind up on bed rest for weeks."

"We'll need to take some of these with us," Gill said. "I hope you don't mind."

"I don't mind, but what do you need them for?" he asked. "Is someone in town hurt?"

Ava and Gillian shared a solemn look.

"Master Gustav," Ava spoke first, "There is no one left in town."

"What?"

"Ava, Ortensia Valborg, the townsguard and the thief from the burgermeister's dinner, and I were kidnapped by cultists that night. We woke up in, and escaped, this sacrificial tomb dedicated to some dark fae named Runden." Gillian's voice grew quiet, "The cultists were the Venzors. They killed their son in front of us."

Ava picked up where he left off, "The tomb's about 10 miles deep into the Shadowfen. It was a long night, and when we came back-" her throat went dry, "there was no one.

Not on my farm, not at the jailhouse. You and that shithead are the only people we've seen."

"The Venzors, huh." Gustav sat down, disappointment on his face.

"I'm sorry, Master," Gillian said.

"It's alright," he sighed, "Better to find out now that they're murderous cult members rather than later. You said they worshiped *Runden*?"

"Yeah," Ava confirmed. "Ortensia even told us about the creepy book her father found about him."

"And where are Miss Valborg and the others?"

"The Burgermeister's Manor," she replied. "Once we've grabbed the potions, we're supposed to meet them there."

"Then let's go." Gustav went to stand, but his knees gave out underneath him.

"Master!" Gill caught his elbow, keeping him from hitting the ground.

"Goddamn lead," Gustav steadied himself, "Don't worry about me. Grab what you need, and I'll teleport us to the Valborgs."

"I have a horse-"

"I am an Obsidian Mage of the Arcane Convocation, and I will travel as such," he lashed.

Ava flinched.

"Sorry." Gustav inhaled deeply to compose himself. "I'm tense, and my pride is a little hurt after being bested by that oaf."

Gillian grabbed some more vigors as Ava pulled her arrows out of the pocked man's corpse before they returned to Master Gustav in the center of the room. Gill handed her a few vials, and she stuffed them into a pouch on her belt.

"Got everything?" Gustav asked.

"Marqui," Ava called and pointed to her shoulder. He jumped up on her back and nestled between her shoulder and neck.

"That's one handsome familiar you've got there," Gustav said.

"Oh no," Ava smiled, "He's just a plain old tomcat. My best boy." She kissed him on the side of the head.

"Alright then," Gustav placed a hand on each of their backs, "Let's go."

And in a flash of purple light, they went.

CHAPTER TWELVE

"Let her go!" Valma snarled. She fought to escape Bolo's touch, but it came out as nothing more than a twitch. Her body too weak to move at her command.

"I don't think so, Stick," Seax said, "but I appreciate the passion. Now, wanna tell me how you got out of that tomb?"

"Go to hell," Valma spat.

"So that's a no from you. What about you, Kaj?"

"W-what are you doing here?" Kaj stammered. "This wasn't the plan."

"This wasn't *your* plan," Seax corrected. "We got hired for a slightly different assignment."

"Same town, two different jobs," Bolo added. "Might as well share a room and save on travel expenses."

"But this was supposed to be-"

"Yes, yes. It was supposed to be your initiation," Seax rolled her eyes. "I'll repeat the question. How did you get out of that tomb?"

Kaj looked down at the ground, jilted and seething.

Seax swiped her blade across Ortenisa's cheek, and the half-dwarf shrieked.

"How did you get out of that tomb?!" Seax yelled.

"How do you think?" Kaj yelled back. He lifted his heavy head and glared at her, "I picked the damn lock!"

"And the cultists?" she said.

"Dead," Valma growled. "Just like you're about to be."

Seax laughed at her threat, "Did you hear that, Bolo? We're about to be heroes of the crown! How much do you think they'll pay us for capturing three noble murderers?"

"Captain Reids would never believe you!" Valma cried.

"I don't need a dead woman to believe me," Seax smirked and adjusted her grip on her knife to press against Ortensia's throat. "I believe this conversation is over."

"Behind you!" Bolo shouted.

Seax whipped around and found another Ortensia behind her, dagger in hand poised to attack. She let go of the true Ortensia to dodge out of the way as the clone swung at her. Ortensia ran, conjuring more clones to attack as she fled. Two joined their counterpart and launched at Seax, but she nimbly dodged their attacks, dissolving the clones to dust in just two swipes.

Another two clones appeared behind Bolo, catching the gaunt man by surprise with two daggers in the back. He let go of Kaj and Valma and swiped his draining touch through the copies. A sickly xanthic light ate its way through them, and Bolo opened his mouth to inhale their pink dust.

Kaj and Valma scrambled to their feet; their strength returned once Bolo let go. Valma took advantage of Ortensia's illusory distraction, drawing forth her blade and driving it into Bolo's side.

Kaj put some distance between them and threw a dagger at Bolo without hesitation. The knife buried deep into his temple, and Bolo chuckled as the acrid glow of his magic spread over the dagger and pushed it in deeper, swallowing the weapon handle and all.

Seax rushed towards Ortensia. Panicked, she summoned five more clones to meet the elf's charge. Her doppelgangers appeared while Ortensia's vision blurred. She paled, breaking out in a cold sweat, and clutched her head to stave off the throbbing ache.

Her illusions attacked viciously, getting a few stabs in, and Seax pushed right through them, treating their jabs as nothing more than mosquito bites.

Valma caught Seax bolting towards the struggling half-dwarf in the corner of her eye.

"Go help Ortensia!" she commanded as she stared down Bolo, "I can handle this one."

"Good luck with that!" Kaj replied as he turned tail to follow her order.

"Awful cocky, ain't ya?" Bolo snarled.

"The word you're looking for is confident."

Valma attacked, her sword quicker than lightning. Bolo went to block the blade with his hands, trying to catch it for his magick to consume. Valma adjusted her strike in the nick of time and sliced it across his forearm, just out of his grasp.

Bolo switched tactics, sending palm strikes, not at her blade but her body.

Ortensia held her arms up to protect her face, and Seax's blade sliced across them. The searing pain and force of her attack knocked her arms down. Seax smirked as she broke her block and raised her knife again, aiming for Ortensia's throat.

Her arm stopped mid-swipe and wrenched backward, knocking Seax off her feet. She hit the ground hard, flat on her back.

Kaj stood behind her with his grappling hook looped around her wrist.

"Nice trick." Seax tossed her weapon to her other hand and brought it down on the rope only to have the blade's edge slip off without so much as fraying it.

"I got it enchanted before we left the city," he stated.

"You're not going anywhere."

"You're right. I'm not going anywhere," Seax stood, a sick smile on her face. "You're coming to me!" She wrapped her arm around the rope and yanked Kaj towards her.

His body rocketed towards her, impaling itself on the point of her blade.

Unarmed and unexpectedly fast, Bolo danced around Valma's attacks.

"Come on, girlie," he taunted. "You've got to be tired."

He swiped his leg towards her head, and Valma narrowly ducked out of the way.

Her shoulder wound reopened, inflamed and seeping blood beneath her leather breastplate, and her bruised ribs scratched against her lungs every time she twisted out of his reach. Despite her best efforts, Valma slowed under his neverending blows. The strength she'd worked so hard to build was failing her, and her mind scrambled to find another way out.

Bolo took advantage of her lapse in focus and uppercut Valma with a citrine-colored punch. She stumbled back, seeing stars as the effects draining touch rendered her legs useless once more.

Ortensia watched in horror as the tide of the fight

turned against their favor, Kaj struggling to pull his shoulder free from Seax's blade while Valma knelt on the ground, tan complexion turning ashen as Bolo's magick flashed over her. Ortensia fought against nausea overtaking her and increasing pressure in her. She willed more clones to come, and the pressure increased, threatening to crush her skull.

She gritted her teeth and diverted her agony to fuel her desire.

Please. Please help them.

An invisible band in her head snapped. Her sense of hearing turned to a ringing static, and a shock wave pierced her mind, voiding out all thought as everything went black.

"My, my," Seax's eyes danced across Kaj's face as he writhed in pain around her knife. "Talwar's going to be so disappointed when I tell him you decided to let a Stick crawl up your ass."

Kaj's clawed at her forearm, failing to loosen her iron grip on the handle.

"We had a pool going back at The Scabbard. Talwar bet a whole five gilt that you'd be the top out of all of his faction's initiates. Too bad you had to fuck it up so badly."

She twisted the knife and smiled as Kaj cried out.

"If it's any consolation before you die, Tal felt awfully guilty having to give ya over to Venzor. But what the client wants, the client gets."

Seax yanked her knife out of his chest with a growl, and Kaj closed his eyes, accepting his fate, only to hear the sounds of a struggle instead of his blood bubbling out of his throat.

He opened his eyes to find Seax thrashing wildly at two of Ortensia's doubles. They held on tightly to the daggers they wedged on either side of her collar bones, and Seax hooked her arm over her shoulder, aiming for the one on her right.

The Ortensias jumped off of her shoulders just as she swung down, letting Seax stab herself in the shoulder blade.

Small hands yanked Valma yanked back across the floor while another pair of Ortensias tackled Bolo, driving his next attack into the ground.

"Fuck these things!" he shouted.

He swung his fist to the side, hoping to hit one of the copies, but met the edge of Valma's sword instead. The speed of his punch driving into the sharp edge of her blade sent his left hand flying through the air, freed from his arm.

"Whoops," Valma croaked, her sword outstretched from where a third Ortensia pulled her back. Bolo's enchanted fatigue faded, and she pushed herself up to stand.

"You bitch!" he launched at her, picking up their deadly dance where they'd left off.

Without being struck, the clones turned to dust, having fulfilled their unconscious creator's last conscious command. Seax panted as she watched them dissolve and grinned through the pain of her self-inflicted wounds.

"Why are you smiling?" Kaj groaned. He gripped his chest, bent over in pain, but managed to hold a dagger at the ready.

"Because now I can kill you without interruption!"

She ran at him and jumped. Her knife came down upon him in a sweeping arch, the tip of its blade pointed at his head. Kaj dodged out of the way, as Seax expected, allowing her to sweep her leg beneath his feet as she landed and knocked him prone onto his stomach.

He wheezed as he hit the ground, the force of the fall knocking the wind out of him. Kaj tried to stand, but Seax drove the back of her heel into the nape of his neck. His head slammed on the ground, breaking his nose against the tile.

Kaj screamed in absolute agony, pulling Valma's attention from her struggle. Fear stilled her sword at the sight of Ortensia unmoving and Seax brutalizing Kaj's body, driving her heel into the back of his head over and over again.

Bolo drove his acrid fist into her jaw once more, much harder and imbued with a stronger enchantment from the last time, throwing her across the room like a rag doll.

Valma tried to catch herself as she bounced across the floor, but her body wasn't hers to control. Searing pain shot through her kneecaps and elbows as they fractured upon impact until her body's momentum slowed. She struggled to remain conscious, tears stinging her eyes as she forced them to stay open with the pain spread across her body, throbbing ceaselessly.

Bolo walked over, ripped the sword from her limp hand, and stood atop her body.

"Now." Bile burned the back of her throat as he leered down at her and ran his tongue over his brown, rotting teeth. "Which hand should I take? Left or right?" He hovered the point of her sword back and forth, deciding.

"You fight with your right, correct?" He lifted his sword, ready to cleave her arm in two, when a bright flash of purple light filled the room.

An arrow snapped the tendons in his wrist, knocking the sword out of his hand.

"My my," Master Gustav chastised, "What do we have here?"

Seax and Bolo turned to find Master Gustav, Ava, and Gillian standing in the middle of the foyer. Looks of absolute terror twisted the latter two's faces at the sight of their friends battered and helpless on the floor.

"Shit," was the only thing Seax could say before a barrage of red arcane bolts knocked her and Bolo off their feet and into the portrait of the Valborgs behind them.

"Heal your friends," Gustav instructed Gillian and Ava. "I'm feeling extra vindictive." His eyes glowed with red magick as he grinned.

"Right," Ava took off towards Valma.

Gillian looked at his master, noticing that despite his intimidating appearance, sweat beaded across his brow.

"Be careful, sir," he whispered and ran to help Kaj, healing, uncorking the vigor in his hand.

"I told you we should have killed him!" Bolo shouted.

Seax didn't bother to respond. She launched herself off the wall and ran at the master mage.

Gustav held his hands in front of him, fingers spread apart, and rapidly fired glowing red bolts of arcane energy as she approached.

She dodged them, a sudden burst of speed causing her to blur, and swung her blade at the wizard's throat. Her knife connected, not with his olive flesh, but with armor, shimmering crimson and conjured instantly. Her attack reflected back at her, and a gash ripped open across her chest. Seax staggered back, clutching at the wound.

"Come now," Gustav chided, "Did you really think I'd leave myself unarmored?"

Gillian turned Kaj's body over.

The elvefolk's face was deeply bruised and bloodied. His broken nose nothing more than a piece of hanging flesh, and his swollen eyes could barely open.

"About time," he croaked.

"Here," Gillian placed the vial to his lips, "swallow." He poured the vigor down Kaj's throat slowly.

Kaj swallowed, relishing in the cool mint of the potion soothing his throat.

The healing effects of the potion took effect immediately. His bruises faded, turning his skin, a deep purple from burst blood vessels, back to its warm, copper sheen. The swelling subsided, his nose returned to looking like a nose, and the multitude of puncture wounds he received, both old and new, turned marginally less gaping.

"Never would've expected you'd tell me to swallow, Wizkid," Kaj quipped.

"What?" Gillian asked.

"Ugh," Kaj rolled his eyes and slowly sat up, "nevermind."

"Valma?" Ava knelt over her paralyzed body. "Here, I've got this for you." She went to place the vial to her lips but stopped when she noticed Valma's eyes darting to the right over and over again, tears falling from them. Ava looked to her right and spotted Ortensia lying on the ground.

"Her first?" she asked. "Are you sure?"

Valma locked eyes with her, gaze fierce and sure.

"Okay." Ava said, "But I'm telling you, she would much rather wake up to the sight of you than me. Marqui, stay here with her." The cat hopped off of Ava's shoulders onto Valma's chest at her command.

She ran over to the half-dwarf lying on the ground, making sure to keep low to avoid any errant bolts from Gustav's attack.

Ortensia laid unresponsive but not as mangled as the others. Ava tilted her head back to help guide the vigor down her throat. In a few seconds, she came roused with a wince and a groan.

Ortensia grabbed at her throbbing head and opened her eyes slowly, "What happened?"

"I don't know." Ava smiled, "You tell me."

"Oh great," she whined, "it's you."

"See, I told Valma you'd rather her wake you up."

Bolo charged toward Gustav's side, yellow fist forward, and punched the magick plates. The armor shattered into a million pieces before being absorbed into the palm of his hand.

Bolo taunted, "Where's your armor now?"

"Urgan's magicks," Gustav remarked, unimpressed, "and poorly executed at best."

Bolo reared back a punch but froze. His goading smile fell from his face, replaced with a grimace in pain that melted into total fear and confusion. Red veins spread from the base of his palm up to his arm before branching across his entire body.

"What the-"

Gustav's red eyes flashed, and Bolo's body popped, his muscles rupturing all at once, sending blood and sinew flying through the air like sparks from a firework. Sweat poured down Gustav's slowly graying face, yet he retained his aloof disposition. He turned his head to face a wide-eyed and embittered Seax.

"Now, I have a couple of questions for you," he snarled.

"Good luck with that." Seax ran her blade across her own throat and stared down Gustav in absolute spite as the life poured out of her. Her legs gave out, and her corpse fell forward into the warm pool of her blood.

The red glow vanished from Master Gustav's eyes, and he folded in half, resting his hands on his knees.

"Thank the gods," he said, relieved. "Any more from her, and I'd be tapped out."

"Who the fuck is this guy?!" Kaj screamed.

Master Gustav looked up to find Gillian gazing at him proudly while his friends stared at him in terror.

"Master, that was-"

"*He's* your master?!" Kaj interrupted Gillian, "He turned a man to pulp with his mind, and *he's* the one training the kid with crazy earth powers?!"

"I'll take that vigor now," Valma called out from her spot on the floor. "And if someone could wipe that asshole's guts off my face and get this cat off my chest, that would be great."

"Give me that," Ortensia ripped a vial out of the stupefied Ava's hand and scrambled to her feet. Her head throbbed even more from the subtle shift in altitude as she wobbled over to Valma.

The blood-spattered feline hopped off Valma's chest and made his way over to Ava's lap. She didn't move to greet him as she usually did, but Marqui was unbothered, taking the opportunity to clean the Bolo's pulp off of himself noisily.

"I apologize that it was a bit... graphic," Gustav moved to sit on the floor, exhaustion seeping in, "but those heathens were about to do the same to you."

"Who were those guys?" Gillian asked.

"Yeah, Kaj." Valma sat up slowly, wiping her lips after drinking the potion. She stared Kaj down, "Who were those guys?"

Sadness, anger, and guilt draped over him. He looked down at his gloves, running his thumb over the hole where his communication pendant once rested.

"Can we have this conversation somewhere else, please?" Ava asked. "I don't-" her gaze fixated on Seax's corpse, "I don't want to be in this room anymore."

"Agreed," Ortensia said. "Let's head to the kitchen. Maybe a cup of tea will help me get rid of this headache."

"Fine," Valma stomped over to Kaj and lifted him to his feet. Her hand locked around his arm, fingers digging into his bicep in a bruising grip, and she pulled him out of the room.

He followed willingly.

CHAPTER THIRTEEN

Ortensia cut the heat from the tea kettle before its shrill whistle pierced her aching mind.

Covered in blood and trying to recover some sense of normalcy, the others sat round a small table nestled in the Valborgs' kitchen's breakfast nook, wiping the gore off their faces.

"Start talking," Valma commanded as she threw her bloodied rag to the ground with a slap. Her already intimidating stature accentuated as Kaj sank deeper into his chair.

Kaj didn't tend to doubt himself. And if others were involved, he would check and double-check that he could only semi-doubt them at the very least. He ground his teeth as he ran through all the mistakes he'd made over the course of the past three weeks, searching for any signs in hindsight of his guild member's betrayal.

"Those people that we fought in there," his voice went small, missing the satiric edge it often carried as he stared blankly at the center of the table, "we're all part of the same group. The Hilt."

"What the hell is The Hilt doing in a podunk town like this?" Valma pressed.

"What the hell is The Hilt?" Gillian added.

Kaj bit the inside of his lip. Was this a mistake? Telling them all this?

He lifted his eyes from the table to steal a glance at Valma, who somehow grew twice her size as she sneered down at him with murder in her eyes.

"We're a collective of underground, for-hire tradesmen."

"They're a mercenary group," Valma spat.

Of course she would know.

"Only some of us," Kaj corrected, then deflected. "You saw my combat skills back there. Do I look like a mercenary to you?"

"Tea's done," Ortensia interrupted, granting Kaj a moment to form his plan of action.

She walked over to the table slowly, her face twisted from the pain of her headache, "Get up and help yourselves."

"Is it black or green?" Master Gustav asked.

"Green."

"A woman of taste," he turned to his apprentice,

"Gillian, get your master a cup of tea, will you?"

"Yes, sir."

"Okay, so you're part of The Hilt, and you're not a mercenary," Valma continued her interrogation. "Why are *you* here?"

"Well," an edge of irritation flared up in his voice. He understood her being upset with the situation, he himself was rather upset with the situation, but a little part of him believed that they were past her seeing him as an outright villain, "I am here for the same reason as I told you upstairs. Some noble contracted The Hilt to obtain sensitive information on Delvin Valborg."

His tongue turned bitter from self-resentment, "As Seax so eloquently stated, apparently they were on a slightly *different* assignment."

"You shatter my window, your friends tried to kill us, and now you're blackmailing my father," Ortensia grumbled as she sipped her tea, "I'm regretting stabbing you less and less."

"And the others?" Valma continued, "That *slightly different assignment.*"

"From what I know, they were supposed to be here to observe me," Kaj swallowed, "That's all."

"Observe you for what?"

"You better not repeat a word of this, alright? This is sacred Hilt knowledge I'm about to drop." It wasn't, but it had to feel like he was giving them something.

Valma stared at him, waiting,

"So," he exhaled heavily, "to become a full-fledged member of The Hilt, you have to complete a job request of import. Other members have to tag along with you just to make sure you actually do the thing and bail you out if you really fuck up."

"But that's clearly not all they were here for."

Kaj bristled, "Clearly."

"Do you think maybe The Hilt told them to do this?" Gill walked back to the table and placed a cup of tea in front of a zoned-out Ava before handing one to Gustav.

The Hilt participated in a number of questionable activities, extortion, bootlegging, larceny assassination, but the mass sacrifice of an entire town of innocents? Not to mention tricking one of their own.

"Never, it goes against our code." Kaj replied and recited, "The good of yourself comes first. The good of the Hilt is a close second. To betray The Hilt, however, will be very harmful to the good of yourself."

"And *this* was a betrayal?" Valma asked. Her implication hurt more than the several stab wounds he'd endured over the past two days.

"Damn right it was!" his voice cracked as he slammed his fist on the table.

"Hey! Watch the mahogany!" Ortensia shouted, her

fingertips pressed against her temples.

"I'm sorry, Kaj." His sudden spike of aggression brought Ava out of her head, "Were you close with them?"

"Seax and Bolo?" Kaj leaned back in his chair, "Not so much."

He withdrew into himself, a small frown and somber sheen covered his face, "but Talwar was one of the thieves I trained under."

"So you're saying we have to keep an eye out for another one of these psychos?" Ortensia grumbled.

"Tell me, young man," Master Gustav spoke up over his cup of tea, "What does this Talwar look like?"

"Big fella, pock marked face," Kaj answered, and Ava paled.

Her blood ran cold as guilt, suffocating and heavier than any passing remorse she had felt in her life, seized her very soul. She looked down at her teacup and slowly picked it up, the heat of the ceramic mug barely noticeable against her numb fingers. She stared at the clear green liquid before taking a sip.

I killed his friend. Murdered him. Tore the life from his body with a single shot.

She swallowed, but the warmth it gave was fleeting.

And I enjoyed it.

She caught a glimpse of her reflection in her tea; her brown eyes turned black and pupilless in its water.

I am a monster. Unforgivable. I should be the one with an arrow through my mouth.

Ava stole a quick glance at Kaj and started to shiver. She turned back to her cup and took another sip to try and abate the chill.

I should say something. I should confess.

"I'm sorry to tell you this," her turbulent mind stalled as Master Gustav broke the silence, "But your friend is dead. He made the poor choice of breaking into my mansion and fell victim to one of my traps after chaining me up."

The tea caught in Ava's throat. She stifled a cough and swallowed roughly.

"If Gillian and Ava hadn't come when they did, it would have been weeks before anyone found me, and I would have been quite dead by that point."

Marqui rubbed his head against Ava's legs, and she set her teacup down to place him onto her lap. She watched Gustav as she did, but he did nothing more than look at Kaj sympathetically.

Or I could never tell him. Her body temperature returned to something more bearable. *That could be alright.*

"That's..." Kaj mulled Gustav's words over, "unfortunate."

His somber state turned to steel, "But if he was one

of these Runden worshiping freaks, then he deserved it."

Kaj doubled down, sitting up taller in his chair, "He deserved it for betraying The Hilt."

See, Ava took another sip and winced as the tea scalded her tongue. *It'll be just fine.*

"Runden…" Master Gustav chewed the name as he said it. "Something about that name doesn't sit right."

"We should look at that folder we found," Valma kept her eyes on Kaj, expecting a challenge.

"Agreed," he stood immediately, ignoring Valma as she squared up for a fight, and pulled out the black leather folder and opened, wax-sealed letter from his pants.

"We really need to get you a bag or something," Gillian remarked.

"Seconded," Ortensia said, "I don't want to touch anything that's been down your pants."

"Well, luckily for you, I don't want you to touch anything in my pants," he mocked.

"Focus! Please!" Valma barked. "God only knows how many townsfolk are being murdered right now. We don't have time for jokes!" She ripped the folder out of his hands and tossed the letter to Ava.

The letter smacked against her teacup, and she scrambled to catch it, splashing tea onto the table as she knocked the cup over.

"Really?" Ortensia scolded, "What did I say about the mahogany?"

"Cici, the goddamn table is already covered in blood," Valma snapped. "A little splash of tea is the least of your worries."

"What's gotten into you?" Ortensia rebuked, "From the way you were dancing around that godforsaken tomb, I figured you'd be overjoyed at the chance to kill a couple of cultists and be the great town hero."

"Just..." she stalled, gritting her teeth as she grumbled, "just shut up and let me read." Valma threw open the folder.

"What do you want me to do with this?" Ava asked cautiously.

Valma didn't respond.

"Why don't you read it aloud, Aves?" Gillian encouraged.

She nodded. Ava ran her thumb over the hourglass sigil set into the seal before she unfolded the pages and read aloud:

Dear Delvin,

I am honored that you have chosen me to be your overseer for the Harvest. Out of the options you presented, I would prefer the week of the 21st of Vesin. Fortuitously, my family and I will be traveling to our villa in Monacor to take up residence for the summer and should be passing through Elvrii during this time.

Additionally, on the topic of a proposal between your daughter, Ortensia, and my boy — I'm not opposed to the idea. If your daughter wishes to meet my boy, I suggest that she send over a dinner invitation. Perhaps she could even schedule the event for when my family and I arrive for the Harvest. What a lovely distraction that would be!

I would also like to deliver the exciting news that my wife and I are expecting not only another child, but twins! Plain Octavin will make an excellent older brother. So, it is of the finest importance that we keep them all safe. We'll be bringing some security of our own. I hope you don't mind.

I'll have a servant dig through the capitol archive for the document details. May your life be blessed with uninterrupted vitality,

Lord Thros Benters Venror

Ava set the letter down, her face taut and twisted with disgust.

"That felt gross to read," she said. "And what harvest are they talking about? There ain't any sort of harvest festival this month."

"Well, here's the festival details he wrote about," Valma slid a well-worn and creased piece of parchment out of the folder and placed it in the middle of the table, away from the blood and where everyone could see it. The details were scrawled in a blocky print, unlike the delicate stroked cursive of Lord Venzor's letter.

Elleri Harvest - Vesin - Bidecennial 957

Pre-Harvest
- Appoint Harvest marshals from town
- Set up night activities
- Ensure peaceful slumber
- Relocate to assigned shrine

- **Forged Shrine**
  - small # of stock
  - 1 spared
  - slow extract after full cull
- **Main Shrine**
  - All other stock, none spared
  - Half-hour extractions, random
  - spare marshals
- **Recite:** "To he who always rises, no matter how time flows, laughing in the face of those who rob us of our rights, we offer you a gift. To feed the source of endless life, we harvest the meager shreds the false gods left behind and claim that which they stole from us."

Post-Harvest:
- Distress marshals
- marshals find the spared
- Discover the extracted
- Report to right authorities

"Sound familiar?" Valma placed a finger on "recite passages".

"That's what the Venzors and their crew chanted before they slaughtered Octavian," Ortensia said.

"Is it now?" Master Gustav picked the note off the table and studied it closer.

"Do you know something, Master?" Gillian asked.

"'To feed the source of endless life,'" Gustav read, "'we harvest the meager shreds the false gods left behind.'"

He threw the note back into the center of the table with the tips of his fingers and snarled in disdain.

"I fear we are dealing with something much darker than some dark fae warrior," he said. "That is a verse of Zozvit."

"It's a-" Gill paled.

"What's a Zozvit?" Kaj asked.

"One of the Destructor Deities," Gustav replied, "The God of the Undead."

Gillian grabbed the ritual instructions from the center of the table and studied them intensely, his hands shaking as he held them.

"Well, that would explain the skeletons," Valma pulled at her ponytail in contemplation, "and the ghosts."

"Are they-" Ava chewed her bottom lip, "- summoning him?"

"No. This seems to be a mass sacrifice to the being, most likely to channel more of his magicks." Gustav looked over at Ortensia, who abandoned her cup of tea to pick at her cuticles, "Miss Ortensia, has your father ever mentioned wishing for immortality?"

"Never!" she answered a little too loudly. She winced and lowered her voice, "Besides, my father doesn't have magicks. I don't see what sort of good this ritual would do for him."

"I see," he said.

"And if you're asking me, this seems to be all Venzor's doing," Ortensia drew blood after pulling at a particularly deep hangnail and crossed her arms to hide the wound. "He was the one who killed his son, not to mention he wrote that damn letter and sent the ritual instructions."

"I have my doubts about that," Gustav said. "Though I'm not intimately familiar with Lord Venzor's handwriting, this symbol on the seal and that folder... they're not the crest of the Sparis Ward."

"If you worshiped a dark god in secret, would you plaster your personal crest all over the place?" Kaj replied. "I sure as all hell wouldn't."

Gillian stood suddenly, slamming his fist on the table with the instructions crumpled inside of it.

"Gill?" Ava jumped.

"We can figure out who's to blame later," his face

flared a brilliant crimson as his eyes darted around the table, landing on each of them, "Did any of you read this? *Really* read this?!"

He pelted the balled-up parchment onto the table, "They're killing someone every half hour, and we're here talking instead of stopping them!"

"Sit down, Gillian," Gustav gave an even warning.

"No! People are dying!" Gillian yelled.

His blood boiled as his lingering frustrations from the laboratory grew. A clock, large and unseen, hung over him, each tick of its hands booming in his ears. At least five innocent people died since they arrived in town, and couldn't fathom how many more passed during the time they lost in the tomb. He promised to protect people. He *had* to protect people.

"How do you expect to find them?!" Master Gustav's shout bounced off the walls. "And if you do miraculously find a clue as to where they are, how do you expect to tackle a cult of potentially powerful necromancers when two of your wizards are drained?!"

Gillian didn't back down, "My magick is fine!"

"But her's isn't!" Gustav pointed at Ortensia.

Ortensia covered her ears, her face scrunched up in pain, "Can we not be so loud?"

"That's magick fatigue. Pure and simple. I'm

disappointed you didn't notice it earlier," Gustav scolded. "And if I go through any more spells, I'll end up just like her. So sit down, and let's come up with a plan of action."

Gustav had a point. Gillian knew he had a point, but that did not mean it was right.

"Another person could die," he growled. Gillian dropped his head, unwilling to concede, his furious stare fixated on the ground in indignation.

"Or hundreds could die from your negligence." His mentor hissed, "Sit."

Gillian stormed out of the room.

Ava jumped up and chased after him, knocking Marqui from her lap. The gray cat collected himself and skittered out of the room to catch up to them.

After a moment, Gustav shook his head, "Fool."

"He has a point," Valma grumbled. "We are wasting time."

"Where did you find this information?" Master Gustav pressed on, ignoring her comment. "Perhaps there's a clue to the main shrine's whereabouts there."

"Valborg's office," Valma answered. "We can take you there."

"My father's office?" Ortensia narrowed her eyes at Kaj.

"Sorry," Kaj shrugged. "Better to ask forgiveness than permission."

"I was there with him," Valma placed her hand on top of Ortensia's. "Don't worry."

Ortensia scoffed and pulled her hand out from underneath Valma's warm palm.

"Let's go then. I'd like to clear my father's character sooner rather than later," she stood up, and the pressure in her throbbing head shifted, making her vision spin. Valma grabbed her elbow, steadying her as she almost fell from the dizzy spell.

"Anyway, to stop this?" she asked Gustav as her vision cleared and she yanked her elbow out of Valma's grasp.

"Time is the only cure, unfortunately, as novice practitioners learn," he stood and went to refill his teacup. "The headache should subside in the morning, but your magicks won't be at their full capacity for a few days. Consider yourself lucky you passed out when you did. It could have been much worse."

Ortensia joined him as he headed out of the room.

"Might I offer a word of advice, Miss Ortensia?" Gustav leaned down to whisper to her as they walked down the hall. Valma and Kaj's footsteps echoed behind them.

"Of course," Ortensia said.

"Don't try to be a hero next time. It's not a role you're

suited for."

"Look, I'm not gonna do anything crazy, alright? Just head back inside." Gill stopped abruptly but didn't turn to face Ava.

They stood on the lawn of the manor. The skies had grown overcast, and the wind had picked up, chilling the air and erasing all traces of spring warmth.

"If I stand here quietly would that be alright?" she asked.

"Fine," Gill sat on the ground and put his head between his knees. He looped his fingers through the cool blades of grass and closed his eyes, trying to calm himself.

While he grasped the grass, the blades in his hands slowly pulled at his fingers. Tugging so gently that he didn't even notice.

We're wasting time. He bit the inside of his cheek, hoping the pain would ground him.

I'm wasting time. People are dying.

The back of his throat stung and swelled, making it hard to swallow.

Ava's family could be dead, and I'm sitting here having a goddamn temper tantrum.

He forced himself to slow his breathing, but the shallowness of his breaths only served to full his panic.

I need to think! I need to-

As his doubting thoughts spread and consumed his consciousness like wildfire, the grass spread open his palms and pulled them down. His hands touched the soil, grounding his body to the land, but his mind remained plagued.

Until he felt a tiny head butt against his back.

"What happened to standing there quietly?" Gillian hissed.

"I said I would stand here quietly," Ava answered. "Marqui made no such promises."

The cat rubbed around his side, squirmed under his arm, and placed two tiny paws on his lap. He stared up at Gillian with two wide golden eyes and purred heavily.

Ava giggled.

"How can you laugh right now?" He snapped. He lifted his head and glowered over his shoulder at her.

"I- I don't know," she frowned and looked away from, "Maybe it's because this all hasn't hit me yet."

She lowered her voice, "It can't hit me yet. I don't have time to cry."

The heat of his anger dwindled, dampened by her somber nature.

His inner turmoil calming, the earth's entreating

trickled through. He sensed Ava through the ground, feeling her tremble against the palm of his hands as her heart raced a mile a minute.

Its tempo spiked.

"How is what Master Gustav said to you any different than what you said to me earlier?" Ava locked eyes with him, sadness replaced with a hard, scathing stare. "I may have had a breakdown, but did I throw a temper tantrum? No. Because I want to save my family."

The sentence hung in the cold air between them before she continued, "My brain won't stop doing the math. Over seventy people are dead." Ava chuckled in disbelief, "I know that's a third of the town, but everything is so crushing right now that that number is weightless."

Her nostrils flared, "So come inside, and let's figure this out together so that number doesn't double."

Goosebumps spread across his arms as he filled with panic at the thought of disappointing her.

"Ava, I'm-" Gill moved to stand but stopped when a rhythmic shaking deep within the ground caught his attention.

"You're what?"

"Hold on," he stilled and focused his senses on his fingertips. The rhythm grew stronger, and he was certain he could trace the source if the small beast on his lap would stop vibrating.

"Call Marqui back," he said, "I'm sensing something,

but he's purring too loud."

"Marqui," she called, and the cat left his lap to trot to her side.

Gill went to move his hands in front of him but found them entangled by grass. He tried to free himself, but the grass pulled back and drove his palms deeper into the soil. His moment of panic at the grass's presumed sentience subsided as the source of the rumbling became crystal clear: something was moving deep beneath the earth.

He closed his eyes and let the rumbling vibrations fill his ears. The rumbling led to a constant squeaking and a low grumble of voices too muffled to be heard clearly.

The light fading through his eyelids darkened, and expecting to see Ava there checking on him, Gill opened his eyes. However, he saw not Ava's honey brown eyes, the gray sky, or the Valborgs' lawn; but a cavern. Somehow suspended on the roof of an underground tunnel, the young mage found himself staring down at a set of metal tracks. The squeaking and voices grew louder as the smallest specs of dirt shook violently at the approach of a minecart, coated in blood and pushed by two hooded figures, rolling into view.

Gill's eyes slammed shut against his will, and the grass released its grip.

"Gillian!" Ava pulled him up off the ground by his collar, her voice quivering with worry. "Quit it! You're scaring me!"

He steadied himself, blinking rapidly as he processed

his surroundings while she yanked him to his feet. Gillian tore her hands off his shirt and held them in his.

Bewilderment twinkled in his eyes as he met her frightened stare, "I found them."

"You *what*?"

"They're here, underground."

"How-" Her eyes darted across his face, "How do you know that?"

"I- I don't know how but I felt it and- and then I *saw* it-" he took a breath and stopped his rambling, "We have to tell Master."

Gillian wrapped his hand around hers and dragged her behind him as he ran towards the house.

"Your family has questionable taste," Gustav judged. He stood in front of the bookshelves in Burgermeister Valborg's office and ran a finger over a bronze bookend cast in the image of a basilisk.

"That hideous thing?" Ortensia looked up from where she searched towards the bottom of the shelves, "That's not one of ours. It was a previous burgermeister's or something."

"I'm talking all of it," he clarified. He glanced down at her, "Your dress is nice, though."

"For someone who was warmly invited over for dinner by my family not two nights ago, you are being incredibly rude." she scoffed—his cold words to her as they left the kitchen still needling at her.

"Have I been?" Gustav walked away from the bookshelf without finishing his thought to check in on Kaj, "Any luck over here?"

"Just a lot of books." He gradually made his way through the books, tipping each one of them forward before tilting them back into place.

"Are you... reading them?" Gustav asked.

"No," Kaj answered.

"Then what are you doing to them?"

"I'm tipping them back to see if they trigger a hidden passage to open."

"Leading to..."

"Leading to the main shrine," he rolled his eyes. "You know, for a master mage, you're not a very creative thinker."

"You think the entrance to a massive sacrifice pit is on the third story of a small wooden manor?" Gustav judged. "Where would it fit? The only thing on the other side of this wall is a bathroom."

"Sure... but there *could* be a hidden panel covering a slide that travels all the way down to Valborg's secret lair." Kaj tapped the side of his temple, "Criminal masterminds always have kooky stuff like that in their mansions."

"My father is not a criminal mastermind!" Ortensia

shouted from the other side of the office.

Gustav closed his eyes and pinched the bridge of his nose between his fingers, trying to relieve his oncoming stress headache. He moved to sit in the chair behind Valborg's desk, having to fold himself nearly in half to fit in the dwarven-sized chair as he did.

Valma walked into the room, a fresh coat of damp blood covering her already bloodstained arms, studying a large piece of parchment.

"I knew it was a good idea to check the bodies. Well, *body*," she stated. "I got us a map."

She laid the map on top of the desk and smoothed it out, stopping as the palm of her hand spread a big smear of blood across the middle of the page.

Master Gustav opened his eyes as Kaj and Ortensia joined them around the desk to look at the hastily drawn and crumpled map.

"You call this a map?" Kaj asked.

Eight rectangles were drawn in two rows on the paper, with an 'X 'marking the third rectangle on the bottom. Another larger rectangle surrounded them with an 'M' and a 'P' written on either side.

"It's not the best map, but it's a map." Gustav sighed, "Now we just have to figure out what it is and where it is."

His comment was met with silence.

"Well, don't all answer at once," he grumbled.

"Don't look at me. I'm not from here," Kaj said.

"I just moved here a week ago," Valma added.

Gustav looked at Ortensia.

"You and I both know the only times I've ever stepped foot in that town is to show face at those homely festivals."

The heavy drumming of frantic footsteps pulled their attention to the hall. Ortensia ducked behind the desk as Kaj and Valma unsheathed their weapons. Gustav remained unphased.

"Master!" Gillian ran into the room, pulling Ava with Marqui struggling to keep up behind him.

"It's a marvel that a beanpole like you has such heavy footfalls." Gustav looked at his apprentice coolly, "Have you come to apologize for your little outburst?"

"Sure. Sorry," Gill panted, catching his breath.

"Not the most sincere apology, but I'll take it," he sighed.

"I found them!" Gillian announced, locking eyes with Valma.

"You did?" she questioned and gestured to the desk, "Alright then, come show us on this map we found."

"You found a map?" he asked. He let go of Ava's hand and joined the rest of the group around the desk. Ava followed suit, lifting her head to peer over Kaj and Valma's shoulders.

"Why do you have a map of the Valborgs' stables?"

Ava asked.

Ortensia popped up from behind the desk, "How do you know what our stables look like?"

"Unless those stables are underground, that's not where they are," Gill interjected.

"No, but that could be where the hidden entrance is," Kaj gave Gustav a smug grin.

The master mage ignored him.

"How do you know they're underground, Gillian?" Gustav asked.

"I- uh," he avoided his master's gaze, "I saw through the earth."

They waited for Master Gustav's response. The master mage stayed quiet.

"Wizards man," Kaj shook his head, breaking the tension, "wild shit."

"We should ride out and alert the Kyresore Garrison, right?" Ortensia asked.

"No, Cici," Valma insisted. "We go down there and save them ourselves."

"What?!" Ortensia looked between her and Master Gustav, "Don't you remember what he said? How are we going to take down a cult of necromancers?"

"We're not. This is strictly going to be a rescue mission." Valma straightened up and addressed the group,

"As far as we know, the other cultists have no idea that we escaped, so we have the element of surprise on our side. With Kaj's expertise, we can sneak our way through the shrine and free all of the townsfolk that we find."

"And what about the cultists?" Ortensia pressed.

"It's highly unlikely we'll encounter all of them at once. Even with us being decently worn out and you without magick, we'd still have the advantage with any Zozvit freak that comes our way in sheer numbers."

"And if you leave me here, you'll have even more of an advantage," Ortensia added. "No need to protect poor, weak, magickless me."

"No, Cici," Master Gustav interjected. "It would be good for you to go."

"Oh, so first you insult me, and now you know what's good for me?"

"I always know what's good for people," Gustav stated. "And I must say, this plan seems feasible. I shall stay here and contact the Kyresore Garrison. That way, by the time you all have cleared most of the townsfolk out of there, the Bastions will be able to clean up any remaining cultists."

"May Marqui stay with you?" Ava asked. On cue, the little gray cat jumped on top of the desk and rubbed his head against Master Gustav's hand.

"Of course." he scratched the cat lightly under his chin.

"Works for me," Valma said, "Everyone else?"

"Absolutely," Gillian replied.

"I'm in," Ava nodded.

"I'm not one for going into necromancer pits." Kaj shrugged, "But you did say I'm essential, so…."

They all looked at Ortensia.

"The Master already decided for me," she mocked. "And honestly, I'd rather get possessed again than be insulted in my own house any further."

"Then it's settled." Gustav looked pointedly at his apprentice, "You best be going. People are dying."

CHAPTER FOURTEEN

As they left her father's office, Ortensia grabbed Valma by the wrist and pulled her towards a spare room. Valma followed along willingly, surprised by the strength of her grip around her wrist.

"What-" Ava started to ask.

"I need a word alone with Valma," Ortensia interrupted.

Valma looked over her shoulder and waved her free hand, "I'll be fine. Go head down to the foyer, and we'll meet you there."

Gillian was halfway down the hall before she finished speaking, but Ava and Kaj nodded in acknowledgment then headed on their way.

Ortensia pulled her into a small bedroom, outfitted for non-dwarven guests with florid furniture and gaudily patterned wallpaper.

"Cici-"

"What the hell are you doing?" Ortensia seethed, cutting off the flirty quip she started to fire off.

Valma rolled her eyes, a bit disappointed that Ortensia was about to throw yet another tantrum.

"We don't have time for this right now. Whatever attitude you have, pack it up and-"

"Fuck you," Ortensia swore, catching Valma off guard. "You're supposed to protect us."

Valma's shoulders tensed, "What?"

"You want to be some big hero, right?" she spat. Her hands balled into fists, and her lips curled into a snarl. "Want to go in there, bust a few heads, and save the day?"

"Yes?" Valma didn't know how to answer the unasked question behind her words or how to handle how all of the good things she said sounded like something to be ashamed of.

"Then why are you bringing us, a bunch of innocent civilians, to aid you on this suicide mission?" Ortensia shoved Valma's thigh, "You're a townsguard! You're supposed to protect us!"

She let her pound against her leg, her punches unbruising against the thick muscle, "What do you mean bringing? They all want to go!"

"And you should have told them no!"

She watched her in bewilderment, trying to piece together what she'd done wrong. Everyone said they wanted to go. Gillian and Ava were adamant, Kaj was apprehensive but agreed, and Ortensia-

Valma grabbed her wrists and knelt to her level.

"Get off of me," Ortensia tugged her arms fruitlessly against her iron grip as Valma ignored her request.

"Do you want to stay here?"

"It doesn't matter what I want-"

"It does," Valma insisted, "I'm not going to make you go down there with us if you don't want to."

"And what will Master Gustav say about that?"

"The fuck do I care what some egghead wizard has to say?"

Ortensia stopped struggling and stared at Valma in wide-eyed surprise.

"You're right. I'm a Berylwood Bastion," she continued, "my duty is to protect the people of this kingdom, not force them to do shit against their will. Honestly, Cici, as much as I want you to be down there with us, if you don't want to go, you can stay here."

Ortensia studied Valma's face with great scrutiny. Her deep brown eyes were honest and widened slightly by her conviction. There was no sign of jest, no flirty quirk in her eyebrow, or cocky smile tugging at the corner of her lips.

"You *want* me to go?" she scoffed.

"I'd think it'd be safer," Valma shrugged and let go of her wrists, but her eyes didn't leave her face, "We don't know who we can trust. And with those damn Hilt members getting the drop on us, who's to say there's not more cult crazies hiding around town. So if you promise to stay in your room, lock both of your doors-"

"No," it came out in a whisper. Ortensia hung her head from the memory of Valma helpless on the floor as Bolo loomed over her, "I'll go."

"You're sure?"

"I said I'll go, alright?!" Ortensia barked, then grimaced at how harsh she sounded, "Just… make sure you do your job while we're down there."

Valma arched an eyebrow inquisitively, taking in the haughty half-dwarf in front of her, nose held high in the air despite her fear, and smirked. She bowed her head low to the ground.

"I will swear to protect you, my lady, on my honor as a Bastion," she proclaimed.

"Ugh. Gods," Ortensia moved past her and headed out the door.

Once Valma and Ortensia rejoined them, and Kaj had a bit of fun winking and wagging their eyebrows at the pair, they refocused and made their way outside to the empty stables, palms sweaty and stomachs in knots.

Ava pointed at the third stall on the right, "This should be the one."

"You think they took the horses down there too?" Kaj asked. His eyes darted around the pens, "Shouldn't there be more of them in here?"

"They probably stabled them somewhere else while they moved everyone," Valma answered. "The last thing you need is a spooked horse kicking you in the face while you're kidnapping someone."

"Yeah, that makes more sense." He hesitated in front of the stall before turning over his shoulder to look at Ava, "I'm not going to get shit on my boots when I walk in here, right?"

"No promises."

Kaj frowned, took a breath, and stepped in. He ran his hands around the wooden walls of the stall, searching for any sign of an opening, and stumbled upon a loose panel under a feed pail.

"Got it!" he announced as he pressed it in.

The bottom of the stall split in two and collapsed in. Startled by the sudden hole in the floor, Kaj jumped on top of the stall's half wall to save himself from falling.

The hay covering the entrance remained on the double doors, a planned camouflage, while the entrance revealed a slight, earthen slope that descended into darkness.

"Still think your father's innocent?" Gillian asked Ortensia.

"Again, this house is nothing but a hand me down," Ortensia replied, "This very well could be the previous burgermeister's doing."

"Sure," he doubted and walked past her to go down the slope. "Let's go."

"Watch out, Stick," Kaj said as he jumped off the wall to follow after him, "Wizkid's coming after your fearless commander shtick."

"I'd like to see him try." Valma placed a hand on Ortensia's back, "Stay by me, alright?"

"How about I stay *behind* you?" she grumbled.

"Sure, I don't mind being a meat shield." Valma shrugged, and the two of them headed down together.

Ava remained at the entrance of the stall.

She looked back, eyes focused on the rafters, hoping to find a pair of green eyes and a mischievous smile looking down at her, but saw only dust and cobwebs.

She unsheathed her bow and descended.

※

It was a steep descent down. From the initial darkness, that blinded all but Kaj, emerged sconces of flickering flame that lit their way as the carved natural rock turned to paved stone tiles. The tiles spread to cover the walls and ceiling as the path let out into a spacious, six-sided room: the antechamber of the main shrine.

"So," Kaj whispered as they entered. "Which way?"

The antechamber was devoid of any furniture or defining markings, only five wooden doors, one on each wall of the room, padlocked and much more foreboding than slabs of wood should be.

"Gill," Ava said. "Do you think you can look through the earth again?"

"I can try." He crouched on the ground and placed his hands flat against the stone. He closed his eyes and focused, trying to feel the earth beneath him but found its familiar call buried deep, suffocated by lifeless marble, tainted and man-made.

"Anything?" Valma asked.

"No." Gillian cracked his knuckles across the tile in frustration, "Whatever this shit is isn't natural."

"Well then," Kaj wiggled his fingers and took out his set of lock picks, "should we start with the first door to the left?"

"I suppose," Valma grumbled. "Ready yourselves and stay vigilant. We'll go Kaj, me, Cici, Gill, Ava. Any objections?"

"It's gonna be hard for me to get a clear shot if I'm behind you all," Ava replied.

"That's why you'll be watching our backs instead.

Anyone who tries to sneak up on us will think twice once they get an arrow through the stomach."

Ava nodded solemnly, unable to hide her disdainful pout.

"Anyone else?" Valma asked.

They all shook their heads.

"Good. Kaj? Do your thing."

"Aye aye, captain," he saluted and set to work unlocking the first door.

With no magic sigils or hidden mechanisms, the pins set into the place quickly. He palmed the padlock as it fell and opened the door just enough to peer through the crack, finding an empty hall on the other side, dimly lit by the same flaming sconces. He looked back to the others and nodded before opening the door a little wider and stepping through it.

Like children sneaking past a sleeping parent, they crept down the hall, rolling their footsteps with their knees bent low. Ava's heels burned as she walked backwards in the squatted position, but the fear of someone like Talwar sneaking up on her overrode the shooting pain.

The first door they came across was unremarkable in make. Kaj checked the handle and found it unenchanted, untrapped, and unlocked. He pressed his ear up against the door and, hearing nothing, gestured for them to follow as he entered.

They found themselves in a storeroom of sorts. Crates

and barrels of all shapes and sizes filled the small chamber. Ava stood by the doorway, keeping watch as the rest of the group perused the cargo. Ropes, handcuffs, mouth gags, chains of lead: packed to the brim with ways to keep a person bound as well as small stores of food and ale.

"Looks like they were planning to be here a while," Valma tapped her knuckle against a keg, "Anybody find anything of note?"

"Good gods, this thing's almost twice my age." Kaj held up a bottle of wine, "Wilderotter Winery Merlot, bottled 917 AB. This shit is from forty years ago!"

He looked at the bottle longingly before asking, "Anybody see a bag in here or something?"

"Leave the damn thing, will you?" Ortensia snapped.

"Oh, come on! We should get something for our troubles!"

"If we get out of here quickly and alive, I'll buy you the fanciest bottle I can find," she picked at a hangnail. There was a waver to the impatience in her voice, "We got a deal?"

"Deal!" He put the bottle back with a smug grin on his face.

"Ava?" Gillian asked, "All clear?"

She nodded.

"Alright, moving on then," Valma directed. "Kaj, lead the way."

The hall remained empty as they continued forward, coming upon two more doors, one to the left of them, marking the end of the path.

Kaj looked back at his companions, asking which one to investigate with a shrug of his shoulders.

Valma pointed to the left door with a stern expression that read, 'no stone left unturned.'

Kaj pouted when he found the door unlocked and silent as well. Giving them a halfhearted thumbs up, he stepped into the room and froze.

The shock on his face urged Valma to move quickly, rushing to his side with her sword at the ready. Her mouth fell agape as she saw the room over his shoulder, and she pushed past him to enter. Gill and Ortensia exchanged a confused look before following after her. Gill gave a quick tap on Ava's shoulder to let her know they were moving in.

Ava bumped against Kaj as she backed into the room. Startled, she whipped around and almost let loose the arrow between his shoulder blades, recognizing his pointed, copper ears just in time to stop herself. She lowered her bow and smacked him on the shoulder.

"What are you doing?" she hissed, "Get in the room!" Ava shoved him through the doorway and took her post, hoping he didn't notice how badly her hands trembled.

Stumbling, Kaj bumped into a frozen Gillian and Ortensia. They were unphased, too focused on the rows and rows of bloodstained and rusted weapons hung up on the walls around them.

On the floor sat more instruments meant to torture and break. Valma walked through them, running her fingertips over tables containing dozens of iron spiders, choke pears, thumbscrews. She wove past the iron maidens and large rack crowding the tiny room towards the weapons on the far wall. Her fingers wrapped around the handle of a giant iron flail and pulled it off its hook. Holding the heavy weapon in her hands, she turned it over, fingertips tracing the bloody fingerprints stained into the handle's wooden grip.

"I thought we weren't taking souvenirs," Kaj squeaked. His innate need to make light of the horror in front of him squeezed the quip out of him.

"These things are old," Valma stated, ignoring his comment. "Really old. A hundred years at least."

"All of them?" Gillian asked.

"Most of them."

"Maybe they're artifacts," Gill suggested, "necessary tools for the ceremony."

"Yeah… maybe…"

"Are you-" Ortensia stammered, "are you going to take it?"

"Gods. No." Valma's voice went quiet, "I just needed to make sure it was real." She placed the flail back on the wall gingerly. She looked down at her hands, flecks of dried blood nestled in the ridges of her palms, and closed her fist.

How many?

Valma walked back towards them, "Sorry. We should keep moving."

"Yeah," Kaj turned around, "this room is... a lot."

"It's only going to get worse, I fear," Valma replied, "All clear?"

Ava nodded and held the door open for the others to step through.

Kaj headed over to the final door, but his hand paused just above the door handle.

"I didn't think the ritual would take this long," an arrogant voice said beyond the door.

"How long did you think it would take?" a low, gruff voice grumbled back.

"Well, I figured I'd be at TOTS working my way through the bar by now."

"Aw. What's so wrong with having a little dinner and drink with me?"

"No offense, but you're not my ideal company, and I much prefer my meals in a less dank environment."

Kaj jumped as Valma placed a hand on his shoulder.

"How many?" she whispered.

He drew his dagger, "Two."

She backed up, looked at the others, and held her sword at the ready. Ortensia moved back to stand next to Ava as Gillian stepped forward.

Kaj slowly wrapped his fingers around the handle and opened the door slightly.

The room resembled a small canteen with a few sets of tables and chairs scattered throughout the space. Two cloaked figures sat at one of the tables, not far from them, their backs to the door as they ate and chatted.

Kaj took stock of the cultists and, considering his advantage, sent a dagger soaring through the air. The smaller of the two jolted, falling face-first into his food as Kaj's blade buried into the base of his skull. His friend stood quickly and reached for his weapon.

He threw the door open and ducked as Valma leaped over him into the room. She planted her feet square into the chest of the man, knocking him back and pinning him to the table. The force of her momentum carried her as her sword arched over her head and into his chest. She pierced through his heart in one blow.

Once the man went limp beneath her, she pulled her sword out and jumped back off of him, landing in a defensive stance, ready to strike again.

Kaj and Gillian stepped into the room, prepared for a brawl, but the cultists didn't move.

"They uh," Valma panted, "died pretty quickly for

necromancers."

"To be fair, we weren't sure they were all necromancers," Gillian noted. He turned back towards the open door, "You can come in."

Ortensia and Ava entered cautiously. Kaj shut the door behind them and propped one of the chairs under the handle to keep it closed.

"That was fast," Ava remarked.

"I know… We had the element of surprise, but even the Venzors put up more of a fight." Valma pulled the black fabric hood off of the man she killed's face.

"What?" Ava gasped quietly.

"You know this guy?" Valma asked.

"Y-yeah, that's-" her stomach knotted.

"Boy. Give the girl some hay and let her be on her way."

"-the stablemaster."

"My stablemaster?!" Ortensia gawked.

"What about this guy?" Kaj pulled his dagger out of the back of the smaller man's skull and turned his head to face the others.

"Wilfred!" Ortensia shrieked.

"Keep your voice down. We don't know who can hear

us," Valma shushed.

"So it's the help who's turned on the town! How crude!" she lowered her voice, but her shock stayed.

"Or your shit heel of a father convinced them to help him," Kaj snapped. All eyes turned to him as his playful nature suddenly shifted to something more damning.

"What did you say?" Ortensia seethed.

"You know it's real fucking convenient that all of the bad shit going on in this fucking hicktown is centered around your family and their capitalizing friends. And that you, his precious daughter, just so happen to be tagging along with us." The notion of another betrayal hardened Kaj's heart and left him on edge. The growing amount of coincidences and signs pointing back to Ortensia were too numerous to ignore, and her callous attitude towards her staff pushed him past the point of tolerance.

That entitled pout sat snuggly on her face, "What are you implying?"

"Kaj-" Gillian warned in vain.

Kaj got up in Ortensia's face before any of them could blink. He grabbed her by the collar of her dress and held her just centimeters from his nose. The look in his eyes was dark and threatening.

"If you stab us in the fucking backs here, I will not hesitate to slide this dagger across your throat."

A sharp metal edge rested gently on the back of his neck. The slick warmth of blood from its last strike dripped down the collar of his cloak.

"Kaj," Valma warned, "we have other things to focus on now. She's no threat to us. She has no magicks. You heard what Master Gustav said."

"You don't need magicks to be a snitch," his stare bore through Ortensia, "and who's to say that chrome dome wasn't lying?"

"Because he's too pompous to lie," Gill hissed in frustration. "Are we done here?"

Valma removed her blade from Kaj's neck, but his fierce grip on Ortensia remained.

The pretentious nature of the half-dwarf flew out the window, leaving a shaken, scared little girl trembling slightly in his hands. He let go of her, stood, and removed the chair from against the door.

Valma placed a hand on Ortensia's shoulder for a moment. Ortensia looked up at her with her eyes glazed over and wide, face ashen.

"I thought we were done here," Kaj snipped.

Valma grimaced and let go of her, following him out the door.

Gill looked at Ortensia, waiting for her to move, to keep with the marching order.

"I got her, Gill," Ava said, soft and kindly. "You go ahead."

"Are you sure?" he arched an eyebrow at her. She looked back at him, for as scared as she was to be down in this dungeon, she tampered the feeling down and smiled warmly.

"Yeah, I'm sure."

He knew better than to ask twice and left the room.

Ortensia didn't move. She couldn't, not with how violently her body shook.

Ava walked in front of her and crouched down to her level.

"I'm sorry about that," she said.

"Why are you apologizing?" Ortensia asked, a quiver in her voice. "I'm sure you liked seeing me put in my place."

"Not like that," Ava replied.

"They really think he did this," she hid her face behind her hair, but Ava heard the soft sobs in her whisper. "They think that I did this."

"I don't."

"Yes, you do."

"No, I don't," Ava insisted, "This is all so terrifying and confusing I don't know what to think." The back of her throat went dry as tears built in the corners of her eyes, "Hell, I don't even want to think right now."

Ortensia stayed quiet. Ava took it as a sign she was listening.

"I know it feels impossible to move forward right now. Everything in you is probably screaming to crawl under a table and just hide, but that's not gonna make this stop. That's not gonna give us an answer," she crouched down even lower, trying to make eye contact. Ava found her face, tears running down it, eyes noticing her but too ashamed to acknowledge it. "Just think about how good it is going to feel when you prove them wrong. You love that feeling, don't you?"

Ortensia's eyes met hers.

"Just imagine how much you'll be able to brag and rub it in their faces," Ava smiled.

"You know your eyes get really red when you cry," Ortensia rubbed the tears off of her face and lifted her head. "You should maybe try to work on that."

"Sure, Cici." Ava stood and wiped her eyes on her sleeve.

Ortensia took a deep breath and headed towards the door. Ava followed after her.

"You know I haven't given any of you permission to call me that," she said.

"Would Orty be better?" Ava held the door open for her to step through, keeping an eye out for danger as she did, "It has a nice ring to it."

"Utter that name in my presence again, and I'll really

raise the taxes on your farm," Ortensia threatened emptily.

"Oh no," Ava feigned horror, "not more taxes!"

CHAPTER FIFTEEN

"Alright, Kaj," Valma whispered to him as Ortensia and Ava rejoined them at the end of the hall, "We're good to go."

He gave a subtle nod and opened the door back out into the antechamber. Kaj jolted and stopped opening the door a quarter of the way. Valma jumped to peer over his shoulder and caught the familiar tail end of a black cloak disappearing two doors down.

"That was fucking close," she exhaled.

"Well, at least we know what door to check next," Kaj grumbled, mad at himself that he didn't listen before opening the door. He double-checked the antechamber before stepping out into it to make up for the mistake.

They crept across towards the door and found it unlocked. The cultist who entered it too hurried to lock it behind him. The other side of the door held another stone-tiled hall. They kept their weapons at the ready as they crept down it, listening intently for any sign as to where the cloaked figure went.

The squealing scrape of a chair sliding against stone and a muffled groan of pain was the signal they needed. They quickened their pace and followed the echoing sounds of struggle.

"Ava!" Valma hissed as she readied herself outside of the door.

Ava ran up to meet her, bow at the ready, "I thought you wanted me in back?"

"After this," she said, "I'm gonna kick open the door, you fire at anything in a cloak that moves."

"Uh-" her throat caught.

"Okay?" Valma asked, impatient. A guttural yell rumbled through the wooden door.

"Okay!" Ava yipped and pointed her bow towards the door.

Valma drove the heel of her boot right above the door handle, caving in the hardware and rocketing the door open.

Ava pulled back her bowstring but stopped. Her racing heart tripled in speed, flitting so fast it threatened to lift her off the ground. Wavy brown hair brushed over moss-green eyes. A black cloak draped over his strong, wide shoulders. The wry smile he often wore absent as a cultist fell limp against him from the sword shoved through their stomach. As the lifeless figure slid off his blade, Ava dropped her bow and ran towards him.

"Kieran!" she cried as she wrapped her arms around him. He stumbled back from the force of her embrace, but she held on tightly, keeping him steady as she buried herself in the familiar warmth of his chest.

"Ava?" Kieran gasped.

"You're alive!" she sobbed into his chest. The slight smell of turpentine wrapped around her, bringing a smile to her face as tears of relief soaked into his shirt.

"Ava!" His sword clattered against the tile as he tightly wrapped his arms around her, leaning forward to plant a kiss on the top of her head.

"What are you doing here?" he whispered into her hair.

She tilted her head up to look at him. Her breath caught in her lungs as he looked down at her in absolute awe. Ava didn't know she could smile any wider, but somehow her face made room, "We're here to rescue you!"

He trailed his hands up her sides and cupped her face in his palms. He ran his thumb across her cheek, wiping away a tear before pulling her into a deep kiss. Ava melted from the tender warmth of his lips, her body relaxing for the first time in days under his touch. She twisted her hands into his shirt and breathed him in.

Kieran was safe, and she would never let him go of him again.

The others stood there frozen, blocking the doorway, the looks on their faces a mix of shock, confusion, and bitter disappointment.

Well, the faces of all except-

"What the hell is going on?" Ortensia asked as she pushed her way through their legs to get a better look. Once she forced her way through the stiff wall of limbs, her jaw went slack at the romantic scene playing out in front of her. A spark of recognition ignited in her at the man swallowing Ava's tongue's mop of tangled, tawny locks.

"So that's how you knew what the stables looked like!" she shrieked.

Ava pulled out of the kiss and looked back to the group with blushing cheeks split by a love-struck smile.

"He's safe!" she giggled.

"The man in the cult robes is safe?!" Kaj guffawed.

"Oh man, this does look bad, doesn't it?" Kieran smiled the type of boyish smile that could make an angry mother drop her frying pan, and a disgruntled father offer to show him his workbench.

He scratched the back of his head, "Sorry. I just thought it'd be easier to sneak around here if I wore one of these things," he pulled at the cloak he wore and grimaced at Ava as she turned around to face him, "Though to tell you the truth, magpie, I'm not exactly thrilled with how I had to do it."

The others looked at the bodies that laid slain on the

ground beside him. Two of them cloaked, the other uncloaked.

"Shit," Valma said, her eyes rested on the braided red hair of Annice, a fellow townsguard. Her throat was slit, and she still wore her leathers from the last-minute patrol Captain Reids called her in for. Valma stepped forward and knelt beside the body.

"You know her?" Kaj asked.

"Yeah." She rasped, "She covered the rest of my shift after the dinner."

"So the townsguard is in on it too," Ortensia remarked under her breath.

Kaj bristled at her comment but swallowed his remarks, "What about the others?"

Gillian stepped into the room, giving a wide berth to Ava and Kieran's continued embrace, and pulled back the hood on the body doubled over behind them.

"I think this is your cook, Cici," he said, gently propping the head up for her to see.

Ortensia swallowed, "Yeah, that's Baretta."

"I can save you the trouble of checking the next one," Kieran's smile faded, his tone somber as he looked down at Ava, his eyes seeking forgiveness. "That's Tomlin, Annice's son and one of the other stable boys I worked with."

"Oh no," she gasped. More tears gathered at her waterline, "Not Tomlin."

"Yeah," Kieran smoothed a hand over her hair and cupped her cheek in his calloused palm, "Tomlin."

"So you killed these guards just to get a cloak?" Kaj questioned.

"Not for just a cloak," Kieran pressed a kiss against Ava's forehead and stepped out of her embrace.

He faced Kaj with a fierce yet faraway gaze, and his jaw tightened, "These people are monsters. They took me out of the cells to take me wherever the hell they've been taking everyone else, but I got the better of them. Stole one of their swords and ran into this hall looking for an exit when I found these two." He gestured to Annice and Tomlin, "The other one came in after."

Kieran took a deep breath to calm himself down before looking back to the woman beside him, "Ava," his big green eyes filled with concern and confusion as he grabbed her hand, "how do you know these people?"

"It's a long story," she smiled sadly at him.

"I mean, Ortensia I can wrap my head around-"

"And Gillian. I've told you about Gill before."

"Have you?"

"I mean- I'm sure I did-"

"Enough," Gill interrupted. He walked past the couple, looking pointedly forward as a cold breeze seemed to roll off of him, "The more time we waste, the more people die. You gonna help us or what?"

"Yeah. Absolutely." Kieran picked his sword off the ground and saluted, "Just tell me the plan."

"We're freeing as many people as quickly and quietly as we can," Valma answered as she stood, running a hand over Annice's eyes to close them. "When you escaped, did you see any other cells?"

"I know where the one I was kept in is," he answered, "but other than that, I have no idea."

"Then we'll check the rest of this hall first, then head there. We've got to make sure we don't miss anyone."

"Have you seen my parents? My brothers?" Ava placed a hand on her boyfriend's shoulder, drawing his attention back to her.

"They weren't in the same cell as me," he sighed, "sorry, magpie."

"Come on," Kaj waved everyone towards him as he checked down the hall. "The coast is clear for now. Let's get moving."

They slipped out of the room and into the empty hall, shutting the door behind them. Kaj took the lead once more, but Gillian fell in step beside him.

"Shouldn't you be in the back with Ava?" he whispered.

"Kieran's got it covered," Gill grumbled.

Kaj shot him a side-eye glare, "Geez. Green is not a good color on you."

"What?" he looked down at his vest, "Are you colorblind or something? This is blue."

Kaj snorted softly, "Nevermind."

After a moment, he continued, "If it's any consideration, something doesn't sit right with me about him. He's got some muscle to him but to take down three people, including a townsguard?"

"Not to defend the guy, but even I could have taken down Tomlin. Sans magick." Gillian grumbled, "So it's not that far-fetched."

"Still," Kaj looked back over his shoulder at Kieran. Sneering in disgust as he watched the kind-looking man smooth a stray hair behind Ava's ear, "He smiles too much for someone who spent almost two days in a torture chamber."

The pair settled into a brooding silence as they crept along before coming upon a door quite unlike the others. Made of heavy iron, the door was buried in the stone wall and boasted a large padlock preventing anything from getting out.

"This has got to be it," Kaj pulled out his lock picks and set to work.

Where hushed chatter would normally rumble through the group as they watched him tackle the intricate lock, silence prevailed, anticipation and worry tying their tongues and knotting their stomachs.

A few heavy seconds later, the padlock unlatched in Kaj's hand, and he pushed the heavy door open. He didn't know what to expect beyond the barred wooden door, nor did he want to let his imagination wander to any potential horrors, but a dark and empty chamber was certainly unexpected.

"What?" he muttered as he stepped into the room. "Wizkid, give me some light."

Gill stuck by the door as the others entered and muttered his illumination incantation. His palms glowed with golden light, and he held them forward, spreading their glow throughout the chamber.

The medium-sized stone room was completely barren: no furniture, no people, nothing. They spread out around the room, looking for some sort of clue or sign as to the space's purpose.

Ava moved to search alongside Kieran but stopped as Kaj pulled her back by the strap of her bow sheath.

"What are you-" she hissed as he pulled her away to check out a random corner of the room.

"What's up with you and pretty boy over there?" he cut her off, looking at her pointedly.

"He's my boyfriend… kind of…" Ava said bashfully, a blush crawled up her cheeks.

"Look," Kaj said. "That promise I made to Little Miss Rich Bitch over there applies to you too. If I find out that you and dreamboat are somehow connected to this shit, I won't hesitate." His eyes were just as cold and damning as they were with Ortensia, "Talwar is dead because of this. Because of them."

"What makes you think I had anything to do with that?" Ava's throat went dry, and the blush drained from her cheeks.

"Because you made out with a guy wearing a black cultist robe in the middle of an underground shrine filled with cultists wearing black robes!" disappointment hissed through his words as he tried to keep his voice down. His eyes darted to where Kieran stood, back turned away from them all as he studied a crack in the wall.

Ava exhaled, the color coming back to her face, and placed a hand on Kaj's shoulder. "Things are super tense right now, so I don't blame you for thinking that way. But," she looked over her shoulder at Kieran. The sturdy shape of his muscular back sent a wash of warmth over her, "Seeing him alive and well has been the only thing to give me some hope that things will be okay. I'm still terrified, but I trust him."

"You trust him." Kaj took a moment to study her face before continuing, "Also, just for future reference, a guy is either your boyfriend, or he's not. There ain't no 'kind of' when it comes to that."

"Hey, I found something," Ortensia's call ended their conversation before Ava could reply.

They all turned to face her as she held up a small gray piece of fabric pinched between her fingers in disgust.

293

"It's like a tiny sock or something," she grimaced.

"A tiny sock?" Valma questioned.

"Fuck!" The room trembled slightly as Gill hit the side of the door frame with his fist.

"You okay, Wizkid?" Kaj asked.

Everything inside Gillian screamed. The stew of rage, guilt, fear, and jealousy that built, silently simmering in the back of his mind, boiled over. The gnawing, emotion-fueled nature of his natural magick begged, *shouted* at him to take action as an invisible force tugged at the roots of his hair, sapping every ounce of his patience to resist the ceaseless urge to bring down the earth and swallow this wretched place whole.

"No. I'm not okay," he seethed, "That's a fucking kid's sock. They had kids in here, and this entire room is fucking empty! You know what that means, right?!"

A light layer of dirt fell from the ceiling, dusting realization across the rest of the group.

"We need to move faster," Valma said, her knuckles went white around the hilt of her sword. "We'll forego stealth to check the rest of this hall quickly."

"Alright," Ava nocked an arrow against her bowstring, "Gill, you want to take the lead?" She looked back to the doorway and found it empty.

"Yeah, we should really fucking go," Kaj spat out quickly and ran out the door after him.

They hustled down the winding hallway, the frantic clicks of their footsteps echoing around the stone chamber.

"Kaj!" they heard Gillian bark as they rounded the corner. He stood red-faced and fuming in front of another barred door.

Kaj scurried to his side and quickly picked the lock. Recalling the motions from before, it came undone easily.

Gill shoved the door open and held a glowing palm into the room.

"Empty!" he shouted. The tunnel trembled in response, and he took off again.

More footsteps joined the percussion of their chase as three cultists charged down the hall in front of them, weapons drawn.

"Stop!" Ava commanded. They all stopped. Her order even cut through Gill's rage to still his feet.

"Ava, stay behind-" Kieran's warning cut off as three arrows whistled past him.

One after another, the charging cultists' heads wrenched back as the arrows hit their marks. They flung lifelessly to the floor, propelled backwards by the momentum of the arrow's impact.

"Keep moving," Ava ordered, "Keep to one side, so I have a clear shot in case more come." They took off running, following her orders, and kept to the left of the hall.

She stepped around a dumbfounded Kieran. "Stay behind me," Ava averted her gaze as she spoke to him, "I couldn't forgive myself if I hit you."

They reached the end of the hall and found the door the cultists came from unlocked. As they threw it open, the light from Gill's palms poured into the room highlighting two bodies strung up by chains.

Dangling by their wrists, the bodies were bloodied and beaten beyond all recognition. Valma was the only one brave enough to approach. A chill ran through her as she placed her fingers against their necks and found no pulse.

"They're gone," she turned around and faced the others.

Gill looked as though the golden glow of his hands was about to erupt into flames.

Kaj's lips pursed in disgust, but his eyes remained locked on the bodies.

Ortensia blanched, eyes cast down to the floor.

Ava hid her face against Kieran's shoulder.

And Kieran stared and the bodies, mouth slightly agape.

"Alright, Romeo." Valma's gaze flashed distant for a moment, firming up as she locked eyes with Kieran, "Lead the way."

CHAPTER SIXTEEN

The horror of those mutilated bodies turned the frenzied fury that pumped through them into focused indignation. Their walk back down the hall was less frantic and more focused on strategy. Valma and Kieran discussed the dangers that lay ahead of them in great detail. The stable hand informed her with as much detail as he could recall about his arrival and time spent as a prisoner of the Zozvit cultists thus far.

They were all angry. A quiet, seething anger, that even silenced the roiling Gillian, though steam still seemed to billow off him.

"Hey," Ava sidled up beside him, "are you alright?"

"I'm fine," he snipped. The chamber around them trembled slightly, and some more dirt fell from between the cracks of the tiled ceiling.

"You don't seem fine."

Ava was right. He wasn't fine. He was disappointed in himself, disturbed and enraged by how casually some of the townsfolk of Elerrï turned on their own, and dealing with the sudden and constant "whispering" of the earth in the back of his mind, loud and irritated now that it found some way to seep through the man-made tiles that blocked it from him earlier. And for some reason, he kept ruminating on how intensely Kieran gripped Ava's face as he kissed her and the terrible case of indigestion that continued to burn in his chest since they rescued him.

"Shouldn't you be up with Kieran?" Gill grumbled.

"No," Ava frowned, "I should be here, in the back, just like Valma told me to."

Gillian felt her gaze on his cheek, studying him, wanting him to look at her to discern his emotions more clearly.

"So you're not fine," she sighed after a moment.

"Of course I'm not fine! People are being slaughtered by the second, and you-"

Dirt fell from the ceiling again, a fiercer tremor this time.

"What about me?" she challenged.

"You-" he stalled, holding back his frustration as much as he held back the earth, "-you shouldn't be fine either!"

"Never said that I was," Ava bit and brushed the pebbles and dirt off her shoulder, "but you don't see me getting upset and shaking the entire earth."

Gillian bristled and ran a hand through his red curls to

shake the dirt from them, "Do you think I wanted to do that?"

"No, but now that we know that you can do that, I need to make sure you're gonna be able to keep calm as we keep moving forward."

He faced her, and his heartburn flared up to sting the back of his throat. He didn't need someone to keep him calm. The cavern around them still standing was evidence of that. Gillian didn't want to be someone Ava needed to take care of. He wanted to be someone she *wanted* to take care of. A desire not a burden, and from the way she was looking at him, he was very much the latter.

"Who said that *you* need to do it?"

The honey of her eyes turned sour. Ava's jaw tightened, the muscles rippling in the same telling pattern as they did before she decked the kids that picked on him on the playground. He readied himself for her strike. He may have grown to stand five inches over her in the years since he left their secondary school, but his height only gave her a clearer shot at his jaw for a knockout.

"You're right," her anger simmered behind her grit teeth, "*I* don't need to do anything."

Ava broke her stare and slowed her pace to drop back behind him.

＊

They stopped in front of the door that led back out into the antechamber.

"Once we leave this hall, we'll need to cross the antechamber and enter the fourth door. That should be the one I came out of," Kieran informed them from the front of the pack.

He looked at Kaj kindly, "Kaj, right? You're the one who can pick locks?"

"Yeah," he mumbled half-heartedly.

"Good," Kieran nodded to himself nervously, "We're probably gonna need that." He took a deep breath that filled the expanse of his chest and summoned up his courage to address them, "Listen, I know things might seem hopeless right now. But you guys can't give up. The fact that you've made it this far is a testament to your strength."

"Thanks for the pep talk," Valma cut off the rest of his speech as he paused to take a breath, "but we're not hopeless."

"Speak for yourself," Ortensia mumbled under her breath.

Kieran smiled softly, clearly disappointed that his half-finished speech was met with such a lackluster response, and opened the door back out to the antechamber, looking both ways before signaling the group forward. They crossed the chamber quickly and approached the fourth door. Kaj got on his knees, ready to pick the lock, but found it already open.

"This can't be a good sign," he said as he showed the group how easily the lock came undone in his hands.

"We can't rush in here," Kieran said gravely. "It's likely they know we're coming."

"Good," Gill snipped, "then we can take them out in one go."

"Exactly." Valma clasped a hand on his shoulder, "These fuckers deserve what's coming to them."

Ortensia tensed at her words.

"That they do," Kieran nodded and led them through the door.

※

They entered yet another winding tiled hall. The hypnotic repetition of tile, uniform and spotless, paired with the echoing, even tempo of their footsteps bouncing off the walls of the empty tunnel lulled their tensed and tired minds under into the waves of their idle consciousness to drown in thought.

Despite the gruesome nature of current events, Valma couldn't help the buzzing excitement pulsing up and down her spine. Her imagination conjured scenes of her cutting down cultist after cultist, smashing the locks to the other cells by striking the hilt of her sword against them, and opening the doors to reveal the rest of the town in tears joyous that they were saved. She thought of Captain Reid's face among them, looking at her in shock then swelling pride, and fighting alongside her as they faced the mastermind behind this evil plot to bring them to justice. Valma wondered even further, picturing a lavish ceremony where the Bastions would reward her with a medal of honor and announce her promotion.

Kaj was no stranger to suffering. If he dwelled on it,

if he let it consume him like it did when he was younger, he would lose himself again. So Kaj set to burying the disturbing intrusions on the past two days into the heavy metal vault he kept locked tight deep in the catacombs of his subconscious. The chained and mutilated corpses they discovered. The pungent scent of sulfur and iron from the pulped masses that once were Bolo and Seax. The squelch that sent shivers down his spine when Gillian's stone slab flattened those cultists against the wall. He sealed the vault and covered it up with the thoughts of returning to Moreacor, of drowning in alcohol and writhing bodies, chasing as much pleasure as it would take to turn this all into just another bad memory waiting to slip out cracks of the vault and sneak up on him on the seldom nights he spent alone.

Ava's suppressed emotions wound the strings of her psyche tighter and tighter. She felt the tension building in the base of her skull, the ache locking her clenched jaw, the crystalline ringing in between her shoulders as her nerves cried out in pain from constant strain. The tune of her turmoil still played distantly, but its minor chords rose in a slow crescendo as shrill screams, a droning, scratchy violin, joined its nagging melody. It demanded to be heard, and she continued to play deaf. Gillian's cruel demeanor added a blaring piccolo to the song, so she focused on Kieran's broad shoulders. The thought of Kieran's green eyes condemning her to damnation for all the lives she'd stolen added the foreboding bass of a cello, and she pivoted to recall the warm embraces of her mother and father. They, too, fell victim to her unwillingly morbid ruminations. Their embraces grew cold as they withered to corpses in her arms and added percussion to the growing orchestra.

As she picked her cuticles apart, Ortensia hoped beyond hope that she would find her father among the captured. Her internal pleads and prayers to any deity that would listen repeated faster and faster the further down the hall they traveled. As selfish and cruel as her father could be to her, Ortensia couldn't picture him murdering others, looming over some poor peasant like Lord Venzor did to Octavian. She envisioned his dwarven form swimming in a pool of the black fabric and almost laughed aloud. Burgermeister Valborg would never be caught dead in such a frock... or maybe he would... if it were tailored right. If the sleeves were taken up enough so they wouldn't get in the way of his strikes. Underneath the hood, his face would be just as hard and gaze just as hateful as it was all of the times he berated and beat her and her brother. Her thoughts stalled on that portrait. Her father could be an angry man, but was he a mass murderer? And what would it say about her if he was?

Gillian's thoughts were anything but his own. The earth's whispers above him grew to screams in the quiet hall as the massive chorus of tiny voices begged him for release. The rock and soil and silt pleaded with him to pull them down and let them swallow everything whole, to reclaim what these vile beings had stolen from them and purify the land. Their desires brought a sense of longing and nostalgia for a time he had not experienced but still wanted to recover, which deepened his fury. It took everything of his willpower not to listen to them, to separate his emotion from theirs, and not let the absolute anger inside him take over. He promised the earth, and himself, vengeance but conditioned that the others must be saved first. Crushing innocents under a ton of rock would only taint the land further.

While they waged their internal wars, stumbled through their mental labyrinths, and pondered the potentials that awaited them, they failed to notice the lack of barred doors and cultists for a place that had been so heavily guarded from Kieran's recount of his escape. Their taxed minds too focused on seizing this fleeting moment of banality and stillness to process and try to repair.

Eventually, they came to a large, heavy wooden door at the end of the hall.

"Kaj," Kieran whispered, snapping Kaj out of his daydreams of warm touches and soft flesh, "Can you open it? This leads the way to the cell I was in."

The elvefolk nodded as he moved to the front and picked the lock quickly.

Not a moment after the padlock came loose and fell into Kaj's palm, a guttural scream of pain ripped through the door. Kieran yanked the door and held it open as the others threw caution out the window and ran through, their legs moving of their own accord.

As they charged down the small hall past the door, it opened up into a large chamber tiled with bright white bones. Intricately arranged into a macabre mosaic, the fibulas, tibias, tarsals, ribs, and skulls spread across the floor and up the walls to cover the ceiling. In the middle of the floor sat a wide, bone basin fashioned from the ribs of some large beast, about two feet in height. Two ducts branched from it to the right and left, the latter noticeably smaller than the other, but both disappeared into the earth.

Atop that pool, facing towards them, stood a rotund dwarven man with splotchy red cheeks and the last of his thinning hairs slicked back against his shiny pale scalp. The beady eyes of Burgermeister Valborg took in the intruders with surprised bemusement as he wiped his bloodied dagger off on his black cloak.

Any waning notion of her father's innocence completely left Ortensia. Horror took its place as her eyes locked on a familiar blonde woman kneeling in front of him. Her limp body slumped against his legs as the blood finished rushing from her opened throat. The light in Cordelia's gray eyes faded slowly as her trembling mouth stopped gasping for breath.

Ortensia's knees gave out, and she fell to the ground, letting out a piercing and mournful scream as she fell.

"You sick fuck!" Valma cried as she raised her sword and charged towards him.

Kaj ripped a dagger from his belt, Ava pulled her loaded bowstring taught, and Gillian bent down to place his palm on the ground.

"Stop."

Kieran's command reverberated through their bodies, tightening their skin against their muscles to lock them into place. Valma tried to keep running, to push past it, but immense pain stilled her as the slightest movement threatened to tear her skin from her body.

"When you said you had a surprise for me, this wasn't what I was expecting," Valborg remarked with a coyly raised eyebrow at Kieran.

Kieran pointed to the slain woman in front of him.

"Sorry, I couldn't wait for you," Valborg shrugged as he kicked Cordelia's corpse off of him and into the basin. A small wave of blood splashed onto the bottom of his cloak and over the edge of the basin as the body fell into it, "Her sobbing was so fucking annoying."

"That's alright," Kieran walked over to the basin and ushered her corpse down the right chute. "You had great timing, sir, checking the surveillance stones in Chamber Two when you did. If I hadn't gone to deal with Baretta and Tomlin, I would have missed 'em."

"I knew that boy didn't have the spine for the job," Valborg sighed, "but the stablemaster did such a fine job with you that I had to give him a chance." He hopped down from the basin and made his way closer to inspect the group.

"Can they speak?" he asked.

"If you want them to," Kieran sat on the edge of the pool casually, not caring about the spilled blood seeping into his cloak. "I won't loosen my hold on the ginger, though.

I don't know what type of magick he's got, but it's crazy strong."

"Oh, I know," Valborg's gaze shifted to Gillian. He snarled, "He's the little shit that wrecked my house."

"Ah," Kieran nodded his head in understanding, eyes not leaving Gill as he did. "You got a preference for which one you'll want to talk to?"

Valborg stood in front of his daughter, "Ortensia will do for now."

"Ortensia," Kieran's eyes emanated a haunting, milky blue light, *"Speak."*

The skin around Ortesnia's jaw and throat loosened.

"W-what are you doing?" a choking sob tumbled out of her mouth.

"That's exactly what I want to ask you," Valborg grumbled. "What happened to the Venzors?"

Ortensia's throat shook out a whimpering cry. Unable to blink, tears streamed down her face in both sadness and pain.

"Ugh," he rolled his eyes, "so dramatic."

She continued her cries, blubbering and heaving, as her paralyzed body tried to expel the twice-fold heartache that threatened to tear her chest apart. Valborg ran his stumpy fingered hand down his reddening face.

"Ortensia! Speak when you are spoken to, dammit!"

he barked, the same soul-crushing bark he used whenever she did something he saw as wrong and struck her across the face. "The Venzors!"

"They're dead!" she choked out through her sobs, like a scolded toddler messily spitting out their guilts after a spanking, "We killed them!"

He turned away from his daughter, meaty hands balling into fists as his body shook with anger.

"Gods!" He kicked a loose skull across the ground and whipped around to face Kieran, "Weren't those Hilt fuckers supposed to take care of shit like this?!"

"They're dead too," Ortensia spat out, desperate to shed the shame that sat like a weight in her stomach but found no relief in her confession. Her sobs turned to hyperventilating wails as her father's back stayed to her. She didn't care about the sting of his palm still lingering against her cheek or the burning of her forced open eyes. She wanted to collapse, to crawl to her father and tug on his robes to ask for forgiveness and beg him to tell her that this was just a nightmare.

Valborg pulled at his thinning hair and stared into the basin.

"Shut her up, please," he hissed to Kieran.

"*Quiet,*" he commanded. With another flash of magick in his eyes, the skin around her lips and throat seized once more, diluting her cries to muffled whimpers.

"H-how-" A rasping whisper slipped out of Gillian. They turned to look at the mage as blood trickled down his cracked lips and emerald eyes filled with piercing rage glared at them, "W-why-"

"See?" Kieran looked at Valborg and shrugged, "Crazy strong." He turned to address Gill, "Did you know that the outer layer of your skin is all dead cells? *Gillian. Hands above your head.*"

Gillian's arms slowly raised. He whimpered in pain as his skin pulled his muscles up to meet Kieran's command.

"The Venzors sent the burgermeister a lot of interesting books," Kieran continued, "He's not much of a reader, but I am. As for the why, I mean, there's a lot of perks to necromancy. What about you, sir?"

"Boy," Valborg barked. "What are you playing around for? He's dangerous, right?"

"Yeah," Kieran smirked at Gill. "But not like this."

"Well, we have a schedule to keep," he let go of his hair and dropped his hands to his side with a slap. "I'll handle the Venzor situation once we're finished."

He turned around, and his beady eyes scanned the intruders' scared faces. He pointed a pudgy finger at Ava, "That one was yours, right?"

"Mhmm," Kieran nodded. His gaze didn't leave Gill's face.

"She's got a steady hold on that bow," Valborg remarked, "She a good shot?"

"The best in Elerrï."

"Have her take care of him then."

Kieran nodded curtly, his gaze finally leaving Gill as his eyes went blue.

"Ava. Come."

Ava stepped forward slowly, her body shaking from the pain of her skin pulling her along. A jumble of pleading, incoherent sounds gurgled out of her as she approached.

"Gods, why must women be so noisy?" Valborg grumbled as he climbed back to his position on top of the basin.

Kieran stood and walked towards Ava, his eyebrow crooked in curiosity.

"Stop," he commanded as she reached him, her terrified eyes searching for any sign of green beneath the glaze of his spellcasting, *"Speak."*

"Kieran, you don't have to do this," her pleas tumbled out at a breakneck pace as her jaw unlocked and tears streamed down her face, "I don't know why he's making you do this, but we can stop him. We can stop him, and we can go back to the way things were. Gill and Master Gustav could help you learn magick if you want." Her voice hitched as she tried to catch her breath, "I love you so much, don't you see? You don't need whatever he's offering you. We have each other."

The clouds retreated from his eyes, and she sighed in relief at the sight of the mossy green that often filled her with happiness. He placed a hand on her cheek, quieting her ramblings with the familiar gentleness of his calloused palm.

Her heart stilled as his gaze darted across her face, watching her, studying her.

Judging her.

"God, you're always so ugly when you cry," he remarked. The glaze spread across his eyes, locking the Kieran she knew behind it, *"Quiet. Turn."*

Ava's mouth snapped shut, and her body twisted unnaturally to face Gill.

"Aim."

Ava lifted her bow and slowly pulled the bowstring back, fingers still hooked with the nock between them.

"Fire."

With a shrill whimper, her fingers let go.

The only sound in the cavern was the whistle of her arrow flying through the air as it grazed Gillian's cheek and buried itself into the bones covering the wall. Blood trickled down the bent wood of her bow, flowing from the palm of her left hand as she fought against the spell that bound her and forced herself to aim wide.

"You useless cunt," Kieran groaned. He raised his hand and backhanded her across the jaw, hard, sending her tumbling across the floor and rendering her unconscious as she landed.

Ava's limp body bouncing on the ground stilled the

boiling rage inside Gillian. The earth's cacophonous calls silenced.

Though his body was frozen, wracked with pain as his skin constricted him, his palms slowly tilted back to face the ceiling by no effort of his own. A warm presence wrapped in between his fingers as a strangely nostalgic pair of unseen hands gently guided him. There was no pain, and no blood poured down his palms as the hands gave him a reassuring squeeze and a soft, warm voice that he knew but could not place whispered:

Bury Him.

And the floodgates of the earth's fury burst open.

Something sharp hit the back of Kieran's head as he watched Ava's body for signs of movement. He twisted around quickly, drawing his sword to face his assailant, but was met instead with a terrifying visage.

Pupilless eyes, emanating a brilliant green light, burned into him, and a fiendish grin crawled upon Gillian's face. The cavern quaked as small rocks around his feet, and Gill's mop of red hair floated up, lifted by the mass of magicks channeling through him.

"D-don't just fucking stand there!" Valborg stammered, his eyes wide with panic. "Kill the little-" his command caught in his throat as a large rock dislodged from the cavern wall behind him and slammed into the back of his head. His body fell forward, landing face-first into the blood-filled basin, splashing blood over the sides and onto the floor.

Rocks, bones, and dirt rained down throughout the cavern as Kieran's eyes went pale in desperation, *"Stop!"*

Gillian's smile grew horrifically wide. He drew forth a large chunk of earth from the ceiling and clipped Kieran's side.

"Stop!" his repeated command fell on deaf ears. A cluster of rock and bone broke free and knocked the legs out from underneath him. Kieran's concentration broke, and he looked upon Gillian with clear eyes filled with terrified indignation.

"I told you," pale blue magick spread over Kieran's palms, "stop!"

The bones, shaken loose by Gillian's tremors, rose at his call and rushed to trap the mage.

The ground beneath Gill's feet broke open as thick roots shot up and wrapped around him, forming thick, brambled armor that shattered the bones as they hit.

Kieran dropped his hands to his side, eyes blown wide in fear and amazement as he watched his attack get swatted away with ease.

A chunk of bedrock shot out from underneath, uppercutting his slack jaw and sending him flying across the room. He landed with a smack against the wall, his skull cracking against it, and he slid down onto the floor motionless. Making sure to truly take care of the nuisance, Gillian collapsed the portion of the cavern above him, burying

Kieran in rubble.

The macabre grip on their skin loosened, but the room did not stop shaking.

Valma, Kaj, and Ortensia regained control of their bodies. The latter collapsed forward, curling into herself while heaving sobs rocked her tiny body. Valma knelt beside her and placed a comforting hand on her back as she watched Valborg's body bob lifelessly in the pool of blood.

"Holy shit, Wizkid," Kaj gasped, "Remind me to never mess with Ava when you're in the room." He turned to look at his friend and staggered back at the terrifying visage of Gillian, wholly consumed by the full force of Nature's magick, looking more mahogany than man.

"G-gill?" Kaj squeaked.

The thorns and roots continued to grow and wrap around Gill, consuming him slowly as large chunks of rock continued to fall from the ceiling, spreading out from the partial cave-in as the earth around them grew unstable.

"Valma-" Kaj warned as he backed away, "Valma!"

She looked over her shoulder and took in Gillian in all his verdant terror. Her limbs went numb as fear coursed through her, and she looked at Kaj for an explanation, but his blanched face echoed her panic and confusion.

A slab of rock crashed to the ground beside them, just shy of crushing their skulls, and snapped them out of their stupor.

"We got to pull him out of it," she instructed.

Kaj nodded and pulled forth his dagger as Valma lifted her blade.

"Come on, Wizkid!" he shouted, "Time to wake up!"

The pair rushed towards him, dodging falling rocks and navigating the earth shifting beneath their feet. Valma swung her sword at the roots, carving away the twisting armor slowly but surely while Kaj swiped at the vines circling his face, trying to clear Gillian's ears in the hopes that he would hear them.

"This is really impressive, man," Kaj grunted as he ripped free another chunk of vegetation, "but I don't wanna be buried alive here!"

Gill gave no sign of recognition. The manic smile faded from his face once Kieran left his sight, rendering him expressionless as the roots continued to bind him.

"I don't think jokes are gonna work right now!" Valma retorted. She cut back a new mass of brambles that sprouted from roots she had already removed. She huffed in frustration. They were getting nowhere.

Having known the mage for only a few days, Valma regretted not insisting Gustav come down with them. They needed someone who knew Gill and his magick better. Someone who-

Valma thought back to the skeleton room, recalling

315

that she caught a glimpse of Ava ripping Gillian from the ground as stone pillars clipped her in the ribs and threatened to tear the room asunder.

"Cici! Cici!" Valma looked over her shoulder and shouted, "Can you hear me?!"

Ortensia's head was clouded, stuffed with the sting of her father's cruelty against her cheek, the fierce need to please him despite how terribly he treated her, and Cordelia's lifeless eyes. She wanted to puke. She wanted to scream.

She didn't know what she wanted.

"Cici!" Valma shrieked, "Cici, come on!"

Ortensia! Her father's voice before he struck her was just as angry as every other time he said her name. That grim and damning look of bitter disappointment in his eyes. The swollen red flesh of his face wrinkling in absolute disgust at her, Ortensia. She knew it well.

Good for nothing, waste of space; *Ortensia.*

Vile, bothersome, nightmarish; *Ortensia.*

Her world was nothing else but his body, gently bobbing in the blood, and his voice battering her with her name over and over again.

"Cici!" Valma's scream was desperate and ear piercing, causing Kaj's ears to ring as he bore the brunt of it beside her.

Sharp and pleading, the desperation in Valma's cry honed its edge enough to cut through the fixated fog that clouded her view, shining a brilliant light that brought her back to reality.

"I'm here!" Cici sobbed, finding her voice, "I'm here!"

"You need to wake Ava up!"

"What?" she turned around, finally seeing Kaj and Valma trying in vain to free their friend.

Valma faced her, narrow eyes wide with panic, "Wake Ava up!"

Her shattered heart dropped into her stomach at the sight of genuine fear on the unwaveringly brave townsguard's face. As Cici's senses returned to her, she took in the crumbling room around her and searched frantically for Ava's body, turning around to find her covered in a layer of dirt a few feet behind her.

She scrambled across the ground and shook her violently, "Ava!"

Ava's face wrinkled as she let out a pained whimper.

"Ava! You have to get up!"

Her eyes opened slowly, "~~Ortens-~~"

Cici clamped a hand over her mouth, her father's voice threatening to return if she spoke her name, "You have to get up. You have to stop Gill."

"I-" Ava's head spun from pounding pain. The ground shook, sending dirt falling from the ceiling into her eyes and bones rattling in her ears. Guilt gurgled up through her stomach as she remembered exactly how she wound up on the floor of the underground sacrifice pit.

"I'm so sorry," she whimpered.

"Ava! You have to stop him!" Cici ignored her apology, "He'll bury us if you don't!"

Ava looked past her, and the cacophony of the crashing room faded to static.

"Gill," she murmured.

The wizard's body was long gone, completely covered in thick vines and brambles despite Valma and Kaj's continued attempts to clear it. Rooted to the ground, Gillian looked more like a tree than a man as the roots climbing up his raised arms carved into the cavern ceiling. The only semblance of her childhood friend left visible was his stoic, freckled face and glowing green eyes.

"How-"

"Do something!" Cici slammed her fists against Ava's chest, clearing the white noise from her ears. "Anything!"

"But I-"

"Come on!" she screamed.

Ava didn't know what to do, what to say, what to think.

Everything hurt, her head, her face, her throat, her heart. The only thing she did know was her guilt. The crushing guilt that blanketed her on the floor of her family's barn grew ten times heavier, and she would do anything to get rid of that weight.

"Gill!" Ava called as she pushed past her pain and got to her feet, "I'm sorry!" Her jaw burned as she spoke, and the back of her eyes stung.

No response. More and more debris still fell from above.

"Did you hear me?" She yelled and stepped closer, "I'm sorry!"

"I don't think he can hear anything!" Kaj shouted back.

They cleared out of the way as Ava approached him. Driven by her need to atone, to be forgiven, she wedged her fingers between the rooted bark and his face without hesitation, clasping his cheeks with bloodied palms as the thorns tore at her wounded hands, "I'm sorry! Please! Stop this!"

His face stared back blankly with no sign of recognition.

The roots spread over her hands, attempting to draw her in with him. She pulled away from his face and looked over the vegetation consuming him, searching for a way to get through.

"We're gonna have to leave him," Valma admitted. "We've got to get the others out before this place collapses."

"No!" Ava shouted back, "We're not leaving him!" Even if she weren't at fault, she never would have left Gill. That would be something she'd never forgive herself for.

Her frantic eyes caught a small glint of pale flesh above his head. She stepped on the bottom roots, lifting herself to get a better look. The vines wrapped around her legs as she did so, but she didn't stop.

"Ava!" Kaj yelled.

"I'm sorry!" Ava cried out again.

As she rose, the sliver of pale flesh turned into a finger, then a hand, then two hands. In the canopy of his entombment, his outstretched palms rested untouched by the roots that so eagerly encased the rest of him. Ava stretched forward, pulling against the vines that bound her legs to grab them.

"Gill! Please!" Ava intertwined her fingers between his, "Let me tell you I'm sorry!"

Gill's fingers twitched subtly, then slowly curled around hers as Ava tightened her grasp.

She tugged his hands down towards her with all of her might.

The brambles around them splintered and cracked, tearing apart and loosening his hands. They fell away as she pulled, sloughing off his body as his arms passed through them. Around Ava's legs, the vines released, sending her slipping down the collapsing vegetation.

She caught herself with a heavy thud and bent knees, gripping his hands tightly, unwilling to let them go.

He didn't know where he was, and he didn't care.

He existed everywhere and nowhere at once.

Though he possessed no sight, he could feel everything: the unseen hands wrapped in his palms warm like rocks baking in the summer sun, the sense of himself expanding, unfurling like a sprout from a seed, the comforting rumble of shifting rock vibrating through him soothing his ails.

In the back of it all, the soft voice sang, its breath tickling against him. It spoke no language he knew, yet he understood the song well enough to calm him, though he couldn't comprehend why.

His serene stupor shifted as the warm river rocks were replaced by soft flesh, slightly calloused.

A shiver shook down Gillian's spine. He had forgotten he had a spine.

He felt the calloused hands shaking as they pushed their fingers in between his.

She's afraid, he thought, *but who is she? Why is she scared?*

He closed his fingers around hers, struggling as he recalled the mechanics behind it.

"You're leaving me." The voice stopped its subtle singing and became all-consuming in his mind, *"I miss you when you're gone. Stay a while longer."*

The shaking hands gripped him tightly.

He couldn't. He wasn't meant to be here.

The hands pulled him forward, leading him back to himself.

"Just a minute more," the voice faded slightly.

Gill felt his arms again, cold and aching as they tore through the air.

"Please." the voice whispered, *"Stay."*

Gillian came back into himself, finding the world collapsing around him and Ava holding his hands with utter desperation on her bruised and battered face.

"Ava?" he whispered, his voice hoarse.

"I'm sorry!" she sobbed, but no tears fell down her face.

The rumbling earth screamed at him to come back. The cavern jolted as a quarter of the room collapsed onto itself, sending them stumbling and knocking guilt into Gillian as he remembered what he did.

"We have to go!" Valma said, "Can you run, Gill?"

"Yes," he answered, shaking his head to clear the

earth's cries from his mind, "I'm so sorry."

"Apologize later!" she replied. "We have to leave now!"

The earth shook again, and Gill sensed it slipping above his head.

"Get back!" He pulled Ava alongside him as he ran towards the center of the room. Valma and Kaj followed his charge as the ground collapsed in behind them, sealing the exit.

"No," Cici whimpered at the sight, "No!"

"Fuck!" Valma kicked a loose skull clear across the room in frustration. She glared at Gillian, "Can you open it back up?"

Stay, the memory of that alluring whisper turned his stomach.

"I don't think I should-"

"Well, we got to do fucking something then, or those prisoners are gonna be crushed to death!" she spat.

"We're going to be crushed to death!" Cici wailed.

"No, we're not," Kaj said. He stood near the blood-filled basin, eyes fixated on the body chute, and jumped down it.

They stared at where Kaj once stood in shock.

"I'm not going in there!" Cici protested.

"Yes, we are," Valma picked Cici up, and she squirmed against her chest, trying to wriggle free.

"Let go of me!" she shrieked.

"Just close your eyes when we get down there," Valma positioned herself above the chute. "Ava, don't let go of Gillian's hands!" She commanded and jumped, sending her and Cici down the bloody slide.

"Ava-" Gill turned to her to apologize.

"We have to get going." Ava dragged him to the basin, the terror in her eyes replaced with something ferocious and protective, "We have to find my family."

"But-" he pulled one of his hands free from hers as they stepped closer to the pool of blood. The earth's screaming split his skull as he did so, and his free hand rose, shaking with longing as it went to connect with the earth once more. He clamped his hand back down into Ava's with what little control he mustered, absolute terror on his face.

Ava gripped his hands tighter and pulled him into the pool, maneuvering around Valborg's body. He sunk down with her. Still warm blood gathered around their knees as she slid down the tube on her stomach and let the weight of her descending body tug him down alongside her.

CHAPTER SEVENTEEN

They fell in darkness. The tunnel around them shook as the smell of blood and decay grew more and more overbearing during their descent. The chute ended abruptly, sending them one after another into a scattered free fall before they landed onto a mass of slick and fleshy forms. Dirt and rubble continued to rain down around them, crafting a cadenza of dull squishes and sudden, hollow snaps that bounced off the walls of the darkened pit.

Holding a trembling Cici, Valma said a silent word of thanks that the only light in the room came from an opening to the far right, preventing any form of definite recognition of the horror beneath their feet.

Kaj was not so lucky. It was not often he cursed his gift of nocturnal vision, but the ocean of mutilated bodies he saw in clear black and white made him wish for blindness.

"T-the w-way o-out," he gagged, "t-the l-light."

They ran towards it, slipping and stumbling over the corpses. Gillian and Ava struggled to keep up, lagging behind as they tried to navigate the blubbery terrain with their hands intertwined.

"Ava," he panted, "You need to let go of my hands."

"No!" she grunted, tripping as something rolled under her foot, "I saw your hand last time! You'll turn into a tree again!"

"I won't!"

"You will!"

"No, I won't!"

The dirt screamed for him.

"I can keep my shit together, alright? We need to go faster, or else we're-"

"Fine!" Ava let go of one of his hands and ran faster, yanking him forward as her grip on the other hand turned vice-like, "But I'm not letting you go!"

Gill let her pull him along without resistance, grateful she led him as it took all his focus to stay in his own body. Ava's hand gave him a foothold to reality while the rest of his body joined the quaking cavern's chorus. The earth around him shifted under his skin, telling him where it was moving, how it was moving, how badly it yearned to move. A piercing scream carried through the vibrating soil. It was far away, and the earth wanted to smother it.

"I'm going to smother it," he muttered.

"What?" Ava's voice rang out through his skull. The vibrations of her voice bounced off the stone, creating and echoed as he heard the question both through the earth and with his own ears.

Gill became himself again, squinting as his senses cleared and the sudden reappearance of light blinded him. He looked down to find Ava grasping both of his hands behind her back once more as they ran down a crumbling mine shaft, leaving bloody footprints in their wake.

"We need to move faster!" He yelled, past Ava to Valma. The memory of the earth craving to bury that scream gave him goosebumps, "The rooms they're in are going to collapse!"

Gill jerked forward as Ava picked up their pace, driven on by his words. He yelped, caught off guard by her surge in strength, and with a quick sprint, they were on Valma's heels.

"Can you hold it back?" Ava panted. She turned over to look at Gill with pleading eyes.

"What?!" Cici shouted at her, overhearing her request, "Are you crazy?!"

"We don't know what that last hall looks like," Valma's heaving breath tickled against Cici's neck. "If he can hold it back for just a moment-"

"And what's the game plan if he goes full willow tree again?" Kaj shouted over his shoulder.

"I'll stay with him," Ava answered. Her eyes bore into Gill, "If I stay with you, you can hold it back, right?"

I can save her, the thought slid through the back of his

mind.

"I can," he said without hesitation.

I can try.

The winding hall came to an end as they barreled through the door and found themselves back in the antechamber, slowly filling with broken rock.

Their pace slowed as they headed towards the final door. Kaj kept moving, kneeling in front of the padlock.

"Can you do it here?" Valma asked. The ground tremored in protest.

"Here?" Ava looked longingly at the last door, "But they're in-"

"If he gets wrapped up again in there, he'll block our only way out-"

"I won't let that happen!"

"We know," Kaj said as he unlocked the door, "But it's better to be safe than sorry. You don't want your brothers to be freed only to get crushed 'cuz they couldn't get past, do you?"

Ava flinched at the thought, and Gillian gently squeezed her hands.

"I can do it from here," he looked at Valma, "Get them out as quick as you can."

"Right," Valma nodded and looked down at Cici, still held tightly against her, hands locked onto the leather of her breastplate as she tried to look anywhere else but at her.

"Do you want to stay-" Valma whispered.

"I'm going with you," Cici stopped her. "I have to. You can put me down, though. I can keep up."

"Okay."

The antechamber bucked, sending a hailstorm of small stones down upon them.

"Now is not the time to whisper sweet nothings, ladies!" Kaj barked as he held open the door, "Murder shrine! Collapsing! Squished children!"

"WE KNOW!" Cici ran out of Valma's arms as she set her down. Valma jogged after her, the two of them disappearing through the door.

"Ava," Kaj called to her, "Don't let go of him, alright? I'll make sure your family is fine."

She looked at him, eyes distant in worry, and nodded.

He bowed his head and disappeared into the dark hall, the door shutting behind him.

"Ready?" Gill asked.

Ava took a deep breath as she bowed her head, unable to bear the sight of nature overcoming him, and squeezed his left hand before letting it go.

Gillian gave himself to the earth. He raised his free

hand above his head, solidifying the connection and falling back into the ether.

The whole of nature wrapped itself around him like a mother reunited with her lost child, whispering in disbelief, **You came back.**

Hell broke loose around them as Cici, Valma, and Kaj ran down the hall. Being surrounded by shifting earth became even more intimidating as the deep rumbling of moving rock accompanied the maddening and soul-seizing shrieks of a woman in deep emotional distress.

The woman's horrid howling grew louder as they ran deeper and deeper down the hall, and soon a jumble of frightened whimpers and cries of protests joined the nightmarish orchestrations.

"SHUT THAT BITCH UP, WILL YOU?" a man barked.

"Dammit!" a shrill woman cut through the cacophony, "Why aren't they answering?!"

The hall curved sharply to the left, and two cultists came into view, fruitlessly shouting commands. The two barred wooden doors kept jumping from the force of something fighting to get out.

Kaj ripped two daggers out from his belt and sent them soaring through the air. They pierced into the sides of both cultists, sending them stumbling back as Valma rushed up and carved her sword through them. They fell to the ground, and she drove her blade down into each of their chests, making damn well sure they stayed there.

"Quit slamming the doors, will ya!" Kaj shouted, "It's hard to pick a lock when it keeps jolting around!"

"Shut the hell up, you monsters!" a voice shouted back.

Kaj bristled, "You want to die in a cave-in or what asshole?!"

Cici brushed past Valma's legs.

"Cici?" Valma questioned.

She paid her question no mind as she rummaged through the cultist's billowing cloaks, drawing forth a ring with a single key on it. She ran towards Kaj and pushed him out of the way, "Move!"

Cici twisted the key into the padlock, and it fell away, barely jumping out of the way before the door busted open and a pile of townsfolk burst through.

"We've got you now!" one man threatened.

"Halt!" Valma commanded, authority deepening her voice.

The earth stopped shaking, and the townsfolk in the hall froze at the stillness, staring at her in astonishment.

"Talk about timing, Wizkid," she muttered to herself.

Gillian let himself relax into its firm embrace, allowing the earth's eagerness and joy at his return to envelope him, all of him, but the trembling hand that kept rubbing her thumb across his intertwined knuckles.

Gill tried to remember how to speak, "Can you hear me?"

"Yes," the world around him sighed.

His heart raced. That was good. He still had a heart.

"You need to stop this."

Nature tightened its grasp around him, its warmth slightly chilled with worry.

"Stop what?"

The trembling hand squeezed.

"The cave-in," he swallowed. Guilt washed over him out of nowhere, driven by a fear of disappointing the force, but he pushed through, "There are innocent people in here with us. They don't deserve to die."

The energy around him shifted, and though there were no bodies in this space, he swore he felt a smiling cheek press against the side of his face.

"Darling, you've always had the power to do so. All you have to do is ask," the voice whispered in his ear. *"Would you like me to show you?"*

"I don't want to stay here," he blurted out but immediately regretted it. Was that the truth? Did he really want to leave? A part of him that screamed at him to remain, to be consumed by the content familiarity of this unknown realm... and it scared him.

Its smile pressed against his cheek fell, *"This will be harder on you then."*

Gillian shook violently as he was thrust from the embrace and became hard bedrock. He felt the stone around him moving, shifting, preparing to fall, as if it weren't in control of his limbs. Their constant scraping and clattering rattled his skull.

Stop, he thought, trying to pull himself together.

The shifting slowed a bit, but more earth crumbled off of him as it did.

He burrowed deeper, focusing his intent. Stopping wouldn't keep the already loose stones from crashing down. He needed them to...

Stay.

Every fiber of his being burned as ten tons of earth rested on his shoulders, hanging from his non-corporal form. His magicks, richer in his veins than he ever felt before, held the crumbling earth in stasis while the strength of his human body quickly waned.

Though the earth stopped shaking, the woman's

screams did not cease. Cici's fingers fumbled, the continued shrieks making her tremble as she unlocked the second cell. She calmed her nerves enough to finally twist the key and opened the door slowly, checking behind her to make sure Valma stood near.

It was another packed cell, but unlike the other one, the townsfolk weren't clamored around the door. Instead, they circled around the room, backs to the door as they tried to soothe the screaming woman. She shifted to try and get a better view through the legs of the crowd and caught a glimpse of a familiar pink nightgown, a beautiful blush against the wearer's deep chestnut skin.

"Mom!" Cici shouted and ran into the room, trying to push through the crowd.

"~~Ortensia~~?"

She froze at the sound of her full name.

"Hey!" a woman yelled, "Clear a path! Her daughter's here!" Mrs. Barncombe, holding a crying boy in her arm, placed her free hand on Cici's back and guided her through the crowd.

"You heard my wife!" Mr. Barncombe barked beside them. His sniffling son, the spitting image of his brother, clutched onto his pant leg and flinched as his voice boomed, "Make room!"

As Mrs. Barncombe pushed her closer, Cici couldn't remember ever seeing her mother so animated; for all of her life, Burgemistress Valborg never expressed an emotion that didn't seem dulled. Her governess, Ms. Sabar, and her housekeeper, Ms. Lari, sat by her side, trying their best to calm the wailing woman, and even went so far as to break decorum and hold Burgermistress close to them in an effort to keep her still.

"Miss!" Ms. Lari called, tears gathered in her eyes as she spotted Cici emerging from the crowd. She turned to the Burgermistress, "Look, Madam! We found her!"

"What's happened to her?" Cici's voice quivered. Her eyes transfixed on her mother.

"I don't know, miss," Sabar replied. "One minute she was sitting here, solemn like the rest of us, then the next she was hyperventilating and screaming like a banshee."

Cici stepped closer to her mother.

"Mom!" she tried to cut through her cries.

The burgermistress' head lobbed back as she let out a gurgling wail.

"Mom!" Cici said louder.

Her eyes were shut, and heavy tears rolled down her face.

"Bernadetta!" Cici screamed. Had she called her mother by her first name any other time, she would have been met by a swift slap on the back of the head by her governess. Mrs. Sabar, however, let the faux pas slide this as her mother's heaving cries slowed. The burgemistress' head lolled forward, and she looked down at Cici with bloodshot and terrified eyes.

For the first time in her twenty years of life, Cici's mother truly saw her. In the back of her mind, Cici always knew something was off about her mother's demeanor. Her complacent nature, no matter the circumstance. Her gaze that seemed a million miles away, even while she looked right at you. How any emotion she expressed seemed like one that would come across the face of someone asleep, recognizable enough to convey the feeling to others but not as strong as those expressed when awake.

And she resented her for it.

We are taught that our mothers are the ones who care for us the most, who will always be there for us, hold us when we cry, share in our joy, protect us from all harm. Cici knew that every child deserved that from their mother, and when she never received it, she questioned herself. Even in infancy, she wondered what she had done to deserve such detachment. When she was scared or upset by emotions her toddler mind could not put a name to; her mother would simply look away, gazing out the window or disappearing in her paintings while Cici writhed at her feet, struggling to understand how something so all-consuming to her could be ignored so easily.

As she grew, Cici thought that perhaps the problem was that she wasn't showing her mother enough positive feelings, that any displays of sorrow or anger were truly as uncouth as her governess said they were. Cici then made an effort to put on a happy face for her mother, only recalling how well her music lessons were going, the latest gossip she read in the local periodicals, and showing her the newest dances she'd learned.

"That's nice," Burgermistress Valborg acknowledged these joys by rote and turned back to her window or her painting. Cici tried learning to paint, thinking that a shared hobby would endear her to her mother, but she might as well have been wallpaper in the room. They'd sat there for hours, painting in silence as every time she asked a question or made a comment on their art, her mother barely responded.

On one particular day, not long after they moved to Elerrï, Cici realized that her mother's incurious disposition was never her fault. Her father was in a particularly cross mood that day, only further aggravated by her and her older brother unfortunately mislabeling some documents he had asked them to sort. His ire rained down upon them in the middle of the drawing-room, his belt stinging their shoulders as he berated them for their worthlessness, and their mother continued her painting as if their anguished wails in apology were nothing more than incidental chamber music.

Afterwards, as a newly hired Cordelia soothed salve over her wounds and consoled her with words a little too cordial between a maid and her mistress, Cici kept coming back to the image of her mother, distant and undisturbed as her children were debased so violently in front of her. She understood why she didn't intervene; to willingly step in the way of Delvin Valborg's wrath would be idiotic, but for her to not even react – to not show an ounce of remorse or disdain, even with Ellsworth being punished alongside her – nagged at her. To escape the sting of her wounded pride and the salve on her back, Cici thought back to all of her mother's interactions and found that there had never been a moment where she wasn't impassive. Her mother had always looked at everyone as if they were nothing more than scenery.

Learning that hurt more than any wound her father dealt.

Yet with one look, one honest-to-god focused gaze at her, Cici's resentment dwindled - giving way to fear as the focus in her mother's eyes turned to turmoil and revolution.

"You have my face…" her mother croaked. "Why do you have my face?"

Cici didn't respond. She couldn't. She was too busy trying to hold back the bile rising in her throat.

"Why do you have my face?!" she screamed. Burgermistress Valborg's face contorted, twisting in neurotic anger. The question became a violent mantra, her voice and panic rising as she thrashed against Sabar and Lari, screaming in a round of madness, "Why do you have my face?!"

A broad-shouldered shadow fell over the four of them, followed by a quick slap that knocked the burgermistress out in a single strike. Sabar and Lari gasped at the sudden act of violence, rushing to catch their mistress as she fell limp in their arms. The rest of the onlookers, however, sighed in relief, reveling in the quiet.

"I'm sorry," Valma's warm voice rumbled behind Cici.

Valma moved to kneel next to Cici, reaching out to place a comforting hand on her trembling back.

"Chan."

Valma stood at attention immediately and whipped around on her heels to find Captain Reids, behind her standing as strong in her nightgown as she did in her uniform.

"The thief sent me over here. Said that before I arrest him, I should speak to you." If the captain disapproved of Valma striking the burgermistress, she didn't let on.

"Captain." A wave of relief washed over Valma. She wanted to hug her superior so badly but decided to save it for when they were truly freed.

"We have a way out of here," Valma informed her, "but we need to move quickly."

The world around them jolted, throwing the townsfolk into a panic as the cavern resumed its shaking.

Valma swallowed her nerves, "Very quickly."

Captain Reids inhaled deeply, nodding as her eyes darted between Valma, the townsfolk, and the crumbling ceiling above.

"Alright, everyone!" she hollered, "Officer Chan will be leading us out of here. Do exactly as she says and move quickly!"

Pride surged through Valma as the captain put her in charge, and she did her best to keep the smile on her face.

"I need half of our strongest in the front, half in the back. The sick, elderly, and children in the center," Valma commanded, and the townsfolk hurried out into the hall.

"We'll run as one unit. Go out there and help get them into formation," she instructed Captain Reids before turning back to the last remnants of the Valborg family still sitting on the cell floor.

Ms. Sabar and Ms. Lari stared up at her, wary yet still awaiting her instruction. Their obvious distrust knocked the pride out of her for a moment. Valma glanced at Cici, expecting her face to echo theirs but found her still hunched over with her back towards her.

"I'll carry her out of here," Valma gestured to the burgermistress. "Can you look after Cici?"

They narrowed their eyes at her. Sabar's disapproving glare, in particular, sent an uncomfortable crawl up Valma's spine. Their silence spoke volumes, but Valma's concern for their discontent vanished as the cavern shook with another massive tremor.

She acted before they choked out a protest, lifting the unconscious burgermistress out of their grasp and slinging her over her good shoulder, "Come on."

"Miss, we have to go," Cici felt Ms. Lari tapping her shoulder; she just couldn't bring herself to lift her head up. Everything was too numb.

"~~Ortensia,~~" Ms. Sabar was much harsher, seizing her arm and pulling her to her feet, "There has been far too much suffering today, and I will not allow your life to end by being crushed underground."

They drug her out into the hall, her toes barely scraping across the ground, and the passing stone floors turned into a gray blur from her tears.

"If you see a child too young to keep up the pace, or someone too weak to run, partner up with them. We all need to work together to get out of here as quick as we can!" Kaj shouted over the tremoring of the earth and the worried cries of the crowd. He scanned the masses, looking for Valma's slick black ponytail or shit brown armor, and instead found two identical sets of familiar honey brown locked onto him. Two young, brunette twin boys stared at him unblinkingly from over their parents' shoulders, catching Kaj completely off-guard with how shocking their resemblance to Ava was.

"Hey," Kaj called out to them, "You the Barncombes?"

The pair turned around to face him, and the twins shifted in their arms, not wanting to lose sight of him.

"Yes, that's us," Mr. Barncombe looked at his wife cautiously.

"Ava's alright," Kaj said.

Tears built up in both their eyes.

"Thank the gods," Mrs. Barncombe sighed.

"Where is she?" Ava's dad asked, "Was she in the other cell?" He started to look among the crowd.

"No, she uh-" Kaj fumbled for a good way to tell her parents that Ava was trying to keep a giant tree wizard from collapsing about a mile's worth of rock onto their heads. Gardening was the first thing that came to mind, but a witty quip probably wasn't the best call. "- she came with us to rescue you. She and Gillian are holding things together just outside of here, so when we leave, you'll see her."

The stone walls of the hall bucked, and a chorus of frightened shrieks rippled through the crowd. A cloud of dirt and debris billowed out of the first cell door as part of the stone ceiling came crashing down into the room.

"Don't talk to her when you do, though!" Kaj added. His heart raced as he realized that Gill may not be as in control as they thought he would be, "Just keep running past her, and I swear to you we'll all make it out alive."

The Barncombes opened their mouths to question him, but he ran away, finally spotting Valma in the crowd.

"Stick!" Kaj called as she stepped out of the second cell. He pushed his way through the masses, covering his head from the dirt raining down upon them. He stopped when he got closer, caught off guard by the unconscious woman slung over Valma's shoulder.

"Who's that?" He peered into the cell behind her, "Where's Cici?"

"Those two got her," Valma angled her head towards a pair of women dragging a despondent Cici. "And this is her mother."

"Can you run carrying her like that?"

"Yup."

"Great. Then we've gotta get the hell out of here." Kaj pointed to the first cell, "That big jolt caved in half of the cell over there."

Valma's nostrils flared, and she snarled.

"Alright, everyone!" She commanded, voice cutting through the pandemonium, "Captain Reids will lead. Move as fast as you can. Leave no one behind!"

The crowd surged against Valma and Kaj as they started their charge down the hall. Another massive tremor shook the cavern, sending large chunks of earth and rock crumbling down. They followed the crowd's current, jogging down the hall at a brisk pace.

"Fuck," Valma swore as a rock smacked the side of her head, "I thought Gill could handle this."

"What are we gonna do if he-" Kaj swallowed his sentence, afraid that saying his fears out loud would make them come to fruition, "It's gonna take a lot to tear him out."

"Yeah," Valma's eyes darted across the crowd, trying to think of a plan, and stopped suddenly. A grin curled at the corners of her lips.

He followed her line of sight and landed on a beast of a man, broad-shouldered and a full two heads taller than the rest of the crowd, wearing a smile despite the pressure of their present situation as he ran.

"Samuel!" she shouted.

The man looked over his shoulder and stopped. The

mob moved around Samuel, and he rejoined its flow to run alongside Valma.

"You're the new townsguard, right?" Samuel asked, his deep voice rumbling as much as the collapsing earth.

If they weren't running for their lives right then, Kaj's knees would have gone weak.

"Yeah," she panted, "We need your help."

"Okay?"

"When we get out of this hall, you're gonna see Gillian and Ava. You know who they are, right?"

"Lil' Barncombe and Ginger Snap?" he questioned.

"Ginger Snap?!" Kaj wheezed, delighting in a new nickname to call Gillian once they made it out of here… if they made it out of here.

"Of course I know who they are!" Samuel cheered, "I'm glad to hear they're okay!"

"Not so okay," Kaj remarked. "They might be a tree right now."

"A what?"

"Look, I need you to get to the back," Valma pressed on. "When we get through the door, you'll see them, or a tree, or a combination of them and a tree... we don't really know. Whatever they are, I need you to grab them and keep running."

"You want me to tear a tree out of the ground?"

"Maybe."

The giant smile on Samuel's face somehow grew wider.

"Done and done," he said and fell away to take his position behind the crowd.

"Good lord," Kaj muttered. He watched Samuel as long as he could before the cheerful brute disappeared into the mob. "I know what I'm doing to celebrate when we get the hell out of here."

"Really?" Valma scolded. "We're surrounded by death and destruction, and you're thinking about that right now?"

"It's called optimism, Stick," he smirked. "Some people think about seeing their families again. I think about getting railed."

"Gross."

※

It took everything in Ava not to collapse in on herself the moment the earth re-encased Gillian. The way his body jolted, the speed in which the roots spread from the ground, and the absence of emotion on his face as his pupils disappeared into glowing green light should have pushed her past her limit. Yet, she remained standing, holding his hand, still human and still recognizably his like her life depended on it.

And when the earth stopped shaking and everything

grew quiet, she realized that it truly did depend on it. The silence that filled the stilled cavern isolated her, giving her nothing but space to think of all the things she did not want to think about.

She went to chew on her bottom lip and stopped as pain shot through her jaw, throbbing and sensitive. Ava raised her free hand to it and winced as her fingertips brushed against the swelling. The pure disgust on Kieran's face before he struck her invaded her thoughts.

Her breathing quickened, and every muscle in her body tensed. Ava's mouth shook open to let out a wail, and her sobs caught in her throat, stopped by the agony that rushed through her jaw. She searched his eyes so desperately in this last image she had of him, looking for the Kieran that smiled coyly at her, kissed her hungrily, touched her tenderly, in the vile visage. That was not the man she knew.

Or had she been a fool this entire time?

Those moments had to mean something, didn't they? The late-night meetings, whispered words under moonlight and bedsheets, hidden touches any chance they could.

Any chance I could, she recalled.

Ava searched and searched her memories for the signs she missed, finding moments that held too many interpretations for her to trust her instincts, and came to one resonating conclusion: she was a fool. And this was all her fault.

The aches from her wounds, the sting of unshed tears

in her eyes, all the pains in her body fell away, faded into numbness as the guilt that kept sinking its claws deeper into her bound itself around her legs and pulled her down to drown her in the fathoms of her mind.

She saw Kieran, his expression twisted and vile, sneaking up behind her parents as they drank their evening sherry. She saw him stalking down the small hallway towards her brothers' room to grab them by their hair and yank them from their dreams. She saw him watching as Valborg held her mother over the basin and ran a knife across her throat as she scre-

The clanging of metal yanked Ava out of the morbid fantasy.

She stiffened, her grip on Gill's hand becoming a vice, and listened.

The metallic rattling grew louder, clamoring down the hall behind them. Her already racing heartbeat doubled its pace.

More are coming.

Ava's eyes flitted frantically between the entranced Gillian and their intertwined hands. She had to let go to protect him, but to protect him, she couldn't let go. She couldn't fire with it sandwiched under her arm, and his arm wouldn't reach between her thighs with him rooted as he was.

She let go of his hand for a moment to turn around, and the cavern jolted. The roots, ravenous, shot down his exposed arm, embedding their thorns into him as they set to consume him entirely, but stopped as Ava, scrambling and panicked, placed his hand between her teeth.

The earth kept shaking, but she wasn't afraid it would collapse. Gill was still in there, fighting to hold it back, so she would fight to keep them safe. Ava grabbed her bow from her sheath, pulled back her bowstring lightly, arrow at the ready, and aimed towards the encroaching mob. The taste of salt on her tongue from the sweat and dirt on Gillian's palm focused her mind and steadied her hands.

The glint of metal twinkling in the dark void of the shrine's entrance signaled her to fire. She sent three arrows soaring towards the emerging steel, one after another, only for them to bounce off the tree embossed breastplate of a member of the Kyresore garrison.

Ava froze as the men stopped at the entrance, staring her and Gillian down, confused and furious, with their blades drawn.

"What is the meaning of this?!" the guard bellowed.

Ava whimpered, paralyzed in horror at what she'd just done.

"They must be the necromancers!" another guard shouted.

"Stop this spell now, or die where you stand!"

Her body trembled. She couldn't move, couldn't set down her bow and show that she meant no harm; she couldn't speak, even if Gill's hand wasn't grasped firmly in her mouth.

The guards stepped forward, "Then you choose death!"

A hundred voices tickled behind her, stopping the guards' advance. With a loud crack of wood, the voices became thunderous, filling the space as the once imprisoned townsfolk rushed past her.

"Move!" one of the townsfolk barked. "It's caving in!"

The guards, stunned, moved to the side as the mob rushed past them, some turning to join them in their exodus. A small part of Ava screamed at her to run with them, to flee, but she couldn't leave Gill.

She wouldn't leave Gill.

And she didn't have to as she was knocked off her feet with such force that her teeth sank into Gillian's hand. The salt on her tongue washed away in the warm taste of copper as she got scooped up by a massive, meaty arm and swept along with the crowd. She spat out Gill's hand as his blood poured down her throat, threatening to choke her.

"No!" Ava shrieked, her voice desperate and shrill, "I can't leave him!"

The world shook violently as the deafening roar of the earth finally consuming the shrine behind them blocked out her bloodcurdling wails. Dirt billowed around them, stinging her eyes and clouding her vision as her captor kept charging towards the exit.

"I can't leave him!" Ava thrashed against the arm

carrying her, "I can't!"

"I've got him, Barncombe!" the man holding her panted. "I've got him right here!"

Ava twisted her bobbing head up and found Samuel sweating heavily with a limp body slung over his shoulder, wearing a blue quilted vest.

"I'm sorry," Ava whimpered, shame washing over her yet again. "I'm so sorry."

Blubbering apologies kept pouring out of her as the dark of the cavern finally gave way to light.

CHAPTER EIGHTEEN

Master Gustav was not the type of mage to be easily concerned. The perfect portrait of calm rationality.

It was an implicit trust in the universe, a trust in balance, and a trust in his own capabilities that allowed him the luxury of being unconcerned. In fact, he could not remember the last time he felt the emotion.

Even fifteen years ago, the prospect of taking in a young ward, whom the Convocation deemed too powerful to be kept in a densely populated area, didn't phase him in the slightest. Gustav knew the young redheaded boy with knobby knees and eyes older than most scholars wouldn't cause trouble, and if he did, that he would be able to handle it.

This level of confidence even extended to the extraordinary events of the past few days. Lesser beings would have shut down, pulling at their hair, drowned by their own emotions. His apprentice and his comrades did, bickering about plans and blame, and he would be lying if he didn't say he was a little bit disappointed in Gillian for getting swept up in it. But the young man gained control of himself, had companions that would keep him in line, made a plan, and set forth to accomplish it, giving Gustav a sense of pride in his own tutelage and the confidence that everything would work out fine once again.

Until the ground began to shake.

The first hour after they left was peaceful. Once he alerted the Kyresore Garrison, Master Gustav poured himself another cup of tea. He set Marqui and himself up outside to watch the sunset while enjoying some cheese and light charcuterie courtesy of the Valborgs.

The cat felt it before he did, dropping a piece of sausage mid-chew to take shelter underneath Master Gustav's rocking chair, letting out a low, rumbling mew in distemper as he ran. Gustav looked at the creature curiously, but his questions about Marqui's behavior were quickly answered as the porch jolted, spilling his tea onto his vestments.

He stood and searched the landscape for the tremor's source but found nothing, and his stomach sank. Elerrï wasn't prone to earthquakes, and after the roots and the seeing through the soil, Gustav knew it was Gillian without a shred of doubt.

As to the cause of the twisting in his gut, Master Gustav thought perhaps it was his magick being so strained that made him uncomfortable, or that the garrison was at the fastest a half an hour away; but more likely than not, despite how much he didn't care to admit it, it was because he was worried about his ward.

"Keep your head, you fool," he muttered under his

breath. "I taught you better than this."

He didn't notice the shallowness of his breathing until the earth stilled again, too many minutes later.

The calmed ground allowed Gustav to hear the thundering hoofbeats of the Kyresore Garrison as they galloped down the road, angling their horses up the path towards the manor.

"Hail!" their bannerman called, raising his hand.

Gustav returned the gesture, watching them sternly as they approached.

"Master Gustav," the broad-chested and well-armored Second Lieutenant Izac Pires dismounted from his steed and greeted the mage with a hearty handshake.

"Lieutenant Pires," he responded coolly, trying his best to hide his disgust at how roughly the man shook his hand.

"You said there was a situation here?" he let go of Gustav. "Something about destructor magicks?"

"Yes," Master Gustav answered. "A cult of Zozvit has infiltrated the town and kidnapped the townsfolk for some sort of sacrificial harvest. I've sent my apprentice and a group of his acquaintances into the underground shrine to help evacuate them while we waited for you to arrive."

"You-" Pires' jaw hung in shock, "You did what? You sent a group of novice civilians down to face an entire cult of necromancers?!"

"They're not novices," he shrugged, "They already handled a few of them in the Shadowfen, apparently. As well as some that were left here in town to keep watch."

"Were you able to identify them?" Pires added.

"Yes."

A moment of silence hung between them.

"And they are?"

"That would be for the Convocation to know."

Pires grimaced, "Is it now?"

"It is."

He narrowed his eyes, "And what happens when we meet the necromancers down there for ourselves?"

"Then you will simply tell me who you saw. I will report that to the Convocation, and then they will advise the Bastions on the next steps after their arrest." Gustav smiled, "As is the standard protocol when dealing with destructor mages."

With a scoff, Pires conceded, "Where is the entrance to the shrine?"

"In the stables," he pointed, "You may want to hurry. That earthquake just now was my apprentice. And as I'm sure you're aware, me saying that is not a good thing."

"Shit." Pires turned to his men, "You heard him, men! To the stables, be on the lookout for any unusual magicks!"

"Sir!" They saluted in unison before taking off en masse towards the stables.

Master Gustav rolled his eyes and headed back into the house to pour himself to refill his mug.

Not five minutes later, right as the kettle whistled, the earth shook again. This time, however, it didn't stop.

"Those idiots," he grumbled. He removed the shuttering kettle and blew out the flame, abandoning his tea on the counter to look out one of the windows facing the stables.

There was no sign of them. The horses the garrison rode in on panicked just like Marqui had, shifting restlessly as they decided whether or not they should abandon their masters. Gustav stared intently at the stables, not realizing how tight his jaw was while he ruminated on how much he hated the amount of stress his ward was putting him under.

That same stress caused him, a man who hardly ever moved faster than a stroll, to break out into a sprint when he saw the first survivors stumble out of the stable.

"Over here!" Master Gustav shouted, "You'll be safer by the house!"

The townsfolk followed his voice, dazed and panicked, and moved to gather on the front lawn of the manor. They watched the stables desperately for their family and friends to emerge and ran to greet them when they appeared.

The heartwarming scenes of families reunited were eclipsed as a crack tore through the shaking ground beyond the stable. The trees in the nearby forest shifted and disappeared, swallowed by the earth crumbling on itself. A sinkhole raced towards the stables, and the people fleeing the shrine below seemed to know, running faster than the first batch who stumbled forward—running for their lives.

Gustav's eyes studied the blurs of faces intensely, searching, and found a billowing black cloak.

"Kaj!" he shouted.

The copper-skinned elvefolk turned and locked eyes with him. Kaj smacked a hand against Valma before leaving her side to join Gustav.

"We were right, Egghead!" Kaj called out.

Master Gustav made a mental note to skin him later for that nickname, "Where's Gillian?"

"He's coming," a look of worry crossed his face. He turned back to look at the wave of destruction quickly approaching the stables, "any second now."

Fewer and fewer people trickled out of the stable, a good sign usually, but it left Gustav frustrated and impatient. The worry stiffened in his chest as the cave-in grew closer. He silently cursed those damned lead chains, those damned Hilt hires, and his own damn self for wasting his magicks. He should be able to do something. He shouldn't be so weak.

A flash of red hair slung over a behemoth's shoulder let him breathe again.

"Bring him to me!" Master Gustav flagged the brute down. His voice, sharp and commanding, hit Samuel's ears just before all sound got swallowed by the splintering crack of the stables folding in on themselves.

Samuel struggled to catch his breath as he handed Ava, mouth covered in blood and rambling like a madwoman, off to her shocked parents before lumbering over to Gustav.

"He's in rough shape," he panted as he placed Gillian gently at Gustav's feet. Samuel gave a quick nod to Kaj while Gustav focused on his ward and walked off to search for his own family in the mob.

"What the hell happened?!" Master Gustav looked back at Kaj before crouching over the battered, unconscious form of his apprentice.

Gill was covered in scratches, with his left side torn up by small sticks and thorns buried into his flesh and his right hand bled profusely from a bite wound. Dirt built up around his mouth, and barely breathing, Gustav pried open his jaw gently. A concerning amount of soil and gravel came tumbling out.

"Shit," he swore under his breath.

"He turned into a tree and nearly brought the entire thing down on us," Kaj said. "Then he turned again into half a tree to stop it."

"That's not an explanation." Gustav reached into one of his robe's pockets and pulled out a small clockwork bird. He handed it to Kaj, "Hold on to Gillian and turn the winding key five times. This will take you back to Verdeer Manor. You have magicks, right?"

"Yes?" he questioned. "But nothing too crazy."

"Doesn't matter how much as long as you have it. When you arrive, say the phrase 'smite the selfish' and snap; that will disarm the traps."

"Traps?!"

"Don't interrupt me!" Master Gustav snapped. "You'll appear in my bedroom. Rest Gillian on the bed and head to the china cabinet; you'll find a few potions in there. There is a milky white one that smells like apples; make sure he swallows all of it, then start picking out the foliage from his wounds."

Kaj paled, "Why can't you do all this?"

"Because," Gustav looked among the crowd, his eyes fell on Lieutenant Pires and Captain Reids discussing something furiously, "I've got to handle things here as the appointed Convocation representative. Plus," Gustav gave a knowing look to Kaj, "Do you really want to be here when they find out your fellow Hilt members were a part of this?"

A cold and scared look came over an already fearful Kaj. He grabbed the bird from Gustav and placed his hands on Gillian's chest, twisting the key as instructed. In a flash of purple light, they vanished.

Gustav let out a long-held breath, relishing in the relief that washed over him.

"Master Gustav," Captain Reids' stern voice fell over him. He stood and turned to her, marveling for a moment at how she could still look so intimidating in a frilly nightgown.

"I'm glad to see you're alright, Captain," he said.

"Lieutenant Pires told me to speak with you regarding the events of the past few days. Said this would fall under Convocation jurisdiction."

Gustav watched the crowd intensely, taking in the cacophony of hysterical emotions: sobs of joy from being freed, tearful hugs of relief, keens of grief, panicked wails.

"Yes, it does," he sighed and rubbed a hand over his scalp. "You know how much I hate these things, Brooke. Let's calm the townspeople first and get healing to those who need it. Then you, the Lieutenant, and I can discuss things over a nice cup of tea."

CHAPTER NINETEEN

Ninety-three people died.

In the following days, the little town of Elerrï dealt with the aftermath of the Harvest as best as a little town could. Families and friends tried to stick together by celebrating life and mourning the dead. Some went back to work, trying to recover a sense of normalcy that would take a while to grasp, especially with the town so much emptier than before. Others struggled with their grief, angry at the events that had occurred, demanding justice that no one knew how to seek.

With Valma's retelling of events, they pinpointed the location of the pit, following the destruction Gillian caused like a map. The amount of debris and the unstable state of the surrounding earth was too significant for them to retrieve the dead, so the town worked with the surviving chaplains of the Temple of Messis to build a memorial. The chaplains used their limited magicks from the goddess to cleanse the ground, removing the darkness that tainted it, while the carpenters and masons set to build benches around it, carving the victim's names into the stone and planks. It would be a place for those who needed to sit and reflect and mourn, and to preserve their history for the generations after.

The wounded town was slowly healing. Trying to live on in the face of tragedy became a salve that helped soothed their hardened hearts.

However, a select few had wounds that ran deeper than their counterparts could ever fathom.

The blue flames licked at the side of her hands, adding the smell of burning flesh to the suffocating smoke that filled the room. Ava tried to move but found her body paralyzed. She knew those lead chains held her to the stable, but how did she get there? When did she get there?

A pock-marked face emerged through the smoke.

"Well, hello again, girlie," Talwar leered over her, blood pouring from his mouth. The blue firelight brought false life to his singular glassy eye while her arrow jutted out of the other, "Remember, you take something of mine-"

Ava blinked, and Kaj took Talwar's place, his expression twisted in anger from her betrayal, Talwar's morning star held above his head.

"-I take something of yours," Kaj seethed and drove the morning star down.

Ava let out a terrified scream as she woke and shoved the sudden weight that landed on her chest.

The object flew off of her, landed with a heavy thud followed by a shrieking child's cry.

"Tallon!" Mrs. Barncombe shouted. She ran into the sitting room and picked up Ava's wailing little brother off of the floor, "I told you that I would wake your sister up!"

"Ava's mean!" Tallon sobbed, his face wrinkled and red as his body heaved with tears.

Immediate guilt slowed Ava's racing heart as she moved to sit up on the couch fully. Her body ached from the dozens of knots and kinks sleeping on it for the past week granted her.

"I'm sorry, Tal," she said. Ava looked at him with tired eyes, "I didn't mean to hurt you. You spooked me, is all."

"See?" Their mom rubbed his back as she cradled him in her strong arms, "Sissy didn't mean it."

Tallon swallowed his tears as he took in the concerned look on his exhausted sister's face.

"Do you forgive me?" Ava asked.

He nodded.

"That's a good brother," Mrs. Barncombe kissed him on the head, "You hurt anywhere?"

"My knee has a booboo," he whimpered.

She looked down at his red and swelling knee. Ava's jaw clenched.

"It's not too bad," she smiled to comfort both her son

and her daughter. "Just needs a little ice from the kitchen."

She carried him out of the room, disappearing behind the kitchen door and leaving Ava to get her bearings.

She placed her head in her hands and took a deep breath, trying to calm her building anger, sadness, and regret on top of the residual fear from her nightmare. Her heart hammered so hard; she felt its beat in the palms of her hands.

"Arow."

The couch cushion next to her sank as a whiskered snout rubbed up against her elbow. She pulled her head out of her hands and turned to scratch Marqui's head.

"I'm alright, Qui." Ava smoothed a thumb over his temple, "Just a little startled."

She took in another deep breath before folding the blankets and putting away the pillow she used neatly. She stretched her arms high above her head, trying to unwork the kink in her shoulder that only got tighter as the week went on. To complete her new morning routine, Ava fluffed the couch cushions and scanned the room for anything else she could fix before having to head upstairs to change. Coming up empty, she steeled herself and walked into the kitchen and found it vacant. Her mother must have taken her whimpering brother outside after icing his knee.

Ava stood in front of the staircase, looking up.

It'll be quick, she thought, *in and out. Just got to get changed. We'll be fine.*

Ava trembled as she willed her leg to take its first step. Her breath became more and more shallow as she ascended, her hand holding the railing in a death grip.

Marqui followed behind. He learned his lesson their first full day back on the farm, having rushed past Ava and scaring her so badly she tripped and slid back down the steps, bruising her knees horribly and biting through her tongue.

Ava paused when she reached the top, digging her fingernails into the railing as she steadied herself. Marqui rubbed across her shaking leg and settled beside her. He thumped his tail against her as she tried to regain some sense of calm.

You're being ridiculous, she scolded herself, it's just a fucking hallway. You've been through worse. Her mental lashings forced her to straighten up and turn the corner to face the hall.

A shiver of relief trickled down her spine as she found all the doors closed.

They must have noticed how jumpy you got when they were open. Her jaw tensed. *You gotta keep that shit to yourself; we hate when they worry.*

Ava pushed on, determined not to let foolish fears stop her, focusing her mind on thinking of anything else but the image of those doors thrown open and bedsheets scattered by their dragged bodies.

Her mental fortitude slipped when she placed her hand on her bedroom's door knob, and Kieran's muffled laugh rang in her ears.

Ava threw open the door, the force letting out a snapping slam as it hit the wall, and found her room empty.

He's dead.

Ava looked at the empty bed, sheets back to their pressed and folded state by her mother, and she couldn't help but picture him there, looking at her with a wry smile as he laid back on her mattress.

They told you he's dead. Her last reminder became nothing more than a whisper in the back of her mind.

"*Really?" Kieran leaned his head back on her pillow and teased, "Your secret knock is a nursery rhyme?"*

"What's wrong with it?" Ava pouted.

He chuckled and flashed that heart-melting smile she loved so much, "Nothing. You're just cute."

"Am I?" she asked.

"You are," the smile didn't leave his face, "You know what else is cute? The panicked look on your mother's face as I watched her scream in that cell."

He blinked, and his green eyes turned pale blue.

"Ava?" her mother called from downstairs, bringing her back to reality. "Everything alright? I heard a bang."

"It's fine!" Ava called back, the need to soothe her mother's worry second instinct, "Just dropped something!"

365

Ava took a deep breath and repeated to herself that her room really was empty. That nobody was there. That-

"Kieran's dead."

※

"Are you sure you don't want to sleep in the house?" Samuel asked. "We've got plenty of beds, and it'd be easy for me to sneak ya in."

Kaj kissed the top of Samuel's head as he laid on his chest and traced his fingers up Samuel's massive bicep. He had been pleasantly surprised the first night they spent together when the dashing giant revealed himself to like being the little spoon.

"I wouldn't want to risk putting your family in danger like that, Sammy-boy," Kaj replied. "You're already taking a big enough risk letting me lay low in your barn here."

Being a criminal was Kaj's favorite excuse. Playing up his "bad boy" persona was not only a great way to get people to sleep with him, but it also served as an easy out to any passing dalliances. Little to no one would risk getting arrested for harboring a fugitive just for a good lay, and honestly, it made them think of him as a sort of chivalrous martyr when he did leave. He always made the reason for his departure sound selfless.

Although, he was highly considering making an addendum to his hook-up rules after his little excursion with Samuel: no large families in the country. Sleeping in a hayloft with rooster crows and the smell of cow shit waking him up

every morning for the past few days almost made the sex not worth it.

Almost.

"It's just..." Samuel's big steel blue eyes gazed up at him, "You did so much to save this town, and now you can't even sleep in a bed for your efforts. I just wish there was something more I could do for you."

"Oh, come here," Kaj cooed as he tilted Samuel's chin back and kissed him. "Don't worry about all that, Sammy-boy. There is still plenty you can do for me."

Kaj heard Ava, Gill, Valma, and Cici's groans of disapproval at his one-liner in the back of his mind and drowned the small ache in his chest it caused with the sweet taste of Samuel's mouth.

"Thank you so much for coming here today. Please take a seat." Captain Reids said as Master Gustav entered her office. He took a seat in front of her desk, nestling stiffly beside Cici and Governess Sabar.

"Can we finally get on with this?" Cici snapped, "I don't even know what I'm doing here."

"Your job," Governess Sabar stated, her harsh tone silencing Cici's impatience.

"We've called you in today to discuss the next steps in restoring order to the town," Captain Reids said. "As is the law of governance, the position of Elerrï's Burgermeister is one of birthright unless there are no heirs to inherit. Then it is up to the lord of our providence to decide the next master. Normally, the duties of Burgermeister would pass on to his wife after his death until the eldest child is ready to inherit, but with your mother's current condition-"

"She's insane," Cici interrupted, "You can say it."

"Let the Captain finish, ~~Ortensia~~," Sabar scolded.

Cici shivered.

Captain Reids continued, "With your mother's condition and with your schooling more focused on etiquette than economics – as Governess Sabar has informed me – your brother Ellsworth will have to be retrieved from Moreacor to come and assume the title."

"He won't be happy to leave his studies," Cici remarked. "I assume he has been notified already. When can I expect him to arrive? I want to have the repairs on the manor completed prior to his arrival."

"No, he has not been notified."

The center of her brow creased, "Why not?"

"Considering the nature of last week's tragedy, Captain Reids, Lieutenant Pires, and I have come to the decision that it is best to keep the details of this event a closely guarded secret for the time being," Gustav answered. "With the Venzors' involvement, it seems that there is more to it than just a small cult forming. We don't know who we can trust."

"Which is why you will need to travel to Moreacor

and retrieve Ellsworth yourself," the captain added.

"We don't have enough staff left to handle that kind of travel!" Cici countered. "You expect me to abandon my post and travel all the way to Moreacor alone?"

"Your duties will be handled between the three of us," Governess Sabar replied. "Just as it has been during your recovery this past week."

"And you will not be traveling alone. I've asked Officer Chan to accompany you, given your existing relationship, and Master Gustav will be sending his apprentice along as well to notify his trusted contacts at the Convocation."

"I'm not going anywhere with that walking natural disaster!" Cici shrieked. "What happens if he loses control again?"

"He won't," Gustav stated. "Gillian's outburst was due to the extreme stress he was under. I highly doubt it will happen again."

"But what if it does?" she retorted.

"It won't."

"You don't know that."

"Miss Valborg," Captain Reids cut through the building tension between them, "Gillian's attendance is nonnegotiable. A small covered wagon will be prepared for you as well as some rations for the journey. You'll be leaving the morning after next."

Cici pouted and sank in her chair, "Wouldn't it be

suspicious if I'm traveling with only a townsguard and a mage to visit my brother?"

"Not if you sell it well," Governess Sabar answered. "I've taught you the fine nuances of conversation, have I not? Don't tell me those lessons were a waste."

They sat in silence for a moment as Cici contemplated her situation.

"May I bring someone else along with us?" she asked.

The captain leaned forward, intrigued. "Who are you thinking?"

Gillian stood surrounded by lush jungle.

Barefoot, he felt the soft grass brush against his toes, shifting gently in the warm and gentle breeze. He took in the nature around him, marveling in the thousand shades of green flecked with bright bursts of color from fruits and flowers. Try as he might, he couldn't see the sky above through the canopy, only the dancing leaves branching off the twisted boughs of tilted trees. Trees leaned so severely it looked as though the entire jungle grew at an angle.

The smell of wildflowers and overripe citrus wafted over him as a pair of arms draped over his shoulders. A chin rested on the top of his head.

"A shame isn't it?" the voice said.

"What happened to it?" he asked.

"The scales are off-balance."

"The scales?"

"Yes. Things are off-kilter," the chin lifted off the top of his head, and soft lips replaced it, "but we'll fix it."

"We will?"

"Yes."

"How do we start?"

"You already have. You sensed destruction, and you acted to stop it. You and your friends make quite the team."

"You saw them?" Gill asked.

"Felt them," she corrected, "but yes. Together you are destined for greatness."

The lips lifted, and the arms held him tighter. A cheek pressed against the side of his face.

"Will you bear the scales, my templar?" she whispered.

He felt her breath on his ear. Gillian whipped his head around, trying to catch a glimpse of her face-

-and smacked his forehead on his nightstand.

"Son of a bitch," Gill swore as he rubbed the pain away and tried to focus his blurry eyes. He shielded himself from the bright glare of the midday sun and looked at the clockwork raven on his nightstand. The clock face embedded in the copper bird's chest read half past noon.

"Shit," he jumped out of bed, "Why didn't Master wake me up?!"

Gillian threw open his dresser drawers and ripped out a change of clothes, shedding his pajamas and pulling his fresh shirt and pants on as quickly as possible. He slipped on his loafers as he left.

"He's going to make me re-grout the golem this time," Gill muttered to himself as he rushed down the hall, "or collect leeches from the lake."

"You cannot be serious!" a man shouted from behind the door to Master Gustav's office, stilling Gillian's hand as he reached for the doorknob.

"Surely, you do not think I am blind? All of us saw him when we were rushing out of that damned crypt! We have spent our lives studying the gospel of the Plough. We are destined to serve her and all of her children. He should be taken in by the chantry and-"

Gill opened the door, acting as flustered as possible.

"I'm so sorry, Master!" he stumbled into the room, stopping in his tracks when he saw Chaplain Cannell.

"Oh!" He bowed his head, "Hello Chaplain. What are you doing here?"

"The chaplain was just leaving." Master Gustav stood up from behind his desk, "Chaplain, it was a pleasure talking with you as always. I will pass your observations over to the Convocation."

"Gustav-" Chaplain Cannell started.

"Gillian!" Gustav's demeanor changed on a dime, becoming cruel and damning as he glared at his apprentice. "Why are you late?!"

"I'm so sorry, Master!" He stepped further into the room, cowering under Gustav's fury, "I forgot to set my alarm!"

"You forgot?!" Gustav bellowed, his voice so loud the room shook. Chaplain Cannell paled.

"I-I'll come back later," he whimpered, running out of the room.

Master Gustav continued, "You lazy, moronic waste of a-"

Gillian shut the door behind the Chaplain.

Gustav let out a sigh of relief and fell back into his chair, "Thank the gods."

"That subtle amplification spell on your voice was a nice touch," Gill remarked.

"Cannell is as stubborn as a mule. It was necessary to get him out of our hair."

"I am truly sorry for sleeping in."

Master Gustav smoothed a hand over his scalp. "For once, I'm grateful for your ineptitude. The Chaplain's been here since this morning. Fate knows how much more of a nuisance he would have been if you'd been awake to encounter him."

Their conversation lulled, and Gillian took a seat in front of the desk, "I had another dream last night."

Gustav looked at his apprentice with tired eyes, "What happened?"

"I was in a tilted jungle."

"Tilted?"

"All the trees were at an angle," he held his hands together, demonstrating the diagonal, "like this."

"Did she speak to you again? The voice?"

"Yeah. She said that the jungle was titled because the scales are off-balance." He searched his master's eyes, "Do you know what that could mean, sir?"

"It could mean a lot of things," he answered. "Did she say anything else?"

"She asked if I would bear them…" Gill looked away and chewed on the inside of his cheek, "and she called me her templar."

"Hmmm…" Gustav sat back in his chair, processing what he said. "I didn't know you could swing a sword."

"Master," he groaned and covered his face, embarrassed by his mentor's poor joke.

"Well, when you meet Archmaster Tansel, perhaps you should tell him about your dreams."

Gillian's eyes widened, "Archmaster Tansel is coming? Your master is coming?"

"No," Gustav replied. "You're going to pay him a visit."

"But he lives in Moreacor."

"That he does."

"I didn't know your teleportation incantation could reach that far."

"It cannot," he smiled.

"Then we're taking a carriage?"

"*You,*" Gustav corrected, "are taking a carriage."

Gillian stared back at his master, trying to piece together exactly what he meant.

"But sir," he doubted, "Convocation rules state that only mages of indigo vestments or higher can travel unaccompanied."

"Unless the travel is sanctioned." Master Gustav opened his drawer and pulled out a small piece of parchment, rolled and sealed with wax twice, "Here is your writ of passage in case you are questioned upon your journey. It bears the sigils of the Archmaster and myself."

"T-thank you," Gillian stammered as his trembling hand reached out to grab it.

Gustav snatched it back. Gill jumped and looked up at his master in confusion.

"My boy," Master Gustav rolled his eyes, "you have asked every question imaginable about this situation yet have left out the most important one. Don't let excitement rush your judgment."

"Sorry." He studied his master's face for an answer and found it cold, clarifying what he needed to know, "Why?"

"There it is," Gustav sat back in his chair, face still grim. "Save any other questions for when I'm done, and listen carefully. You will be traveling with Valma and Cici to visit her brother in the city. Once you are settled, you are to pay a visit to Archmaster Tansel. The writ has his personal address listed on it. Do not send word you are coming; arrive unannounced."

"Okay."

"You are to tell him every last detail about the Harvest, including what happened with your magicks and your dreams, but only when he is alone. Do not speak to him unless he is alone, and do not speak about this with any other member of the Convocation. You are also to give him the letters from Venzor that Kaj found at the manor."

Gillian nodded.

"You leave tomorrow morning. Questions?"

"Yes."

"Out with it then."

"Is there a reason why Cici's brother wasn't summoned by letter?"

"Yes. Besides the citizens of this town and the Kyresore Garrison, no one knows what happened here."

Gillian swallowed nervously, "So, you believe there is something bigger going on because of Venzor's involvement?"

"Clearly."

He bit the inside of his cheek once more before looking back at his master, "Couldn't I just deliver the message to Ellsworth? I'm sure Valma and I could handle it on our own."

"It'd be very strange for a no-name mage and a no-name guard to travel weeks to stay at the home of an up-and-coming young noble. Escorting a sister to see her brother? Not so much."

Gillian grumbled in frustration. He was excited to venture out on his own, but bringing Cici along with him dampened his zeal.

"Any more questions?"

"No."

"Good," Gustav tossed the writ to Gillian, who fumbled to catch it. "Now go down to the cellar and start gathering some ingredients. We'll have a nice meal tonight to celebrate your first solo journey as a mage of the Arcane Convocation. Pick whatever you'd like most, and I'll make something happen with it."

"Of course." Gillian's mood brightened. Master Gustav rarely cooked, and when he did, it was always a treat.

Gill stood with a smile and bowed his head, "Thank

you so much, Master."

"Yes, yes," he shooed him away before turning his chair to look out the window.

Gill paused outside the door when he reentered in the hall, running his thumb over the crests pressed into the wax. A swirling red wax bore his master's mark, and a deep orange bore the Archmaster's.

To keep it safe, Gill headed back to his room and buried it where he kept all the things he held precious: his underwear drawer. He lifted a bunch of wrinkled garments and placed the scroll carefully against the drawer's wooden bottom. He covered it and moved to another section, revealing a small communication pendant.

Glowing green and wrapped in leather to form a necklace, he held it in his hand and spoke wordlessly.

Cici hated everything about this.

She hated the smell of the livestock, how long it took to get to this godforsaken farm, and most of all that the only person who could help her more than likely hated her guts.

She took a deep breath and knocked on the Barncombes' front door.

"Ava?" a voice called in the house, "Can you get the door?"

"Sure!" Ava called back.

Cici's stomach clenched as Ava's footsteps grew closer.

"Hello?" Ava asked as she opened the door, looking forward before looking down to find Cici at her doorstep. The pleasant mask she wore to greet strangers dropped away.

"What are you doing here?" Ava grumbled.

Really? Is that how you greet a person? Cici wanted to say but thought better of it, "Can we talk?"

"About?"

"Things."

"What things?"

"Barncombe, I'm trying my best to be cordial here."

Ava rolled her eyes, "Fine. Come in," and held open the door for her as she entered.

"Ava? Who is it?" Mr. Barncombe shouted from another room.

"Cici!" she shouted back.

"Cici?" he questioned.

"Valborg!" she replied.

Cici winced at Mr. Barncombe's lack of response and took a seat at the kitchen table.

Ava sat across from her, "Talk."

"Aren't you going to offer me a cup of tea?"

"Nope."

Cici ground her teeth, "Fine then." She took a deep breath to curtail her irritation, "I would like to hire you to accompany me as one of my guards while I travel to Moreacor."

"No."

"Ava-"

"I said no. I am not a guard," she stated.

"The fact that you can slay three men in mere seconds with that bow of yours would suggest otherwise," Cici challenged.

"Why are you going to Moreacor anyway?" Ava scoffed, "Don't you have to take care of the town after your father destroyed everything?"

Cici lowered her gaze and pulled at her hangnails at the mention of the former burgermeister, "I am visiting my brother, Ellsworth, to alert him of the burgermeister's passing and to bring him here to take the title as his own."

"Okay?" she questioned, "Just send a letter or something. Why the hell would you travel all the way there when you can send a hawk?"

"Because no one outside of the town knows what happened, and for Master Gustav and Captain Reids to make sure it doesn't happen again, things need to stay that way."

"Ask Valma to go with you then."

"She already is."

They stared at each other in silence.

"Well?" Cici asked.

"Well, what?" Ava retorted.

"Are you coming?"

"Hell no! I can't go to Moreacor. I've got things to do here: animals to attend, crops to harvest, horses to reshoe-"

"Ava," Mr. Barncombe made his way to stand in the doorway between the kitchen and the sitting room. He stared at the pair of them with a furrowed brow that only served to accentuate his sun-formed wrinkles.

"Don't worry, Pa. I told her no."

"You shouldn't have," her father said.

Ava glared at her father in stupefied betrayal, "What do I mean I shouldn't have?"

"I mean that you should go."

"But I have to chores to do here I-"

"It's high time that your brothers started pulling their weight and learned how to run this place. Hell, you were gathering chicken eggs and feeding the livestock much younger than they are now."

"What about-"

"What about what?" Mr. Barncombe spat, his tone shifting from playfully concerned to harsh and authoritative. "Chickadee, ever since that awful day, you have been nothing but a wreck. You can barely get up the stairs without shaking like a leaf. So as much as I love knowing you're safe at home, having my family whole, you need to get out of here. Put some space between you and all that misery."

Ava couldn't look at him.

"Plus, you've always wanted to see the ocean, haven't you?" He eased off of his scolding, "The beaches near the city are beautiful, so I've heard."

Ava turned to Cici, "How much is it?"

"It's not so much an amount in coin," she answered. "I will foot the bill for all of your food, accommodations, and necessary essentials on our journey as well as charge your family no land taxes for the next two years."

"That is too kind of you, Miss," Mr. Barncombe smiled, "Two years land tax free will do a lot of good for our family."

Ava clenched her jaw, "When do we leave?"

"Tomorrow morning," Cici smiled at the disdain on Ava's face, ecstatic that she'd gotten her way, "My apologies for the late notice."

"You promise me you will go straight to Moreacor and will not leave Miss Valborg's side?" Captain Reids stood tall, arms folded sternly over her chest.

They stood in the receiving area of the jailhouse, the pale light of early morning barely illuminating the room as it poured in through the windows.

"Well, we'll have to stop and rest a few times, Captain," Valma said. "So I can't promise straight there, but I can promise I won't leave Cici."

Valma was having a great week, all things considered. She could barely walk down the street on her patrol now without being stopped by some very grateful townsfolk. Her tab at TOTS was almost always covered, either by one of the patrons or by the tavern's owners, and she'd gotten so many baked goods and handmade gifts sent to the jailhouse for her that she could successfully open her own bakery and secondhand shop if she wanted to. Top if all off with her assignment as Cici's escort for an undercover mission that was basically a paid beach vacation, and Valma was practically skipping for the past few days as she readied the provisions for their journey.

Captain Reids continued, "Even if her attitude becomes intolerable?"

"There's nothing about her that's intolerable to me," she shrugged. "And come on, Capt, do you really think I would disobey a direct order?"

"It's not that I think you'll disobey," she stared her officer down, "I just want to make sure you remember this conversation before you do something rash again."

"I get it," Valma bristled. While Valma soaked up the town's praises the past week, Captain Reids delighted in keeping her from getting too big a head. "I should have gotten the garrison as soon as we noticed the town was empty instead of trying to handle things myself. You've beaten me over the head with it enough times."

"Good."

"But you have to admit it was a good plan-"

"Chan," she warned.

Valma shut up.

The captain sighed and uncrossed her arms, "Remember your goal, alright? You have to escort them all there safely over anything else that comes your way. I don't expect any trouble on your journey, but ya just never know."

"Don't worry," she placed a hand on her captain's shoulder. "I won't let you down."

"Did you really bring the cat?!" Cici's shrieks of annoyance from outside shook the room.

"And that starts right now," Valma laughed and extended her hand, "I'll see you soon, Captain."

Captain Reids clasped her hand against Valma's forearm, "Make me proud."

⸻

Ava tightened the last belt connecting Jasper to the covered wagon. She smoothed her hand over his dapple coat before moving to address the chestnut and cream-painted mare hitched next to him. She held up a hand to let the horse smell her. After a few sniffs, the mare bowed her head, encouraging Ava to pet her snout.

"That's a girl," Ava cooed softly. "Now, you're going to be very nice to my Jasper, alright? He's a gentleman, but if I notice he's letting you do most of the work, I'll make sure to keep him in line."

Jasper snorted, offended. Ava turned to look at him, raising an eyebrow.

"Oh really?" she wryly questioned. "Guess I'll just eat all the carrots I packed for you then."

Jasper nickered, shaking his mane like a scolded child.

Ava smirked, "That's what I thought."

"Hey there, Aves!" She turned to find Valma leaving the jailhouse, waving, "Long time no see!"

She waved back, "Hey, Valma."

Valma walked towards her and slapped a hand on the side of the mare, "I see you've met Begonia. She's a doll, isn't she?"

"She doesn't like when you do that," Ava stated.

"Do what?"

"Smack her," Ava petted Begonia's snout, "You might want to apologize."

"Yeah, girl?" Valma leaned over to look the mare in the eye, "You don't like when I do that?"

Begonia trilled her lips.

"I'm real sorry," she smoothed her hand across the spot she hit. "I didn't mean anything by it." Valma turned back to Ava, "Where's Cici?"

"Pouting in the wagon."

Valma sighed and ran her hand over her face, "It's been five minutes."

"She knew what she was getting into when she hired me," Ava shrugged. "I'm not gonna coddle her pretentiousness."

"I'll go talk to her."

Valma headed to the back of the caravan. She pulled open one of the canvas flaps and found Cici sitting inside, arms crossed in frustration as she glared at Marqui. The cat didn't look back at her. He was too busy cleaning himself on top of one of the crates.

"What are you doing?" Valma sighed.

"She brought the cat," Cici spat. "This is a stealth mission, and she brought the cat."

"She brings the cat everywhere, right?"

Cici huffed and crossed her arms tighter over her chest.

"Well, then wouldn't it draw more attention if she didn't have the cat with her?" she continued.

Cici turned her ire towards her, but the smirk the townsguard wore didn't waver.

"I'm not sitting back here with her," she stated.

"There's plenty of room on the driver's bench next to me," her smirk curved into a smile. "I'll take the first few hours; then she can take the next shift."

"Fine," Cici stood. "Let's get on with it then."

Cici climbed out of the caravan and walked alongside Valma.

"Aves, I'm gonna drive the first half of the day. You mind taking the second?" Valma called as they made their way to the front of the carriage.

"Fine by me," Ava answered, kissing Jasper on his snout before heading to join Qui in the back.

Valma hopped up on the driver's seat and slid into the empty spot next to Cici, still pouting with her nose wrinkled in disgust from the smell of the horses. With a soft crack of the reins, they headed down the soft dirt of Kyresore Road.

"You called this a stealth mission," Valma remarked after a few minutes. "You a fan of mystery novels then? Or is it spy thrillers?"

Out of the corner of her eye, she saw Cici look up at her; her eyes narrowed as she tried to discern some type of hidden agenda behind her question. Valma imagined that it wasn't very often that she held a casual conversation with someone.

"Spy thrillers," she said after a moment. "Though I have enjoyed the occasional mystery."

"You ever read 'Vexed by Vipers'?" she asked.

"I have not. Is it any good?"

"It is, and it has some pretty steamy romance scenes if you're into that sort of thing."

"Steamy? What do they kiss in a sauna or something?"

Valma's eyebrows shot up, and she looked at Cici in disbelief.

A mischievous smile spread over her face, "Oh, this is going to be a very fun trip."

Valma slowed down the horses as they approached Verdeer Manor, spotting Gillian's wild terracotta curls shaking in the breeze as he stood outside of the main gate, travel bag in hand. He waved at them as they stopped and made his way towards the back of the caravan.

"Hey," Ava called from the back, "why did we stop?"

Valma shot a stern look at Cici and whispered harshly, "You didn't tell her he was coming?"

"What does it matter if I told her?" Cici whispered back. "They're friends. It'll be fine."

The no answer from Valma set Ava on edge. She stood in the back of the caravan, bow readied, and aimed at the canvas opening. A hand reached in to grab the flap, and she pulled her bowstring back to fire, only to freeze as Gillian's head appeared.

His blue eyes widened, and his freckled cheeks blanched, "H-hey, A-ava."

"Hey, Gill." Ava slowly loosened the tension on her bowstring and lowered her weapon, "What are you doing here?"

"I was going to ask you the same thing," he replied.

"Everything alright back there?" Valma shouted.

"Y-yeah!" Gillian yelled back.

"Well then, hurry it up!" Cici snipped, "We're wasting daylight!"

Gill stepped into the cart, and as his weight made the wheels bounce, Valma snapped the horses' reins. The carriage jolted forward, sending him stumbling back before he overcorrected and fell forward, right on top of Ava.

"Will you stop shaking the cart back there?!" Cici shrieked, "All this motion is making me sick!"

"Sorry!" he apologized before looking down at the soft object pinned beneath him. Ava's big brown eyes blinked back at him. His face grew hot as a blush rushed to his cheeks.

"You alright?" she asked.

He shot up off of her, "I just lost my footing! I didn't mean-"

"It's fine," Ava sat up and fixed her clothes before turning to inspect her bow for any damage from the impact.

Gillian felt a familiar snout rub up against the back of

his head. He looked over his shoulder to find Marqui sitting on the crate he leaned against. "Hey there, Qui," he whispered to the cat and reached up to scratch behind his ear.

Marqui happily leaned into his touch, purring in delight.

"So," Gill cleared his throat and looked back at Ava, who inspected her bow a little too intently, "heading to Moreacor, huh?"

"Cici hired me," she stated, not bothering to look at him as she answered.

"Really? What for? The Master and Captain Reids said we'd have plenty of rations. Did she want a hunter for fresh meat or-"

"She hired me as a guard."

Gill was taken aback, "A… guard?"

Ava put her bow back in its sheath and sighed, "Yeah, I don't get it either. But she said she wouldn't charge my family land taxes for the next two years, so-" she gestured to the caravan, "-here I am."

"Here you are." He looked Ava over as she stared off. Dressed in her hunting leathers, demeanor tense, if she wasn't washed up and if her wounds weren't healed, Gillian would have thought they were still under the threat of the Harvest.

"What about you?" Ava relaxed a little, leaning back against the side of the cart and tilting her head up to look at the canvas covering, "Cici didn't mention you were coming along."

"Huh," Gillian noted. "I'm meeting with Master's master to tell him about the Harvest."

Ava tensed, frowning slightly, "Ah. Sounds fun."

Gillian redirected the conversation, "It sucks that it's under these conditions, but I'm excited to meet Archmaster Tansel. Maybe I can convince him to give me a few lessons while I'm there. Plus, it'll be-"

"Open the back. I'm coming in hot."

Gill sighed as the disembodied voice filled his head.

"What's wrong?" Ava sat up at attention, his sudden sigh bringing her to finally look at him, though more out of worry than anything else.

"Nothing," he stood and made his way to the back of the cart. If he stayed calm, perhaps it would spread to her as well. "Just move to the side and get ready to deal with a very angry Valma and Cici."

"What are you gonna do?" Ava warily followed his suggestion.

"Something stupid," Gillian grumbled as he tied the curtains of the canvas back.

Ava tilted her head to peer out the opening, and the color drained from her face as a fluttering mass of ratty black fabric billowing around the eat shit grin of Kaj swung through the air towards the moving cart at a breakneck pace.

Kaj let go of the rope in his hand and propelled his body forward into the back of the cart. He tucked his knees to his chest as he fell, protecting himself as he rolled across the wooden floor of the wagon. The entire carriage shook from the force of his landing as he smacked against the wall separating them from the driver's seat.

The canvas slit above Kaj's head flung open.

"I said quit the shaking! If I vomit, I'll make sure to aim for you ingrates!" Cici shouted. She panted furiously, her face pale from nausea.

"Oh good," Kaj said, "you're still as terrible as ever. I'm glad to see nothing has changed."

Valma's head appeared beside Cici's, her eyes searing with anger.

"You!" she seethed.

"Hey, Stick! Good to see ya-" his speech choked off as Valma pulled him up by the collar to face her.

"Where the fuck were you?!" she snapped, "Do you know how much shit I got for letting you escape?!"

"Valma, the reins," Ava cautioned.

"What the hell else was I supposed to do?!" Kaj retorted.

"Come back to the station for questioning! We weren't going to arrest you, not after you helped save all those people!"

"Do I look like a fucking snitch?!"

"Valma," Ava called louder, "the reins."

"The kingdom would've protected you! Hell, maybe they would have made you a detective or something! A special informant on criminal undergrounds!"

"And step on the necks of my friends and family like you imperialist lap dogs?" Kaj spat, "Fuck you!"

"Jasper! Begonia! Halt!" Ava shouted.

The carriage rocked violently as the horses stopped in their tracks, sending Valma forward and knocking her and Kaj's heads together. She let go of his shirt to touch her aching forehead, and Kaj collapsed onto the floor of the wagon.

Rubbing his forehead, Kaj whined in pain, "Whatcha do that for, Bullseye?"

"I'm not having my horse's ankle snapped just because you two got beef," Ava scolded.

"Well, she started it!"

"You're the one who ran!" Valma spat, "Why the hell are you even here?"

"Because I need a ride back to the city. The sooner I get out of this hicktown, the better."

"And why should we help you?!"

"Because if it weren't for him, I'd be dead!" Gillian

interjected.

They all turned to look at him.

"I owe him, alright?" The bravado Gill displayed faded as he drew everyone's attention. He rubbed the back of his neck nervously, "I promised I'd get him back home somehow, and well... this is somehow."

"You could have told me first," Cici snipped.

Ava scoffed, "Says the girl who didn't tell me Gill was coming."

"Yeah, what was that about anyway?" Gill asked.

"Wait, she didn't tell you either?" Valma glared at Cici in disapproval.

Cici sputtered, "She didn't tell me about the cat!"

"Gods," Kaj groaned loudly and hung his head between his knees, "I can't believe I was actually looking forward to seeing you guys."

A moment of silence fell between them.

Kaj's words eased a bit of the tension in Ava's chest. The soft sincerity in his voice was quite the opposite of the damning vision her nightmares crafted.

She watched the others react to his confession. Cici's pout unfurled a bit, Valma's frustration melted away with a snicker, and a twinkle glittered in Gillian's eye. Marqui even jumped off his crate to greet the elvefolk, rubbing against

Kaj's leg as if they were old friends.

"You can stay," Cici grumbled after a moment, "but only because we are wasting precious travel time sitting here and arguing."

Kaj leaned forward, bowing low to the ground, "Oh, thank you great and merciful Cici!" His tone dripped with sass, "I shall be forever in your debt, my liege."

"I know you're joking, but it is still nice to see you lying prostrate on the ground," she smirked,

"Valma. Remind me to tell the guards when they inspect us at the garrison that Kaj is my fool."

"Gladly," Valma smiled and turned back to take the reins, giving them a slight crack and driving the cart forward.

Kaj snapped his head up and glared at Cici with a childish pout, who stuck her tongue out in return. Their immature bickering pulled a wheezing laugh out of Gillian that Ava hadn't heard in a very long time. She couldn't help the smile that came upon her face at the joyful sound.

Perhaps her father was right; perhaps some time away from home would do her some good.

THE SCALEBEARERS

ELSEWHERE

    Nimble fingers rubbed dark wax over a fraying thread, binding the worn fibers together, making it strong, making it whole once more...

    ...and waking him up.

THE SCALEBEARERS

ACKNOWLEDGMENTS

First and foremost, thank you for reading my book. Books are meant to be read and for you have to have chosen to read mine is amazing. Whenever you have read this book (or reread this book) I hope that your next few days are filled with delights, whether it be small things like the warmth of the sunshine streaming through your car window at a stoplight or big things like winning a Nobel Peace Prize.

Now onto thanking the people, places, and things that made *The Scalebearers* possible.

Thank you to:

- The Universe
- My editors/beta-readers: Dr. Alison Korn, Courtney Bundens, Kristen Cleaver, Hayeley Norris, Melissa Tevlin. You are all wonderful. Thank you for seeing the things I didn't.
- My cats
- My friends
- My family
- My junior year english teacher, my high school latin teacher, my college professors: Mote and McGee, and Jamie
- Mythology and Folklore
- Ray Bradbury
- The casts of Critical Role, Dimension 20, and The Adventure Zone

- Green Day, Delta Rae, and The Oh Hellos
- Driving with the windows down on fall and summer days
- Fall and Summer
- Stained Glass
- Black tea with honey in mugs that make me smile
- Margot. I'm sorry they trapped you in that closet.
- Computers and the internet
- My imagination
- Dancing
- Naps on the beach
- Butterfly stickers
- *The Artist's Way*
- *The Mirror Visitor Quartet*
- Cece Elliot
- Dean DeBlois
- Cheese aand crackers
- Pizza bagels
- Shrimp tempura rolls
- Soft sweaters
- Sewing scissors
- Crop top
- Pens. You know the ones that right real smooth?
- Warm baths
- The sheer existence of fanfiction and fanart
- The moon
- The sound of leaves rustling in the wind
- Cedar water
- Shakespeare
- Anime

GLOSSARY

Locations:

- **Elerrï** *[el-er-ree]* - A small village located off of the Kyresore Road in the Kingdom of Berylwood. Known for their lumber, farming, and animal husbandry.

- **Krosten** *[kross-ten]* - A town located in the northern part of Berylwood, between the border of the Arid Frosts and the Shadowfen. Known for their furs and big game hunting.

- **Moreacor** *[more-uh-core]* - The Kingdom of Berylwood's largest port city on the Durmez Sea. Home to the Arcane Convocation's head citadel. Known for their imports, exports, fishing, fashion, and entertainment.

- **Cirvain** *[sir-vein]* - The captial city of the Kingdom of Berylwood.

- **Carran Bay** *[karen]* - A seaside city on the southern coast of Berylwood. Known for its resorts.

- **Kyresore Road** *[kear-sore]* - The main road that runs across the expanse of Berylwood from east to west. Connects Moreacor to Cirvain.

Objects:

- **ikiwort** *[icky-wort]* - A bush known for the numbing

and antiseptic properties of its sap.

Months:

- **Vesin** *[ves-in]* - The Évanvicht equivalent to April. Named after Ves the Goddess of Water.

Deities:

- **Messis** *[mess-is]* - Goddess of The Land, nature, and earth. Plants and minerals are her domain. The second born of the Creator Deities. Known sometimes as the Doe or the Plough. Islat's daughter.

- **Wakorin** *[wah-core-in]* - God of Time. The sixth born of the Creator Deities. Islat's son.

- **Prakari** *[pruh-kar-ee]* - Goddess of Righteous Vengeance. The fourteenth born of the Creator Deities. Cinnvaya's daughter.

- **Ves** *[vess]* - Goddess of Water. The third born of the Creator Deities. Islat's daughter.

- **Laeth** *[layth]* - Goddess of Death. The twelfth born of the Creator Deities. Islat and Cinnvaya's daughter.

- **Osla** *[oss-la]* - Goddess of Revelry. The tenth born of the Creator Deities. Islat's daughter.

- **Zozvit** *[zahz-vit]* - God of the Undead. The twelfth born of the Destructor Deities. Berreux's son.

- **Urgan** *[er-gahn]* - God of Wastes. The second born of the Destructor Deities. Berreux's son.

SWEET

Portrait by Lou (Twitter: @asdfghjkiri)

Sweet can't remember a time where she didn't have a story in her head. Works that tell evocative, emotionally driven stories in a unique light hold a special place in her heart. She collects copies of fairytales, folklore, myths, and most any old book that sparked the imagination. The top books in this collection currently are a 126-year old copy of *Beauties of Shakespeare* and a very worn paperback copy of *Treasure Island* she stole from her grandmother's basement.

You can find her at her website (storiesbysweet.com), on Twitter (@sweetdiscords), on Tumblr (sweetarethediscords.tumblr.com), and if you would like to see more of the Scalebearers' adventures you can join her Patreon where she posts canon and non-canon short stories as well as lore for the realm of Évanvicht, and content for her works outside of *The Scalebearers* series.

Lightning Source UK Ltd.
Milton Keynes UK
UKHW010725130123
415295UK00001B/219